CRUSADE
FALLEN ANGELS – BOOK 3

Terence West

CRUSADE
FALLEN ANGELS – BOOK 3

DOUBLE DRAGON

A DOUBLE DRAGON PAPERBACK

ISBN 978-1-78695-467-1

Double Dragon
is an imprint of Fiction4All

Published 2020
Fiction4All
www.fiction4all.com

Dedication

This book is dedicated to my grandmother, Ada Russell, and my father, Herman West. You two never took any of my nonsense and always kept me on the straight and narrow path. Thank you.

You mean everything to me.

Acknowledgments

As this is the final book in the Fallen Angels Trilogy, I want to thank everyone for making this possible. When I started writing *Fallen Angels* in the fall of 1994, I never realized what the book would turn into. Now here I am, years later, finishing the third book in the series. It's strange to sit down and recall the trials and tribulations that all of my novels went through to become what they are now. This had been one of the most wonderful experiences of my life thus far, and it is my pleasure to share it with you, the reader. From Jake, Alex, Griggs, and myself, thanks for taking the journey with us and joining us on *our* crusade.

Chapter One

THE DISTANT PAST....

The armada of silver saucers hovered ominously above the lush green world. Clouds wrapped around the blues and greens of the oceans covering the majority of the planet like a blanket of soft, white linen. The armada had traveled vast distances from their home world to reach this fertile planet, the fourth planet in the Sol Solar System. They had gone through the furthest reaches of the known universe on their trip here to the outer arm of this spiral shaped galaxy. This, to them, was literally the backwater of the galaxy. Compared to the rest of it, the small, fragile creatures that inhabited this planet were mere new-borns.

The machine race was here for a purpose, though. This was not just another routine surveillance mission. Over the past thousand years, they had begun to detect violent changes occurring in the planet's make-up. The civilization that lived here was completely unaware. They assumed their gods were angry and they were being punished on some unknown whim. The machine race had come here to protect their investment. They wanted to ensure this civilization would continue, if not on this planet, then on another.

The lead saucer gave the signal to the rest of the armada to ascend into the atmosphere. The mighty ships slowly sank below the clouds of the blue- green world. They hovered, undetected, while observing the civilization in its final days.

Massive crowds had gathered around three

large structures: massive pyramids built on a grassy plain surrounded on both sides by two rivers. The area was known as Cydonia. They were holding rituals on the steps, trying to appease their gods. Humanoids were on their knees bowing before the giant structures, while priests led them in prayers. The humanoids were sparsely dressed, only wearing a few light cloths around their chest and waist. The priests, on the other hand, were lavishly garbed in silver and gold with flowing red and white robes billowing around them. Blood from their sacrifices stained the steps of the pyramids.

Turning away, the armada of ships traveled a small distance across the planet to another huge monolith. The humanoid civilization had taken an entire mountain and over a period of years, carved it into a face that peered off into space. Workers were still completing it standing on their immense wooden scaffolding. Chipping and cutting into the rock, the massive ornate headpiece the face would be wearing was starting to take form.

This baffled the machine race. Why had the civilization determined the need to recreate their likeness on a massive scale? Did they need to show future generations they were indeed here? Or was it to please their gods so they would show favor when the spring harvest came? The machine race knew they had made a good choice to save this civilization. There was still so much they wanted to know about them.

Alarms started to blare inside the saucers. They had detected an immense upheaval in the crust of this planet just beginning. The machine race knew this planet's life was about to end in a fiery blaze.

They watched as a quake rocked the land, sending the wooden scaffolding and the workers tumbling to the ground. Next to the face, the ground split open spewing molten lava everywhere. The fragile humanoids tried to run from the burning substance, but were quickly swallowed by it.

Accessing its scanners, the main saucer pulled up a geothermal map of the planet. Volcanoes were forming and erupting all over the surface. The sky had begun to darken due to the thick ash being tossed into the atmosphere. The main saucer quickly relayed orders to the other ships:

TAKE EVERY SPECIMEN YOU CAN FIND.

The saucers rapidly shot off to different areas of the globe on their mission, while the main saucer still loomed over the face. Turning its attention away from this dying planet, it slowly rose out of the atmosphere into space. Accessing its scanners again, it looked across the millions of miles to another planet in this system. It was the third planet from the star, another small blue and green world with one small moon orbiting it. Life was just beginning to evolve there after a major cataclysm with an asteroid, and just like here, it was experiencing a few growing pains. The saucer scanned the planet's core. It seemed much more stable than the current planet. The machine knew it would be a suitable home, though not quite as hospitable as this one.

A beep sounded inside the machine signaling the other saucers had completed their mission. Relaying the coordinates of the new planet, the armada set off toward the tiny world. It began searching through its records. The databanks returned several entries on the planet. It had been catalogued under the heading 'BCE-121887-3'. That wasn't fitting for its new inhabitants, though. It began to search again for a more fitting label. Quickly, its memory came upon the perfect name. One used previously by the being that originally constructed the machines and gave them life. The machine thought it would be appropriate to call this new world "Earth" in honor of the creator. It saved the file as it continued on its way.

***

THE PRESENT....

The great machine whirred to life beneath the miles of layered ice. A distant transmission had cued its auto-start systems. It knew they were coming, and they would expect the data. As a precaution, the great machine began to cycle through its systems performing a complete diagnostic.

It stopped.

There was something wrong. Checking....

Its transmission relays had been damaged somehow over the past five thousand years. It tried a self-repair. It tried again. Nothing. It was unable to remedy the problem. It knew, however, that the machines would make every effort to repair the damage once they arrived. Performing one final diagnostic, it decided it was futile. It quietly powered its systems down. There was nothing to do now but wait for their arrival.

Chapter Two

Built deep within Cheyenne Mountain in Colorado, NORAD was bustling with activity. Air Force personnel were scurrying around the floor busily. The command center was, for the most part, dark. Three immense screens were at the front of the room constantly displaying tactical information. In front of them, rows and rows of consoles were monitoring all air traffic, civilian, commercial and military.

"Sir?" a young Lieutenant asked from his station near the back. He tried to wait patiently for his CO to reply, but he knew this was too important. "General Summers!"

Four men were standing in the corner of the control room, apparently discussing something. A man with dark hair turned from his conversation toward the Lieutenant. "What?"

"I'm sorry, sir, but I didn't think this could wait." The young man turned back to his console and pressed a series of buttons. "I've got something really strange here," he said, pointing to his monitor.

General Gregory Summers turned and strode briskly toward the young man's terminal. Laying one of his hands on the top of the workstation, he leaned in close to the monitor. "What've you got?" he asked with a slight Texas accent. Gregory Summers was a large man. Almost as wide as he was tall, but everyone knew he was all muscle. He had been growing a large black beard for several months, adding to his already intimidating appearance.

"I've got something strange on the radar." Lieutenant David Stewart, on the other hand, was a small, wiry man with fire red hair. "As you know, General, I've been tracking and cataloguing all the debris in space around Earth."

Summers nodded.

"Well, just a few moments ago, I caught a strange blip on the outermost fringe of my radar."

"What was it?" Summers asked.

Stewart shook his head. "I don't know, sir, but it was big and looked to be headed this way. It was there and then it just disappeared."

Summers immediately straightened up. "Where was it when you last saw it?"

"Just beyond the orbit of Mars, sir."

"Keep an eye on this thing," Summers commanded him. "I want to know the moment it comes back on our scopes."

"Yes, sir," Stewart turned back to his console.

Summers took a long breath as he started 'The Walk'. He hated this part of the job. 'The Walk' referred to the path the general or commanding officer had to make as they moved toward the Command Station. It was located near the front of the rows of consoles. It consisted of a tall metal table with two phones and a monitor. Summers grabbed the receiver from one of the phones and pressed it to his ear. It had only one button on it. Pressing it, Summers heard the phone begin to ring. After two short rings, he heard someone pick up on the other end.

"Mr. President," Summers greeted. "I may have some alarming news."

The shot glass made a hollow thud as it hit the bar. This place was a dive. Nothing more than a hole in the wall, it was one room with a long brown wooden bar running down the entire length of it. It had no room for tables or chairs, just a row of stools. Only the flicker of several neon lights illuminated the place. Currently, four patrons occupied stools.

Lifting his glass, Jake Silver signaled to the bartender for another round. Walking down the long bar, the bartender pulled a bottle from under the counter and slowly filled Jake's glass with thick amber liquor. The bartender shot Jake an ominous glance as he turned to attend his other customers.

"Leave the bottle," Jake instructed him hoarsely, pulling a half mashed cigar out of his beaten brown leather jacket. He looked like hell. He had black rings under his eyes from lack of sleep, and he hadn't shaved in almost three weeks. His black t-shirt was tattered, and the blue jeans he was wearing had a hole in one knee.

The bartender, a portly older man with a thick brown beard, snatched the bottle away from Jake's grasp. "I think you've had about enough, mister. Drink your last shot and go home."

Lighting the cigar, Jake picked up the glass and dumped the alcohol down his throat. Standing up, he leaned over the bar toward the man. "I said, leave the bottle."

The bartender took a step back. "I think you better go home. Let me call you a cab," the bartender said politely as he picked up a small black

14

cordless phone from behind the bar.

Jake reached over and slapped the phone from the man's hand. "What the hell is wrong with you? I just want to sit and have a nice quiet drink in your establishment, and you want to get rid of me? That's not very good customer service." Jake stumbled back for a moment before he regained his balance. He knew he was getting drunk, but he wasn't ready to leave. He wasn't drunk enough yet.

"Go home and sleep it off, or I'll call the cops and they'll toss you into the drunk tank." The bartender was trying to keep his cool, but it was slipping very quickly.

Jake began to raise his voice. "Why don't you just shut the hell up, you pudgy bastard, and give me the bottle?"

"That's it." The bartender looked down the bar at two large men watching a football game on a small color TV. They were both dressed head to toe in black leather. Handing Jake the bottle, he swiftly made his way toward the men. "Guys?"

The two gruff men looked up. "Yeah?"

The bartender leaned over on the bar in front of them. "I'll give you both free drinks for the rest of the night if you get rid of that man sitting at the bar over there."

The two men looked at each other and smiled. "Free drinks and we get to kick someone's ass? I like this bar." The two men stood and began to walk toward Jake. The first man looked to weigh at least three hundred pounds. He had a scruffy blonde beard and tired blue eyes. He had on a black shirt with a picture of the confederate flag on it with a black leather jacket and black combat boots. The silver spurs on his heels jingled as he walked. The second man, though not as big, was no less intimidating. He stood at least a foot taller than the first with raven black hair and steely blue eyes. He was wearing a long black leather trench coat that hung to his heels. The two men took positions on either side of Jake, who had retaken his seat.

Jake looked up. "What can I do for you two," he hated to use the word, "gentlemen?"

The first man snatched the bottle away from Jake and smashed it on the floor. "You've been fucking with our friend," he said in a growl. "I think it's time you leave."

"Is that so?" Jake asked, turning his attention to the second man. The man had pulled a pair of brass knuckles out of his pocket and was sliding them onto his tattooed hand. "What if I refuse?"

"Then we kick your ass," the second man replied with an almost Brooklyn accent.

Jake lifted his half empty glass to his mouth and swallowed the last gulp of alcohol. "Well, if it has to be that way," Jake said as he set the glass down. With quick reflexes, he sent his left elbow into the second man's stomach and swung around and hit the first man squarely in the jaw. Both men stumbled back from the unexpected attack.

"You're going to regret that, you son of a bitch!" The first man charged Jake.

Stepping aside, Jake grabbed the first man's head and slammed it against the bar. Spinning on his heels, he ducked just as the second man threw a high punch. Retaliating, Jake sent a vicious uppercut into the second man's midsection. Grabbing his head, Jake kneed the second man hard in the nose.

The second man stumbled back holding his bloody nose. "Mother fucker!"

The first man caught Jake off-guard. Wrapping his meaty arms around Jake, the first man held him tightly. "Fuck him up!" he shouted at the other man.

The second man quickly moved up to Jake and sent a jab into his chin with the brass knuckles. "How'd that feel?" Reeling back, the man hit Jake hard in the midsection knocking the wind out of him. "You want some more?"

Jake shook his head as he caught his breath. "No, I think I've had plenty." Kicking hard, he smashed his booted foot into the second man's knee sending him to the floor. Throwing his head back, he hit the first man in the nose. Quickly spinning around, Jake sent another punch into the man's nose. The big man toppled to the floor, his nose a broken, bloody mess.

Stepping away from the two men, Jake grabbed his lit cigar from the ashtray on the bar and took a long drag. "I suddenly don't feel so welcome here." Pulling a fifty dollar bill from his pocket, he tossed it on the bar. "Keep the change," Jake said with a smile as he walked through the exit.

Chapter Three

"I love you, too," Faith giggled as she rolled on top of Tyler. The two kissed passionately for a long moment, but were interrupted by the ring of the telephone.

Reaching over to the nightstand next to their bed, Tyler grabbed the phone. "Hello?"

"Hi, this is Tina, can I talk to Faith?"

"Yeah, hold on." Tyler handed the phone to Faith. "Hello?" Faith asked.

Tyler got out of bed. "I'm going to go and get a glass of juice. Do you want something?"

Faith shook her head.

"Hi, Faith, its Tina," the girl's voice was filled with exuberance. "I hate to call you on your day off…"

"But?" Faith knew what was coming next.

"Jennifer just called in sick and we need you to come into work."

"Sorry, Tina, but I haven't had a day off with my husband since our honeymoon, and I'm determined to spend today with him."

"Is there any way I can persuade you otherwise?" Tina asked. "Nope, sorry," and with that, Faith hung up the phone.

Tyler walked back into the room with a tall glass of orange juice and slid back into bed. "They wanted you to come in and work on your day off again?" Tyler asked with a frown on his face.

"Yeah," Faith replied. Setting the phone aside, she ran her hand over his bare chest, "But I told them no. I want to spend my day off with my husband."

"That's very sweet of you."

"I know." Faith looked out the bedroom window of the small house they were renting in Elko, Nevada. The morning sun was shining through their white shades. "I wish we had more time together."

"I'm sorry," Tyler said while running his hand through Faith's hair.

"Between our jobs and my college classes, that just doesn't leave us a lot of time together."

Faith sat up and smiled. "Well, at least we have today together, and I'm going to make the most of it, but first," she kissed Tyler's forehead, "I have to use the bathroom." Faith lifted herself off the bed and walked toward the bathroom door. She was only wearing a long, white t-shirt.

Tyler smiled as he watched her. He had never been so happy in his entire life than he had been with Faith. After Jim Durard had released him from the FEMA offices in Las Vegas, they had returned to Tyler's hometown and rented a small apartment. Faith, with her nursing experience, had gotten a job at the local clinic, and Tyler had concentrated on graduating high school while working as a night freight loader at one of the local department stores. Tyler finished his senior year of high school only three months later, and had started college later that same year. The summer after his sophomore year of college, Tyler and Faith had gotten married. Now, less than a year later, they were still struggling to find a balance. Tyler knew all newlyweds went through this, and that they would be fine.

Faith returned to the room, and pressed herself seductively against the doorframe. "Hello, Mr.

Mitchell," she said in a sexy voice.

Tyler smiled. "Why, hello, Mrs. Mitchell."

Faith laughed out loud. "I don't think I'll ever get used to hearing that!" She ran toward the bed and jumped in. Quickly drawing the shades, the two began to make the most of their day.

***

He pulled another stack of papers from his inbox and placed them in front of him. Placing his elbows on his desk, he leaned over and held his head in his hands. It had been a long day already, and it was only one o'clock in the afternoon.

Jim Durard looked down at the papers and began to fill them out.

Dropping his pen on his desk, he pushed it away and leaned back in his padded leather chair. This wasn't what he thought it would be when he accepted the promotion. Durard loosened his tie and unbuttoned the top button of his shirt.

Turning around in his chair, Durard rubbed his hands through his blonde hair, then clasped them behind his head. He stared out of his twentieth story window over San Francisco. He had held this new position of Assistant Regional Director of the Pacific Area for the Federal Emergency Management Agency for over a year now. Durard had been promoted shortly after he had helped eradicate "The Yellow Death" in the Southwestern United States. His superiors at the time felt that because of his performance during the 'TYD plague', he would make an exceptional director. Staring out at the skyscrapers and buildings of San

Francisco, Durard began to question that decision.

A knock on his office door startled him. "Yes?"

A small brunette poked her head into Durard's office. "A.D. Durard, your one o'clock appointment is here," she smiled softly.

Durard spun around in his chair and began to straighten his tie. "Thanks, Clarice, send them in."

Clarice nodded and opened the door wide. "Assistant Director Durard will see you now," she said into the waiting room.

Durard watched a man enter the room. "Good afternoon."

Durard stood and shook the man's outstretched hand.

"My name is Jeff Tulley and I'm with *The High Desert Reporter*, a newspaper based out of Reno, Nevada." Tulley was a man of average height, and looked to be just slightly overweight. He had a full head of thick, brown hair and a neatly trimmed brown goatee. Tulley was wearing a faded pair of blue jeans with a white polo shirt and black sport coat.

"What can I do for you, Mr. Tulley?" Durard asked as he returned to his seat.

"We're running an investigative series on 'The Yellow Death', and the people involved with it," Tulley said while sitting down in a chair in front of Durard's desk. "I would like to do an interview with you, Mr. Durard."

"My official statement and reports are available through the records department," Durard said with a sigh. "I have no wish to comment beyond that."

Tulley snapped open the brown briefcase he had with him. Grabbing a handful of papers, he

21

placed them in front of Durard. "I've already requested your statement, and your reports," Tulley pointed to the papers. "As you can see, they don't explain a whole lot."

"What?" Durard knew his statement and field reports were extremely thorough. He began to leaf through the packet of papers and was shocked to find that sections of them had been blacked out, while entire pages had been deleted. "I don't understand. Why would these files need to be censored?"

"That's what I was hoping you could tell me," Tulley admitted.

Chapter Four

Jake awoke in the same position he had fallen asleep in. Lifting himself off the couch in his living room, Jake tried to rub the sleep out of his eyes. He slowly began to peel off his leather jacket as he stumbled toward the bathroom. Stopping in the hallway, he leaned up against the wall and pressed his hands to the sides of his head. He had a throbbing hangover from the night before. Straightening up, he kicked off his boots and dropped his jacket in a heap on the floor.

Summoning the will to move again, Jake carefully traversed the hall toward the bathroom. *Why does the bathroom have to be the last door at the end of the hall?* Stepping through the doorway, Jake stopped in front of his bathroom mirror. Placing his hands on the cold porcelain sink counter, he stared motionless at the man in the mirror. A three day beard was growing on his face, and dark bags hung under his eyes. Turning on the tap, he cupped his hands under the cold running water and splashed it on his face.

Grabbing a towel off the rack next to him, he pressed it against his face. The soft linen felt very good. Dropping the towel next to the sink, Jake dunked his head under the running water. He let the cool water run through his dark hair. Reaching over, he again grabbed his towel and wrapped it around his head. Rubbing hard, he dried off his hair. Tossing the towel on the floor, he pulled off his t-shirt and deposited it in a small wooden hamper in the corner.

Turning away from the mirror, he looked across

the hallway at his bedroom. His bed looked very inviting. Jake decided he needed some more rest. He staggered across the hallway into his bedroom and sat down on the edge of his bed. He looked around his room. The walls and carpet were bare white. A lone window hung on the far wall allowing a sprinkling of morning light throughout the room. A large, wooden dresser stood next to the window and just across from the closet. His queen-sized bed sat alone in the middle of the floor, only accompanied by a single wooden nightstand on one side of the bed.

Lying back, Jake turned his head to look at the clock. It read eight forty- seven. He knew he had to be at a stakeout that night, so he might as well sleep in. He didn't want to botch the first case he'd had in over six months. Jake unzipped his jeans and pulled them off. Tossing them on the floor, he slipped into his bed and pulled up the covers.

Rolling onto his left side, Jake stared listlessly at the alarm clock next to the bed. Next to it, he noticed a small white envelope and suddenly remembered why he had gotten drunk last night. Lifting the envelope, he stared at the return address in the upper left-hand corner: Cairo, Egypt. *Alex.*

Jake's first instinct was to rip open the letter and read every word, but he quickly had a change of heart. Four years ago, she'd left him lying alone in the hospital with a bullet wound in his chest. She left him. He still hadn't forgiven her for that, nor did he intend to. Jake had lost so much to help Alex, and she'd done nothing in return.

Jake knew that wasn't the real reason he was angry with her. Over the course of a year spent running from the government, he and Alex had grown very attached to each other, or at least he thought so. When Alex walked out of that hospital room four years ago, it became very clear to him that she had other priorities. Jake knew from the instant Alex wrapped her arms around Jason Griggs on that rooftop in Las Vegas that she was gone. Alex loved Griggs. That was it, yet Jake couldn't get past it. He hated to admit it, but he loved Alex, too.

Tearing open the envelope, Jake pulled out several folded pieces of paper. Unfolding them, he instantly recognized Alex's sloppy handwriting. He started at the top and slowly made his way through it.

"Jake, I was just wondering how you were," she started.

Griggs and I have been in Egypt for the past three and a half years. We've signed on with a dig on the Giza Plateau that's very exciting. We're unearthing some kind of burial chamber in the Valley of the Kings. Jason and I are having a wonderful time. We try and spend as much time as we can in Cairo. It's a beautiful city with a rich culture. I think you would like it here. You know what the most wonderful thing is? The elegant mixture of the old world and new as the edge of Cairo has spread all the way to the foot of the great pyramid. It's a rather interesting sight. I hope you're doing all right, and I hope to talk to you very soon.

Love, Alex

Jake refolded the letter and set it on his nightstand. Folding his arms behind his head, he stared at the ceiling. He missed Alex terribly.

***

A brisk wind was whipping across the Valley of the Kings in Egypt, kicking up sand. It was making it very difficult for the team to see. The three large pyramids on the Giza Plateau behind them were barely visible. Several members of the team had already tied their handkerchiefs around their mouths and fastened their sunglasses tightly to their eyes. The team leader signaled for the group to move down into the first chamber.

Dr. Alex Robinson was near the rear of the group. Jason Griggs had his arms wrapped around her and was leading her toward the entrance to the first chamber. The team had been excavating this location for almost four years now. It had been a very interesting find, especially since it was in the Valley of the Kings. Most archaeologists speculated that no more tombs remained to be opened. The entrance was dug down at least ten feet in the desert sands. A set of makeshift wooden stairs had been laid to help the team move in and out of the tomb more easily. Griggs was holding Alex's hand as he began to lead her down the stairs. "We're almost there," Griggs soothed.

"I still can't see," Alex whimpered. "I've got sand in my eyes."

"Hold on." Griggs guided Alex carefully over the final few steps and finally, into the chamber. "We're in."

Pulling off her sunglasses, tears were streaming from Alex's eyes.

"Damn," she said as she tried to rub the sand

26

out of her eyes.

Griggs pulled her hands away from her eyes. "Don't rub them." Griggs looked around the room and over the team standing inside. He spotted a nearby man with a bottle of water. Reaching over, he snatched the bottle and pulled off the cap.

"Hey! That was mine!" the man argued.

"Sorry," Griggs said as he began to lift the bottle toward Alex's face. "Tilt your head back and open your eyes."

"I can't," Alex cried.

"Okay, then just hold still." Griggs gently opened her right eye with his fingers and held it open. Tipping the bottle forward, he began to rinse the sand out of her eyes. Repeating the process with her left eye, he sat Alex down on a chest that was behind them. "How does that feel?"

Alex was holding her hands over her eyes. "Better, but my eyes still hurt."

"It'll pass, just keep them closed for a minute." Griggs stood and handed the empty water bottle back to the man. "Thanks," Griggs smiled. "Sure," the man said angrily. "Anytime."

Sitting down next to Alex, Griggs looked around the chamber. This was actually the first time he had been down here. It was a large room, with pillars supporting the roof about every fifteen feet. Each square pillar was elaborately decorated with hieroglyphs and pictures of various gods. Alex had taught him these kinds of chambers were usually the burial sites for a pharaoh's queen and her family, or for his high priests. They weren't sure which was the case with this one yet. No mummies or treasures had been found.

Griggs turned his attention back to Alex and started to rub her back. She was wearing a pair of khaki pants with a white shirt and a pair of tan hiking boots. She had decided to straighten her long brown hair last week, and Griggs still wasn't sure if he liked it yet or not. He had always seen her with it done in curls or slightly wavy. Griggs, on the other hand, was wearing a pair of blue jeans, a green t-shirt and his black combat boots. "Are you okay?"

Alex got up and slowly opened her eyes. "Yeah, I'll live," she said while rapidly blinking her eyes.

"Can I have your attention please?" a voice with a British accent asked from the middle of the room. Griggs looked up to see their team leader, Professor Byron Scott, trying to get the attention of the group. "Hello?" he said, waving his arms. Scott was an older man with bright blue eyes, a gray mustache and short gray hair. He was wearing an outfit that was more akin to the 1930's than today. Tan jacket, tan trousers and knee-high brown boots. Griggs smiled every time he looked at Scott.

The team quickly turned and fell silent.

"Thank you," Scott said. "It's seems we've encountered a bit of bad luck with this sandstorm. Bloody thing just seemed to come out of nowhere, but we're not going to let that slow us down. While we have some time down here in the first chamber, why don't we go about translating some of the text on the pillars?" Each member of the team pulled a small notebook out of his or her pockets. "That's right. Everyone pick a pillar. There's plenty to go around." Scott turned and spotted Alex and Griggs sitting on the trunk near the entrance. "Are you all

28

right there?" he asked while walking over.

Alex looked up through blurry eyes. "Yeah, I'm okay, Professor Scott. I just got a lot of sand in my eyes."

"Good," Scott sounded relieved. "When you get the chance, why don't you two start working on the pillars with the rest of the team? No rush," he added as he walked away.

Chapter Five

She stared at her lover's face, tears streaming from her eyes. She couldn't believe he had done this to her. She had thrown her marriage away because of him.

"Why are you doing this to me, Bruce?" Jennah asked while holding the covers tightly over her naked body.

Bruce turned away from Jennah. "Look, I never meant to lead you on." He pulled on his shirt.

"The hell you didn't!" Jennah leaned over and grabbed a blue silk robe off the floor. Pulling it on, she stood up. "Tom and I had eight wonderful years of marriage together before you showed up! I left him for you!"

"I didn't make you do anything," Bruce nonchalantly said while standing. "Why didn't you tell me that you were married?" Jennah cried as she took a step closer. "Why?"

Bruce turned to face Jennah. "I'm sorry. I honestly never meant for any of this to happen. I," Bruce stopped when he felt a lump begin to well up in his throat, "I just wanted to see you again."

Jennah's anger subsided as she stared into Bruce's sad brown eyes. Lifting her hand, she carefully caressed his face. Ten years ago, they were in love, but then it all fell apart. Back then, Jennah couldn't see herself with anyone other than Bruce, but now, things were different. Jennah's gaze hardened as she slapped him hard across the face. "You selfish bastard." Jennah spun around and walked out the door.

Bruce stood alone in the room. Dropping down

30

to his knees, he held his face in his hands. Looking up, he stared into the heavens. "I still love you, Jennah."

Applause erupted from the crowd as the curtain was lowered on the stage. The house lights slowly came up in the theater. The applause grew louder while shouts of "encore" echoed above the cheers. A bright spot hit the red velvet curtain as it slowly began to pull open, revealing the assembled cast.

A man in a black suit stepped to the front of the stage. He lifted the microphone to his mouth. "Thank you," he said to the cheering audience. "My name is Walter Fredrickson, and I wrote and directed this play." The crowd applauded again. "I want to introduce the cast of 'The Road Not Forgotten'," he turned to look at his crew. "The best damned cast a director could ask for." The director introduced his cast one by one as he led them up to the star. "Ladies and gentleman, it's my pleasure to introduce this next woman. This was her first time on stage, and I think she handled it like an old pro. Playing the part of 'Jennah', it's my pleasure to introduce," he paused for dramatic effect, "Samantha Silver!" The crowd stood to their feet while they cheered wildly.

Samantha pushed her long brown hair behind her ears and stepped forward. For the first time all night, she looked at the crowd and smiled. She had made it. Letting out a sigh of relief, Samantha took a bow, then turned to re-join the cast. Standing next to each other, the entire cast bowed as the curtain closed for a second time.

Backstage was filled with smiles and hugs. The entire cast and crew was celebrating a spectacular

31

opening night. Bottles of champagne were being handed out. The director pulled a folding chair into the middle of the group and stepped up on it.

"I want to say thanks," the director said, holding the green champagne bottle above his head. "You have all allowed me to see my dream come to fruition. Thank you." He took a drink from the bottle. "I want to thank one more person." He scanned the crew for Samantha. Spotting her, he smiled. "To Samantha Silver, the talented young woman who poured her heart into the part of 'Jennah'. I see a bright future ahead of you."

Samantha's green eyes sparkled as she smiled. "Thank you, but I couldn't have done it without the rest of the cast and crew." She raised the bottle, then took a drink of her champagne.

A young woman with a headset and a clipboard tapped Samantha on the shoulder. "Ms. Silver?"

Samantha spun around to see the woman. "Yes?"

"You have a phone call," the woman reported.

"Thank you," Samantha replied. Turning back to the group, she quickly said her 'goodnights' and then retreated to her dressing room. Passing through the door, she seated herself at a small chair in front of a large lighted mirror. To her left on the vanity sat a small, black phone. "Hello?" she said in a soft and sweet voice.

"How's my little girl?" a woman's voice asked.

"Hi, Mom," Samantha said with a smile. "I'm fine."

"I'm sorry I missed opening night, Sam, but I have a major client I have to give a presentation to in the morning, and I just wanted my team to be ready." Lindsay Chase, Jake's ex-wife, was a busy ad executive for a prestigious New York advertising firm.

Samantha sighed. "It's all right. Did John make it?"

"I don't know why you just don't call him 'Dad'?"

"Because he's not my dad, he's my stepfather."

"I don't want to get into this with you again," Lindsay said with exasperation in her voice. "I'm afraid John didn't make it either."

"Well, that's a shock," Samantha said spitefully. "What was his excuse this time?"

"He didn't have an excuse," Lindsay answered sternly. "He just had to work late."

"It just boggles my mind," Samantha admitted. "Whenever there's something important happening in my life, you two are never around. The only person who ever took any interest in me was Dad, and he lives halfway across the country in Nevada!"

"You know that's not true, Samantha. John and I have been very good to you," Lindsay argued. "I've been the best mother that I could be since your father left." Her tone was beginning to turn harsh.

"What do you mean 'when Dad left'?" Samantha shot back. "If I remember correctly, it was you having an affair, and it was you that left Dad."

"I don't have to take this garbage from you," Lindsay said angrily. "I just wanted to call and congratulate you on your first performance."

Samantha sighed again. "You're right, I'm sorry. It just hurt my feelings a little when you weren't here."

"I know, and I'm sorry, Sam."

"Thanks for calling, Mom."

"Anytime," Lindsay replied. "Before I go, I was wondering if you wanted to come over for dinner this week?"

"Yeah," Samantha said with a smile. "I'd like that."

"Okay. I better let you go. You probably have a cast party to go to. I love you, sweetie, and I'll talk to you later."

"I love you too, Mom. Bye." Samantha hung up the phone and leaned back in her chair. She stared at herself in the mirror, at her long, straight brown hair, her green eyes, her well defined cheekbones and her full lips. She knew she was a very good-looking girl. Samantha smiled. She was twenty-four years old, a talented actress in her first starring role, and for the first time in her life, happy.

Samantha heard a knock on her door. "Yes?"

"Sam?" Her co-star peeked in her door. "What's up, Craig?" Samantha asked.

Craig Jeter, the actor who played 'Bruce', was a tall muscular man with short dark hair and dark eyes. Samantha could see some of his Italian heritage in his face. "A bunch of the cast and crew are going out to celebrate. You want to go?"

"I don't know," Samantha said, turning back to the mirror. "I really need to get home and get some rest."

"Come on, this was our opening night, and your first performance ever," Craig argued. "Everyone wants you there."

Samantha thought for a moment, then smiled. "Yeah, I guess I'll go."

"Great," Craig responded. "I'll go tell the others. We'll meet you in front of the theater in a few minutes."

Looking in the mirror one final time, Samantha laughed quietly to herself. *I could really get used to being the star.*

***

Night had fallen over Reno, Nevada. Jake had been sitting in his blue, late model sedan for longer than he cared to think about. Hamburger wrappers and old newspapers littered the floors and seats. He was parked on a quiet rural street. Midlevel apartment buildings sat silently around him, only a few random lights were scattered about.

Jake lifted his small black digital camcorder off his lap and set it on the dashboard in front of him. He rubbed the stubble on his rough face, then leaned his head back. He was here on a stakeout. About a week ago, a woman had come into his detective agency with a problem: she thought her husband of fifteen years was cheating on her. The woman wanted Jake to tail her husband and take photos of him in the act. Jake didn't usually take cases of this nature. He felt this was dirty work, meddling in other people's lives, but he had been without work for a long time and the bills were beginning to pile up.

Jake glanced down at the clock in his dashboard. It was closing in on two in the morning, and there was still no sign of his subject. Rubbing his weary eyes, Jake reached over to the glove compartment and removed a silver flask.

35

Unscrewing the top, he pressed it to his lips and took a long drink of the alcohol inside. It burned as it rolled down his throat. Wiping the excess off his mouth onto the sleeve of his black t-shirt, Jake closed his eyes for a moment. He couldn't remember the last time he had a decent night's sleep that wasn't alcohol induced. Taking another drink from the flask, Jake reached down and pulled the recline lever on his seat.

Staring out the driver's side window, he watched a man and a woman slowly walking along the sidewalk in front of him. Neither of them was his target, but he couldn't take his eyes off them. They were apparently in love. The man and woman were both Caucasian and probably in their late twenties. They were smiling and talking while they strode along. It was a cold spring night, but that didn't seem to be bothering them. Jake remembered the sensation of being in love for the first time. No matter what he was doing, or where he was, he felt as if he had all the time in the world, and nothing else mattered. Jake envied them. He envied them, because they had normal lives. Something he hadn't had for the past six years. He watched them holding hands as they rounded a corner and moved out of sight.

Smiling for the first time in a long time, Jake slowly lay back in his seat and closed his eyes again. Every time he did so, he only saw one face: Alex's.

He needed her. Trying to shake her from his mind, Jake slowly let himself drift off to sleep.

Chapter Six

Alex carefully pulled a wide paintbrush across a line of hieroglyphs, removing the sand and dust. Leaning close, she blew the last bit of residue out of the carved relief. Alex took a step back and began to decipher the markings.

"And Isis and Osiris returned to the sky, taking with them the knowledge they brought with them," she read out loud.

"What did you say?" Griggs poked his head out from behind a separate pillar.

Alex pulled away from the hieroglyphs to look at Griggs. "I was just reading this," she said, pointing at the pillar.

Griggs walked over and stood beside her. "What does it say?"

"It's very strange," Alex admitted. "Usually all references to the god Osiris have him returning to the underworld, where he rules, but in this passage, it says he returned to the sky."

"Are you sure you're reading that correctly?"

Alex nodded. "Yeah." Alex stepped closer to the pillar and wiped off a second line with her brush. "Look here," she pointed to a group of symbols. "I think these are supposed to represent stars," Alex said while looking at several asterisk shaped glyphs, "but this...." her voice trailed off. She ran her fingers slowly over the carving. "I've never seen this symbol before."

Griggs stared intently. "It looks really familiar," he admitted finally. The disc shaped symbol had one thick outer ring, with two smaller rings inside. It appeared to be hovering over a small group of people emitting a beam from the bottom. "You're going to think I'm insane," Griggs laughed, "but I really think that looks like a UFO."

Alex looked at the symbol for a moment. "You know, it does look a little like a UFO."

"What have we found?" Scott asked from out of nowhere.

Alex was startled. She didn't hear him approaching. "I'm really not sure, but I've found some strange hieroglyphs."

"What do you mean?" Scott asked.

"Well, look at this line of text," she pointed to the top line she had cleared. "That is very strange," Scott said. "May I borrow your brush for a moment?"

"Sure." Alex handed her brush to Scott.

Leaning closer, Scott carefully cleaned off the next few lines of glyphs. "This is strange," Scott admitted. "I really think this is a prophecy."

"What do you mean?" Griggs asked.

Scott pointed to the line below the UFO symbol. "Well, roughly translated, it says that Osiris will return."

"What does that mean?" Alex wondered.

"I don't know, but in the next few lines, the prophecy worsens." Scott ran his fingers over the next row of hieroglyphics. "It says that when Osiris returns, if he is not happy with the state of the world, all humanity will be brought to their knees." Scott stopped for a moment before continuing. Disbelief swept over him as he began to translate the remaining hieroglyphs. "The skies will burn and the seas will boil, and mighty floods will swallow every trace of civilization."

Alex gasped. "The apocalypse."

"This is talking about the end of the world?" Griggs asked. "Apparently," Scott speculated. "Osiris was the Egyptian god of the underworld. That's their equivalent of our heaven. In most ancient texts, Osiris is thought of as a benevolent god, not a vengeful one." Scott rubbed his beard while he thought.

"So why would he coming back to pass judgment on us?" Alex wondered. "I have no idea," Scott admitted. "This is probably just another of the Egyptian's many stories to scare off grave robbers."

"Perhaps," Alex said, "but perhaps not." She caught sight of another interesting hieroglyph. "What the hell is that?"

"It looks like a face," Griggs knelt down to get a closer look.

"Right, but it's not Egyptian in style. It's too," Scott searched for the word, "blocky."

Alex suddenly realized what the symbol represented. "I know what this is. It's one of the giant heads on Rapa Nui," Alex said excitedly. "It's one of the Moai."

"What?" Griggs asked.

Alex stood up. "On Rapa Nui, *er,* Easter Island, there are dozens of these giant stone monoliths scattered around the island shaped like heads. They're known as 'Moai'. This hieroglyph looks exactly like one of them."

"That can't be," Scott argued. "There was no civilization on Rapa Nui at the time this tomb was constructed. This tomb dates back almost five thousand years, and the earliest Moai found was only around thirteen hundred years old."

"So how is this here?" Griggs asked while staring at the symbol.

"From what the text says," Alex quickly translated, "it looks like Rapa Nui was one of the many places Osiris visited." Alex smiled. "It says that he also left a repository of his knowledge there."

"This is highly unlikely," Scott argued. "There is no proof that the ancient Egyptians ever visited Rapa Nui, let alone left some kind of temple or tomb there."

Alex was quiet as she carefully considered the text, and the strange hieroglyphs. "It all adds up."

"What?" Griggs asked.

"All the clues are there," Alex said excitedly. "It said Osiris returned to the sky, we found a picture of what appears to be a UFO, and there's proof that he visited other places."

"I'm afraid I'm not following you," Scott admitted.

Alex smiled. "They weren't referring to Osiris, but rather an alien race that influenced the Egyptian Culture."

Scott scoffed. "I've been hearing this alien rubbish my whole life," he said disdainfully, "but I have yet to see any compelling proof that aliens have been visiting us, let alone influencing our culture."

Griggs began to open his mouth and retort, when Alex stopped him. "You're probably right, Dr. Scott. Now, if you don't mind, I think Jason and I are going to take a break."

"Sure," Scott smiled. Turning around, he walked away.

Griggs was puzzled. "I don't understand why you caved like that. We know aliens exist."

"I know," Alex reassured him, "but it's just easier to agree than to try and convince anyone otherwise." Alex wrapped her arm around Griggs' waist and began to move away from the rest of the group. "This is the moment I've been waiting for."

"What do you want to do?" Griggs asked.

"I think it's obvious," Alex smiled. "We need to go to Rapa Nui. We will find the answer to this puzzle there."

Neither Alex nor Griggs saw the solitary man standing in the corner listening to their conversation. Trying not to draw attention to himself, he carefully moved further into the tomb. Once he was out of sight, he pulled a small black satellite phone out of his pocket. Quickly dialing a number, he waited for an answer. He heard a click on the other end of the line, but no answer. He knew this was his signal. "Easter Island," he said with a thick Middle Eastern accent, then hung up. Dropping the phone on the stone floor, he smashed it with his booted foot. The man reached into his pocket and pulled out a small medicine bottle. Twisting off the cap, the man dropped a small yellow pill into his hand. Taking one final look around, the man popped the pill into his mouth and swallowed. The poison quickly went to work. A moment later, the man lay dead on the floor.

***

Durard tossed a handful of papers on the floor in anger. He was extremely frustrated. After what seemed like hours of digging through his field reports, he had found more omissions and blackened passages than in any congressional expense report.

It was late. Durard turned and stared out the small window in the rear of the records room. The lights of San Francisco were shining brightly, even though it was close to three in the morning. Slipping his fingers around his tie, he slowly loosened it and undid the top button on his shirt. He dabbed the beads of sweat on his forehead with the sleeve of his white dress shirt. It was extremely hot in this small room that consisted of four sets of black filing cabinets against the walls, a lone copy machine and a phone sitting beneath the window. Durard began to wonder if they turned off the air conditioning in the building at night to try and cut costs.

Turning back to the cabinets, Durard opened the second drawer. He let his fingers leaf over the brown file folders before coming to his target. Using his left hand, he spread the folder open and removed the papers inside. He laid them flat on top of the outstretched drawer and began to flip through them. This was his main report he filed three years ago on "The Yellow Death", or "TYD" as it had come to be known. Thick black lines cut through every page of his report, omitting key lines and even entire paragraphs. Even his name had been removed from the top of the file.

Durard slapped the file shut in frustration and slammed the drawer closed. "Why would they censor my reports?" he wondered. "Reports of TYD were all over the media for years after the initial incident four years ago. I didn't think any of this was sensitive material."

Squatting down on the floor, Durard began to scoop up the pages he had thrown there. Standing up, he haphazardly arranged the small stack into a pile on top of the filing cabinet. Durard reached behind him and grabbed his jacket off the copy machine. He turned and began to walk toward the door, but was startled when the door was thrown open.

"What are you doing here?"

"I...." Durard was stunned for a moment. "Sir, I didn't know you were still here."

Mark Jameson nodded. "I had a few projects I had to put the finishing touches on." Jameson was the Regional Director of the Pacific Area for FEMA, and Durard's direct superior. Jameson was an older man, with short brown hair that had begun to gray at the temples. He was always clean-shaven and had piercing gray eyes. He was dressed in his usual attire of a suit and tie. Jameson looked around the small room and smiled. "May I ask why you've decided to let loose hurricane Durard in the records room?"

"Sir, I," Durard stopped for a moment. For his entire duration as Assistant Regional Director here, Durard had always had a very good working relationship with Jameson. He didn't want to lose that now, but he needed answers. "I need to know why my field reports on TYD have been censored."

The smile quickly faded from Jameson's face. "I'm afraid I can't answer that question, Mr. Durard."

"Why?" Durard pressed.

Jameson shook his head. "Jim, you and I have

43

always gotten along pretty well, right?"

Durard nodded.

"You know I wouldn't lie to you, right?" Durard nodded again.

Jameson took a deep breath and slowly exhaled it. "I can't tell you why your reports were edited."

"What do you mean you can't tell me? Do you mean that you don't know, or you just can't tell me?" Durard asked, growing more frustrated by the minute.

Jameson smiled again. "Let's just leave it at that, shall we?"

Durard shook his head. "That's not acceptable. I need to know why my reports were edited. I thought our work on The Yellow Death was public domain. After all, we were the ones who found the cure to the plague, and it was us who administered that cure. I didn't think it was FEMA's policy to hide the truth from the public."

Jameson was starting to lose his patience. "I suggest you lower your tone and drop this, Mr. Durard." The old man looked Durard in the eyes. "Some things are just meant to stay secrets," he whispered. "Look, I'll level with you. This office wasn't responsible for editing your reports."

Durard was stunned. "I don't understand."

Jameson smiled again and patted Durard on the shoulder. "I can't say anymore." He checked his watch. "It's three thirty in the morning, and you have to be back here to work at eight. You better get home and get some rest. At least go home and get cleaned up."

Durard wasn't satisfied with the answers he had been presented with, but he knew Jameson was right. "All right." Pulling his jacket on, he walked past Jameson and through the door. "I'll see you in the morning, Mr. Jameson."

Jameson nodded. "All right." Durard turned to leave. Jameson watched him move down the hallway and stop in front of the elevator. The elevator doors dinged as they slid open. Jameson waited until the doors slid shut before turning around. Stepping back into the records room, Jameson snatched the phone off the wall. Punching in a quick number, he heard the other phone begin to ring.

"Yes?"

"Durard is beginning to question," Jameson reported grimly.

"That's very unfortunate," a female voice answered. "He must be dealt with."

Chapter Seven

Craig already had too much to drink. He was stumbling around the small pub with a pink feather boa wrapped around his neck and singing, "Turn, turn, turn", by the Byrds. The large group of cast and crewmembers that started the night had dwindled down to less than ten people. They had broken off into several smaller groups and had separated into different corners of the bar.

The pub was a large, brick building with windows lining the front wall. The room they were in was split away from the rest of the establishment by a small divider. The bar was decorated with the team logos of the local sports teams. On the far side there was a big screen TV that had been playing sports all night, but was now playing the local morning news. A few patrons, besides the cast and crew, were peppered throughout the dimly lit establishment.

Samantha was sitting in the corner slowly sipping her glass of merlot. She had changed into a long black skirt, white blouse and white jacket. She glanced down at her watch. It was just past five thirty in the morning in New York. The night was slowly fading as the sun was beginning to rise. They had arrived here just before midnight. She didn't know why she had stayed so long. She knew she had a long day ahead of her, plus a performance that night.

Craig caught sight of her and began to make his way over to her. Pulling the boa off his neck, he wrapped it around Samantha's shoulders. "Are you having a good time?" he asked.

Samantha could smell the alcohol on Craig's breath. "Yeah," she replied sarcastically, "I'm having a great time."

Craig crumpled down into the seat next to her. "What's wrong?"

"I was just thinking about my mom," Samantha confessed. "Why?"

"She's always got an excuse."

Craig looked confused. The alcohol was slowing down his mental capacities. "An excuse for what?"

"For not showing up." Samantha took a sip of her wine and held the glass in her hand. She slowly swirled the alcohol around, admiring this vintage's legs. "She didn't come to our opening night."

"I'm sorry," Craig tried to comfort her.

Samantha shrugged. "It's no big deal. This wasn't the first time she's done it, and probably won't be the last."

"Well, what's her problem?" Craig asked angrily.

Samantha knew he was drunk off his ass. Craig was generally a really egocentric person, only caring about himself and his problems. For him to be bothering with someone else's plight was a rare occurrence. "I just don't think my mom was really cut out to raise kids. She's just never been very good at it."

"Well, what about your dad?"

Samantha took another sip of her wine. "I haven't seen him in years."

"Why not?" Craig asked in a caring voice.

"Well, he and my mom divorced when I was only eight years old," Samantha confessed. "For a

47

while, my mom and I stayed in New Orleans where my dad lived, so I had the chance to see him at least once a week, but then my mom was offered a good job in Baltimore, so we moved. I saw my dad one more time after that when he helped us move. Shortly after that, my dad quit the FBI and moved to Nevada. I haven't seen him since."

"So he wasn't the greatest father either, huh?" Craig speculated.

"No, that's not it at all," Samantha corrected. "I really like my dad. I just don't get the chance to talk to him all that often. I don't think we've spoken on the phone for probably six years now."

"Oh," Craig replied solemnly. "I'm sorry. I just assumed—"

"Don't worry about it." Samantha patted him on the back. "I would probably think the same thing if someone else had just told me that story."

There was a long, uncomfortable silence between the two. They had known each other for about six weeks now, after meeting on the opening day of auditions, but this was the most personal conversation they'd ever had.

A smile suddenly crossed Craig's face. "You smell really good." Samantha stood up in disgust. "We were having a really nice conversation, and then you decided to hit on me. What's wrong with you?" Craig leaned back in his chair and shrugged. "Beats me."

"I'm going home now," Samantha declared. "Want some company?"

Samantha just glared at Craig. By the look on his face, he was already deep into fantasizing about her. "Good night, Craig," she said as she stood up.

Grabbing her purse off the chair next to her, she headed for the door.

A rush of cold air washed over her as she stepped through the front doors. It was a brisk morning in the Big Apple. She stood quietly for a moment outside the bar. The streets were already jammed with cars, and the sidewalks were quickly filling up.

Her apartment was only a few blocks from here, but she didn't feel like walking. Stepping to the curb, she raised her hand and tried to hail a cab. She spotted a yellow taxicab amidst the sea of traffic and tried to flag it down. The taxi went right by her, unable to get to the curb.

Samantha quickly spotted another cab. She raised her hand high in the air again, and this time, the driver noticed her. She waited patiently for the taxi to weave through traffic toward her. Before the taxi could reach her, a long black sedan screeched to a halt in front of her. Samantha quickly took a step back from the car, startled. To her dismay, the front doors shot open and two large men dressed in black suits stepped out. Samantha turned and began to hurriedly walk away. Before she could get far, the two men were upon her. Samantha screamed at the top of her lungs as the two men began to drag her toward their car. Tears began to stream from her eyes.

Fighting against the two men, Samantha tried to break free of their grasp, but they held tightly. Before she could scream again, the two men had pushed her into the back seat of the car and slammed the door closed. Samantha frantically searched for a door handle, but couldn't find one.

There wasn't even a seat in the back, just an empty space between the front seats and the trunk. A thick grate separated the front and the back of the vehicle. Samantha reared back and kicked the grate as hard as she could. The two men quickly piled back into the black sedan and sent the car careening away from the curb.

Craig suddenly emerged from the bar with a female member of the crew on his arm. He spotted the black sedan and Samantha screaming in the back. "Hey!" he yelled at the top of his lungs, but he was too late. The car was quickly pulling out of sight. Craig charged along the sidewalk trying to keep pace with the car, but was quickly falling behind. He tried to catch a glimpse of the men in front seats, but he couldn't tell very much. He glanced down to try and get a license plate number, only to find the car was without plates. He was drunk and exhausted. Slowing to a halt, Craig fell to his knees and tried to catch his breath. He watched the red taillights of the car speed around a corner in horror. "They took Samantha!"

"Why are you doing this to me?" Samantha screamed.

Neither of the men answered. They both just stared forward at the traffic ahead of them.

"Let me go!" Samantha screamed again. Lifting her feet, she kicked hard against the passenger's side window. The glass shattered, sending shards in all directions. Sitting up, she quickly tried to push herself out the window. She suddenly felt a sharp pain in the back of her neck. Reaching back, she ran her fingers over a small dart embedded there. "What the…?" She quickly realized she had been injected with a tranquilizer. Struggling to stay conscious, she groped at the door as she tried to pull herself out. She felt her body start to become heavy as the drug kicked in. Falling back into the car, she stared helplessly at the two men in the front seat. "Why are...?" She hadn't even finished her sentence when she passed out.

***

"Colonel, we've just heard from our field operatives in New York. We have Samantha Silver."

"Good. Any reports from our spies in Egypt?" the colonel asked.

"Yes, sir. Our man in Cairo reports that Dr. Robinson and Mr. Griggs are leaving Egypt and heading toward Easter Island."

"Why Easter Island?"

"We're not entirely sure, sir. Following orders, our spy reported in, then terminated himself. The general doesn't want to leave any loose ends this time."

"Very good, Captain. It looks like the general's plan is going off without a hitch. Dismissed." The colonel watched his junior officer salute, then exit his office. Laying his hands on his desk, the colonel thought for a moment. *It's been a long time coming,* he thought. *Finally, we'll end this.*

***

Jake leaned over onto his desk and rested his face in his hands. "Look, I'm really sorry. I don't have an excuse."

"No you don't!" Jamie Land screamed. Jamie was a tall redheaded woman with well-defined features. Her hair was pulled back from her face, allowing her angry green eyes to sparkle. She was dressed entirely in black, from her skirt to her blouse. "I followed my husband and that little floozy to her apartment, and what do I find when I get there? You fast asleep in the driver's seat of your car. You obviously didn't get the photos I wanted!"

Jake looked up at the woman. "Pease, Mrs. Land, if you'll sit down, I can explain."

Jamie lashed out, knocking the small metal chair in front of Jake's desk onto the floor. "I paid you a great deal of money to get photos of my husband being adulterous. I needed those photos for my divorce. I was going to take everything that bastard has, but now, I can't! I owe all the thanks to you, Mr.

Silver."

"Mrs. Land, would you please sit down?" Jake asked.

Jamie looked at the second chair in front of Jake's desk for a moment. In a huff, she plopped down into the chair and stared angrily at Jake. "I'm listening. Hit me with this great explanation."

Jake started. "I haven't been sleeping well lately—"

"Are you kidding me?" Jamie screamed. "I'm going to get shafted during my divorce, and you claim to be having sleeping problems?" Jaime stood and glared at Jake. "You assured me that you were very professional when you took this case. I see

52

now that you were lying." Jamie turned to leave. "I expect a full refund of my deposit, Mr. Silver, otherwise, expect a call from my lawyers." With that, she stepped out of Jake's office and slammed the door.

Jake exhaled a deep breath and leaned back in his weathered brown leather chair. After rubbing his eyes, he glanced around his office. It had wood floors and fake wood paneling on the walls. His desk stood in the middle of the room, and behind him was the only window. Through it, Jake had a great view of Lake Tahoe. Papers were beginning to pile up in the corners, and on his desk. He had months of backlogged files waiting to be completed. Even a few from before the Anderson Case six years ago. Grabbing a handful from his desk, Jake tossed them angrily on the floor.

Standing up, Jake moved briskly toward his office door. He didn't care what time it was, he just wanted to go home. He was angry with himself for botching the case. Even a first year rookie could've snapped off a few photos without falling asleep. Jake began to reach for the door handle when he heard his phone ring.

Walking back to his desk, he spun the white phone around to face him. He pressed the 'line one' button and lifted the receiver to his ear. He didn't know why he had multiple lines on his phone. He never received more than one call at a time. "Hello?"

"Jake?"

Jake was startled to hear the voice on the other end of the phone. "Alex?"

"Yeah, hi," Alex said softly.

Jake smiled. This was the first time in four years he heard Alex's voice. "How have you been?"

"Been doing good," Alex admitted. She paused for a moment. "How are you?"

"I've been doing good," Jake replied cheerfully. "The business has been going well. I haven't even had any time to sleep, I've been so busy."

"That's great! I'm really glad to hear that," Alex replied. "Hey, listen, I've got a bit of a proposition for you."

"Well, I haven't been propositioned by a woman in a while," Jake laughed. "I've missed your sense of humor, Jake."

The statement caught Jake off-guard. He didn't know how to respond. "Thanks."

"Have you received my letter yet?" Alex asked. "Yeah, I read it yesterday morning."

"Well, like I said in the letter, Jason and I have been working on this dig in Egypt for almost four years now, and we just finally gained access to the main chamber of the tomb," Alex admitted proudly. "Once in there, we found the most interesting prophecy inscribed in hieroglyphs. It prophesized the return of Osiris."

"I'm not following you. Who's Osiris?"

Alex, for the past three years, had only been talking to Egyptologists. She had forgotten that not everyone knew the Egyptian mythologies. "Osiris," Alex began, "was the Egyptian god of the underworld, but in the text I found, we think the Egyptians were referring to an alien race as 'Osiris'."

"What?"

"We even found a hieroglyph that resembles one of the heads on Easter Island." In Alex's excitement, she was beginning to speed up. "It's just incredible!"

"That's great, Alex, but what does this all have to do with me?" Jake wondered.

"I need your help."

Jake was quiet for a moment, as if waiting for the punch line of a joke. "For what?"

"For an adventure!" Alex announced grandly. "The adventure to end all adventures. To finally discover the truth."

"What truth?"

"*The* truth," Alex emphasized. "We know aliens have been visiting this planet since the dawn of man," she said excitedly, her voice slightly quivering, "but now, we can finally find out if they've been influencing our evolution."

Jake was astounded. "Let me get this straight, after all that's happened to us in the past five years, you want me to go on another wild goose chase after aliens? After all we've been through?"

"Yes," Alex answered without missing a beat.

"Are you out of your mind?" Jake asked seriously. "I don't understand, what are you saying?"

"I'm saying that I'm not going with you this time. I've finally started to get my life back in order, and I don't want to ruin that."

Alex was dismayed. "I thought for sure you would go with us."

"Are you kidding?" Jake asked angrily. "Weren't you the one who told me four years ago that you were tired of running? Didn't you say that?

You said you wanted your life back. Did I misunderstand you?" Jake paused for a moment. "Why now do you want to go chasing after these things again?"

"I said that I was tired of running from the government." Alex stopped.

She hadn't expected that she would be having this conversation with Jake. "I'm a UFOlogist, Jake. This is what I do." Alex tried to think quickly. "I think you owe me this."

"Alex," Jake said with a sigh of exasperation. "You walked out on me four years ago. You left me lying in a hospital bed with a bullet wound in my chest. I don't *owe* you anything. I think it's you who owes me everything." Jake had no idea he had so much pent-up frustration aimed at her. "I've rescued you more times than I can count on this little crusade of yours."

"Crusade?" Alex echoed. "You think I'm on some kind of damned crusade?" she asked angrily. "I'm trying to find the answer to a question that has plagued humanity since it became capable of reasoning: why are we here? I," she stopped and corrected herself, "*we* need an answer."

"I'm sorry, Alex, but I just can't seem to care." Jake hung up the phone. He stood in silence for a long time, just staring at the phone. A burst of anger gripped his body. "We haven't spoken in four years and all she can think about is aliens." Jake lashed out and dumped everything off his desk. Straightening up, Jake spun around and walked toward the door. Pulling it open, he stepped outside into the cool North Tahoe air. Even though it was the middle of summer, the temperatures rarely grazed the upper eighties. Closing his office door behind him, Jake walked to the curb and stopped. He slumped down onto the concrete. Lifting his head to the sky, he watched the white clouds roll by in the blue sky. "Could things get any worse?"

Chapter Eight

Durard laid his suit jacket over the back of his couch. Pulling off his tie, he slumped down onto the thick brown leather couch. He quickly kicked off his shoes and leaned his head back onto the cushions. He hated this couch. He could never understand what possessed him to purchase it. It was the most awful thing to sit on during the summer, and not the most comfortable thing to sleep on.

Leaning forward, Durard grabbed his remote control off a small wooden coffee table and clicked on the television. It was close to ten thirty in the morning. He had gone back into the office for about two hours after getting no sleep the night before. He had told his secretary he was sick and had a doctor's appointment. Truthfully, he just didn't feel comfortable at work at the moment.

He glanced around his apartment. It was huge, measuring almost four thousand square feet, and lavishly decorated. For the first time in his life, Durard had the money to buy the decor he wanted. *That's one nice thing about being the Assistant Regional Director of FEMA,* he told himself. *The only thing....*

He turned his attention back to his sixty inch television. He hit the volume button on his remote. Durard had been watching "The Dating Game" before he had left for work this morning, and hadn't changed the channel before he left. He was apparently now in the middle of one of those annoying daytime talk shows. Durard read the caption at the bottom of the screen: "Midget transvestite hookers, and the albino men who love them." He smiled. This was his kind of show after all.

Placing the remote back on the coffee table, Durard stood and walked into the kitchen. It was separated from the living room by a large archway and a bar that ran from the wall into the center of the room. Opening the refrigerator, he quickly scanned its contents. Pushing a half empty bottle of white zinfandel out of the way, he reached for a tall bottle of orange juice. Standing up, Durard peeked through the arch at the television, trying not to miss the program. Opening a tall wooden cabinet above the bar, he pulled out a glass and set it down. Intently watching the show, Durard poured himself a glass of juice. Leaving the orange juice on the counter, he grabbed his glass and quickly made his way back to the couch.

Sitting down, Durard took a sip of the orange juice before placing it on the coffee table. Leaning back, he sprawled out over the couch. *Maybe this is what I needed,* he told himself. *A good day off.* The ringing of his telephone startled him. "Damn."

Standing back up, he traversed his carpeted floor toward the kitchen, where his phone hung next to the bar. Durard reached out to answer the phone, then stopped. "Ah, to hell with whoever it is. The machine can get it." Durard turned to walk away when he heard the familiar beep of his answering machine.

"Jim? Are you there?" It was Jameson. "If you're there, could you pick up? Pick up please." He waited a moment. "Well, I guess you're not home yet. I just wanted to, *uh,* remind you about our, *um*, meeting this morning."

That's very odd, Durard thought. *For someone who's known for his coolness under pressure, he sure sounds agitated.*

"It's important you get a hold of me," Jameson continued. "I really need to know where you are."

Durard heard the click of the receiver as Jameson hung up. "That was damn strange," he admitted, "but I'm not going to let it ruin my day off." Turning around, he quickly made his way back toward the couch. As he walked by his living room windows, he glanced through them out of habit. He had done this a thousand times before. He only had a view of the next building, so he wasn't sure why he kept doing it. Walking by, Durard suddenly stopped. Turning around, he quickly moved back to the window. Looking across the way, he scanned the balconies on the opposite building. He could've sworn that he had glimpsed three men dressed in black, but now there was nothing.

I must be more exhausted than I think, he told himself. Shaking his head, he began to move away from the window. Suddenly, he heard the crack of a high-powered rifle, and the panes of glass shattered. Durard instinctually dropped to the floor and covered his head. He heard a second crack, and then a third. He heard one final crack, then silence. Lifting his head, Durard skittered away from the window toward his couch. Grabbing his shoes off the floor, he frantically began to pull them on.

Durard looked up just in time to see his front door explode off its hinges. Durard watched patiently for a moment, not moving. He was shocked to see a small gray canister roll into the room and start to emit a noxious gas. The yellow smoke rapidly flooded the room, stinging Durard's eyes and throat. He tried to take shallow breaths. He knew it was tear gas.

He watched two men dressed in black fatigues enter as the smoke thickened. Their faces were covered by gas masks, allowing Durard to see only their eyes. Making a quick decision, Durard sprinted toward his kitchen. From there, he could get to the door to the balcony, and to fresh air. The two men lifted their weapons and began to fire. Bullets tore through the walls around him as he dove behind the bar. Bottles of liquor shattered, spilling their precious contents everywhere. Grabbing one of the bottles, Durard haphazardly threw it back over the bar toward the two men, missing them by a long shot.

Durard quickly weighed his options. Grabbing a can of cooking spray off the counter next to the stove, he spun around and opened the drawer behind him. Rummaging through the drawer, he came upon his quarry. Pulling out a small lighter, he flicked it with his thumb. A small flame sprung from the igniter. Holding his breath, Durard jumped up and sprayed the cooking oil through the flame. The gas ignited, sending a ball of flame into the face of the first man. The black vest he was wearing caught fire. He struggled wildly to put it out.

Durard turned the lighter toward the second man and pressed the button. To his horror, nothing came out. Durard pressed the button again. Still nothing. He watched the man begin to bring his weapon up to bear. Tossing the can of spray at the soldier's head, Durard leapt over the bar and tackled him.

The two men struggled on the ground for control. The soldier delivered a heavy uppercut into Durard's ribs that stunned him. Rolling off, Durard tried to catch his breath, but the smoke was growing thicker. The soldier took advantage and rolled onto Durard, pinning him to the floor. Durard flailed wildly, trying to roll the man off of him. Durard accidentally succeeded in knocking the soldier's gas mask off. He watched the soldier press his hands over his mouth in an effort to filter out the gas.

Durard seized the opportunity, and knocked the man off. Grabbing the gas mask, Durard pressed it to his face and took a deep breath. Tossing it aside, Durard threw a punch across the man's chin. Retrieving the mask, Durard stood up and took another deep breath. He needed to get out of his apartment.

Starting to move toward the door, he felt a hand clamp around his ankle. Turning around, he saw the second soldier holding on to him. The soldier smiled as he reached into his vest pocket and pulled out a small device that resembled a lipstick tube. Durard watched the man press a button on the top of the device. Kicking the man hard in the face, Durard wriggled free of the man's grasp and bolted for the door. Making a right, he hit a dead sprint as he neared the elevator doors. Durard heard the device detonate behind him. A shockwave knocked him off his feet and sent him flying headlong into the still closed elevator doors. He impacted with a sickening crunch. Sitting up, he felt his limp left arm. He knew it was broken.

Glancing behind him, he saw fire spreading

down the hallway. The grenade had incinerated the walls of his apartment, and part of his neighbor's. Fighting off the pain, Durard lifted himself off the ground and looked around. He spotted the emergency stairwell just a few feet away. He needed to get out of the building, and out of San Francisco. Looking to his left, he grabbed the handle on a fire alarm and yanked it down. Alarms began to sound all over the building. Opening the door to the stairs, Durard began to make the arduous journey down.

***

The man waited for someone to pick up on the other end of the phone. He was standing in a small phone booth just outside Jim Durard's apartment. He checked his watch again. It was almost eleven in the morning. He was relieved when someone finally answered.

"Newsroom," a gruff male voice announced.

"Yeah, this is Tulley, I need to speak with Joanne."

"Hold on," the voice relayed. Tulley was promptly put on hold and subjected to the soft melodies of easy listening. He looked above him at Durard's apartment building. Smoke and flames were billowing out of the upper floors. He had to admit that this music wasn't calming him at all.

The music abruptly stopped. "This is Joanne."

"Joanne," Tulley said excitedly. "It's Jeff."

"What now, Jeff?" his editor asked unemotionally.

"You know that story I'm working on? The one

about Jim Durard, FEMA, and The Yellow Death?"

"Yes," Joanne answered. She sounded distracted. It was no secret that she didn't like Tulley. She always felt his style of reporting was very 'tabloid'. He always wanted to do stories on UFO sightings or conspiracies.

"Well, I've been trailing Durard, and his apartment just exploded! I swore I heard gunshots too!"

Joanne perked up. "Is Durard alive?"

"Yeah, I saw him stagger out of the building and get into his car."

"Why are you talking to me then?" Joanne asked. "Follow him and find out what the hell happened. This could turn out to be a big story."

"I'm on it, but I need some more expense money."

"What happened to the three hundred I already gave you?" Joanne asked seriously.

"Hey, it isn't cheap staying in San Francisco," Tulley admitted.

"All right," Joanne replied reluctantly. "I'll authorize your company credit card for another five hundred dollars. Now get going!"

"Thanks, boss." Tulley hung up the phone and ran toward his dilapidated late model sedan. Hopping over the driver's side door, he pressed his key into the ignition and started the car. Slamming the gas pedal to the floor, he sped off just as a fleet of fire trucks and emergency vehicles began to arrive on the scene.

***

64

Alex sat alone on the balcony of her hotel room. She was naked, except for the gray silk robe she had wrapped around her. It was a quiet night in Cairo. For the first time in days, the wind had stopped blowing. She turned her head skyward and stared at the stars. They seemed so strange here. Alex knew they were no different, but they looked odd on the other side of the world.

Taking a step forward, Alex wrapped her hands around the black metal railing and leaned over. She looked across this ancient city. She liked it here. From the bustling city to the tombs and pyramids filled with remnants of one of the greatest civilizations to ever live, this was history.

Straightening up, she brushed an errant lock of brown hair away from her face. Reaching into the pocket of her gray robe, Alex pulled out a pack of cigarettes and a lighter. Flipping open the package, she pulled out a single cigarette and placed it in her mouth. Igniting the lighter, she quickly lifted the flame to the end of the cigarette and took a drag. Alex exhaled the smoke through her nose as she returned to a small metal folding chair. Crossing her legs, she stared out over the city.

She had starting smoking again this afternoon. Earlier today while she was in the store buying groceries, for no reason, she picked up a pack of cigarettes. She had always been fascinated by the Hollywood cliché of the rough and rugged man with a cigarette hanging out of his mouth. She had smoked in high school and through much of college, but had quit when she graduated. She took another drag then flicked off the ash.

"What the hell are you doing?" Alex jumped.

"What?"

"You're smoking!" Griggs exclaimed as he walked out onto the balcony. He was wearing only a blue pair of boxers. His usually well-kept blonde hair was a mess on top of his head.

"I know, I meant to tell you." Alex had been hiding it from him. It felt dangerous; like sneaking into the girl's restroom in high school for a quick smoke in between classes.

Griggs seemed disappointed. "Why are you smoking?"

Alex took another drag off the cigarette. "I don't really know. I just saw them in the store and they looked really good."

Griggs sat down next to her. "Do you know how bad those things are for you?"

Alex nodded. "I've been told."

"Then why?"

Alex shrugged. "I guess I've just been a little stressed lately."

"Stressed about what?"

"I—"

Griggs suddenly realized the truth. "Jake turned you down, didn't he?" Alex frowned. She hadn't told Griggs that either.

"Yeah." Alex took another puff. "He's still very angry about us leaving him in the hospital alone."

"Can you really blame him?" Griggs asked. "In retrospect, we did kind of abandon him."

"Can I ask you a question?" Alex quickly changed the direction of the conversation.

"Sure," Griggs replied sympathetically.

"Do you think I'm on a crusade?" Alex asked meekly.

Griggs grabbed a second chair and placed it next to Alex. Sitting down, he rubbed his hand on her back. "I think we're all on a crusade of some kind. It's just that some people are more consuming than others."

That didn't make Alex feel any better. "Is my crusade all consuming?" Griggs shook his head. "I don't think so. Look at it this way: if yours was all consuming, you wouldn't have time for me."

Alex smiled. "Yeah, I guess you're right." Alex lifted her arm and flicked her cigarette over the railing. "You know, we're going to need help on Rapa Nui. Do you think we should call Tyler, Faith or Durard?"

Griggs smiled. "You're still obsessed with this whole 'Easter Island' thing, aren't you?"

Alex nodded. "I have to know, Jason."

"I don't understand why."

Alex thought for a moment. "It's just one of those things. Remember when you were a kid and you wanted to know if there was a Santa Claus? This is the same thing. I have to know if it's true."

Griggs smiled. "Well, I think you're old enough now to know the truth." Alex was puzzled. "What are you talking about?"

Griggs' expression grew very serious. "I'm sorry, Alex, but there is no Santa Claus."

Alex laughed. "You know, you can be a real ass sometimes." She quickly stopped laughing when she heard a knock on the door. "Will you see who that is at this ungodly hour?"

Griggs nodded and walked back into the room. Alex could hear muffled voices talking inside. A moment later, Griggs returned. "It's for you."

67

Alex stood up and wrapped her robe tightly around her body. Stepping back into the room, she saw Professor Scott standing in the doorway. She smiled and walked toward him. "What can I do for you, Professor?"

Scott stood dressed in his familiar khaki shirt and shorts. He was holding his hat by the brim in front of his chest and running his fingers nervously along it. "I apologize for not announcing my visit," he said in his proper British accent, "but I've just received two very important pieces of news." He lowered his head for a moment, then looked back up at Alex. He was behaving like a teenage boy asking a girl to the prom. "I was wondering if we could discuss them over a cup of coffee?"

Alex smiled. "It's a little late for coffee, Professor. Can you just tell me here?"

Scott frowned. "I'd rather not."

Alex looked over at Griggs. "Do you mind?"

"No," Griggs said. "Not at all."

"Let me put on some clothes, and I'll meet you in the lobby in five minutes, okay?"

Scott nodded happily. "Indeed." He turned around and grabbed the handle of the door. Opening it, he smiled again and exited the room.

Alex turned to look at Griggs. "I'm not sure how long this is going to take." Griggs slumped down into a chair on the far side of the room and grabbed a small black remote control off the table. "It's all right, Alex. I'll be here when you get back." He smiled as he flipped on the television.

Chapter Nine

A claxon sounded, then stopped. Lieutenant Stewart felt the hairs on the back of his neck stand up as he stared toward the main viewer. The President had just upgraded to DEFCON three. NORAD, and the military, was now on full alert.

"What's the status of the 'intruder'?" General Summers asked from behind Stewart. He had been sitting there ever since he had gotten off the phone with the President.

Stewart checked his radar screen. "Still approaching, General. They've just gone through Jupiter's orbit," Stewart paused, "and, General, we've confirmed it. The 'intruder' is on a direct course for Earth."

"Damn," Summers said while rubbing his eyes.

"I may be out of place, General, but I think you need to get some rest." Stewart looked at his superior officer. "You've been here in control for over twenty hours."

Summers shook his head. "I don't have time to sleep."

***

Jake sat quietly on the couch staring at a blank television screen. It was dark in his living room, except for the small lamp sitting on the table next to him. Lifting his bottle of beer off the coffee table, Jake took a long drink. Jake sighed as he leaned back. Taking the last drink, Jake tossed the bottle on the floor. He glanced around the living room of his house. It was a disaster, but it was always this way.

He pulled his feet up and rested them gently on his makeshift table made of milk crates and a piece of plywood.

Jake closed his eyes. He couldn't picture Alex's face. He knew exactly what she looked like, how the light played off her beautiful features, but he couldn't see her face. He wasn't sure what that meant. A sudden noise startled him. His eyes shot open and he sat straight up on the couch. He was staring down the barrel of a loaded .45. The person holding the gun had a ski mask covering their face so Jake couldn't make out any details. He watched in horror as the person pulled the trigger. Jake felt a surge of pain as he fell back against the couch. Looking down, he saw a gaping bullet wound in his chest. Jake looked up at the person with terror in his eyes. "Why?" he asked. The person began to laugh out loud. Jake recognized that laugh. His attacker lifted her hand to the ski mask and slowly pulled it off. Jake was fighting to remain conscious. "You!" he declared angrily. Anne looked down at Jake and smiled. Lifting her weapon, she pressed it hard to Jake's head. Her green eyes glimmered with evil as she pulled the trigger.

Startled, Jake jumped up from the couch. He quickly ran his hand over his chest. Nothing. No bullet wound. Jake let out a long sigh of relief. He was just dreaming. A knock on his front door startled him again. *What's got me so spooked tonight?* he wondered as he moved toward the front door. Jake grabbed the handle and slowly opened it. "Oh, hi, Rachel."

Rachel Wills, Jake's next-door neighbor, was slightly shorter than Jake with long, curly reddish

70

hair and green eyes. She was wearing a pair of faded blue jeans, a white t-shirt and a black leather coat that hung almost to her knees. "'Oh, hi, Rachel'? Is that all you can say?"

Jake looked confused. "What did you expect?"

Rachel smiled. "I haven't seen you in almost two years, Jake. For god's sake, we live next door to each other and we even work across the street from each other."

"I'm sorry." Jake stepped out of the doorway. "Would you like to come in?"

Rachel nodded and came inside. "So, to what do I owe the honor of this visit?"

Rachel was slowly peeling off her jacket as she walked toward the living room. "I'm actually here to collect on an old debt," she admitted.

Jake walked into the living room behind her and turned on the main light. "Old debt?"

Rachel sat down on the edge of Jake's couch and rested her coat next to her. "Remember, oh, about five or so years ago, when you asked me to watch your house while you went to Las Vegas to work on a case?"

"Yeah, I remember that."

"I also remember you saying that you would only be a couple days, at the most."

"Rachel, where is this going?" Jake asked with a smile.

"Well," Rachel started, "it turns out that you weren't gone for a couple of days. You were gone for over a year!"

"I know, I'm sorry," Jake admitted. "I got really tied up on that case I was working on."

"It seems so." Rachel slowly stood up and

slinked toward Jake, who was still standing in the entrance to the living room. "You said you would return the favor some day." She placed her hands seductively on his chest. "I think that day has come."

Jake laughed out loud. "What the hell are you doing?"

Rachel smiled. "I'm bored to death, Jake," she said, taking a step back. "It's Friday night and I want to go out and do something."

"Why don't you just go out with a couple of your girlfriends?" Jake asked. He wasn't in the mood to leave the house.

"Most of them are at work," Rachel confessed. "Come on, Jake, it'll be fun. Besides, you owe me big."

"But—"

"Ah," Rachel said, placing her hand on his mouth. "You don't have a choice in the matter. Now go put on a pair of shoes and a coat, and don't forget your wallet. You're buying."

Jake smiled. He knew this was a battle he wasn't going to win. *Maybe a night out would do me some good. Might help me keep my mind off Alex for a while.* "You're on, Rachel."

Rachel threw her arms around Jake and hugged him. "Thanks, Jake." Jake returned the embrace. He hadn't had a woman in his arms since Alex left, and Rachel was suddenly looking very appealing. "Just let me go grab my coat." Turning to walk out of the living room, Jake heard his telephone ring. He looked at Rachel. "I better get that. I'll only be a minute." Jake snatched his cordless phone off the couch and pressed the talk button. "Hello?"

"Jake, it's Lindsay."

Jake's mood turned darker. He hated it when his ex-wife called. She usually wanted something. "What, Lindsay?" Jake asked abruptly.

"I don't know how to tell you this," Jake heard Lindsay trying to hold back her tears, "but...."

Jake's darkness quickly faded. He sat down on the couch and listened to the phone intently. "What, Lindsay? What's the matter?"

"I couldn't do anything," Lindsay blurted out amidst her sobs. "I couldn't help her."

Jake suddenly had a sinking feeling in his stomach. "Is it Samantha? What's wrong with Samantha?"

"She's gone, Jake!"

"Gone? Gone where?" Jake asked worriedly.

"I—" Lindsay was sobbing so hard, she couldn't even finish her sentence. "Lindsay, listen to me. You need to calm down. Take a few slow, deep breaths, okay? When you're crying, I can't understand you. Now just calm down and tell me what happened." Jake listened as Lindsay started to take a few deep breaths.

"Jake," she started to sob again, but tried to stop. "Samantha's been kidnapped."

"What?" Jake roared. "Someone kidnapped my daughter? What happened?"

"The police don't know who did it. All they have is the testimonial of one eyewitness."

"What did he say?" Jake asked hysterically.

"He claims two men grabbed Samantha and pushed her into a dark colored sedan."

"Did he catch the license plate number?"

"No," Lindsay cried. "He said there wasn't

73

one."

"The car didn't have plates on it?"

"That's what he said."

Jake thought for a moment. "Is that all he saw?"

"Yes."

Jake's mind was too frazzled to comprehend what he had been told so far. "Lindsay, I need you to fax me a copy of the police report."

"Okay." Lindsay had started to sob uncontrollably again. "I just want my baby back, Jake."

"I know," Jake consoled. "I'll find her. I promise." He turned to see Rachel still standing next to him. "I'll call you first thing in the morning, okay? You just try and get some rest tonight."

"I will."

"Everything's going to be all right," Jake promised.

"I hope so, Jake," Lindsay said. "I don't know what I'll do without my daughter."

"You can't think that way. Samantha will be found, and she'll be just fine." There was a short pause. "I love you, Jake," Lindsay said timidly.

The response startled Jake, but felt comfortable all at the same time.

"You too, Lindsay. Goodnight." Jake clicked the off button on the phone and set it down carefully on the couch next to him. His mind instantly started to wander. Images of Samantha when she was just a little girl flooded his thoughts. He latched on to the memory of Samantha riding her tricycle on the driveway of their house in New Orleans. She was only four at the time. She'd hit a rock and crashed her bike. Jake swooped in like an angel of mercy and comforted her in a way only a father could. He took her inside; tears rolling down her dirty face and sat her on the bathroom counter. There he applied a bandage and kissed the cut on her knee better. She stopped crying and wrapped her little arms around his neck and hugged him.

"Jake?"

"Huh?" Rachel pulled him out of his stupor. "I'm sorry."

Rachel smiled. "That's okay. So are we still on for tonight?" Hope was all she had left.

"I'm afraid I'm going to have to give you a raincheck," Jake said quietly. Rachel sat down next to Jake on the couch. "What's the matter? What happened?" she asked sympathetically.

"My daughter Samantha has been kidnapped."

***

Alex and Scott were sitting in a booth in a small American themed coffee shop in downtown Cairo. Scott had ordered a cup of black coffee, while Alex was enjoying a cup of hot chocolate with whipped cream on top. The coffee bar was done in red and gold, and resembled an old-fashioned malt shop more than anything else. There were two other patrons scattered across the small shop, but they seemed more interested in their copy of the day's paper than anything else.

Scott took a sip of his steaming cup of coffee and set it down in front of him. "Alex," he said thoughtfully, "I've heard that you are planning on leaving."

Alex made no quick denial. "I am."

"Why?" Scott asked. His usually blue eyes seemed more tired than usual. For the first time in the three years Alex had worked with him, he was beginning to show his age.

"It's complicated," Alex said quietly. She was cradling her mug of chocolate between her hands, enjoying the heat. "I have to find out if the prophecy is real."

"For god's sake," Scott said angrily. "You really believe in that rubbish?" Alex looked up at Scott. "Why is that so wrong?"

"The vast majority of the scientific community completely debunks the idea that aliens are visiting our planet."

Alex leaned close to Scott. "I know they are."

"How do you know?"

Alex smiled. "I've seen them with my own eyes."

Scott was a bit taken back. "What?"

"That's right. I've seen the ships, I've seen the technology, and I've been party to the government's cover-up."

Scott took another sip of his coffee. "How?" he asked uneasily. He didn't like talking about UFOs and aliens. He felt only cranks discussed this topic, and he didn't want his long and illustrious career as an archaeologist to be tainted by it.

"I found an alien artifact under the Sphinx five years ago."

"Bull," Scott shot back. "No one's ever been allowed to dig under the Sphinx. The Egyptian government won't allow it."

"I never said I had permission." Alex took a sip

of her chocolate and let the words sink into Scott. "Minutes after I found the artifact, I was taken by soldiers belonging to the United States Air Force. They took me to Area 51, along with the device. The whole time, I was being used as a stool pigeon."

"How?"

"The brass at Area 51 apparently knew the device existed beneath the Sphinx, they just couldn't go in and get it themselves. They used me for that. As soon as I got the artifact, they came in and took it. Apparently, they explained to the Egyptian government that I stole it and they didn't know of its whereabouts."

"So they took you and the device and blamed the whole thing on you?" Scott asked, not believing the words coming out of his own mouth.

"Yeah," Alex laughed, "but it ended up biting them in the ass."

"What happened?"

"The alien device was actually a doomsday weapon. Through a sequence of events, it was activated and ended up destroying one of their top secret bases in the Nevada desert."

Scott sat back in his seat, all the while keeping his eyes on Alex. "I don't believe this."

"Why not?" Alex asked in frustration. "I was there. I saw the whole thing with my own eyes!"

"That's the problem, and will be the problem with UFOs, aliens and abductions until they decide to come down and land on the White House lawn and give a press conference," Scott stated. "You know as well as I do that the scientific community relies on fact, not first-hand witnesses. They need to be able to prove something before they believe it."

"They need to learn how to take some things on faith," Alex shot back. She thought for a moment. "Hell, most of the scientists in the government's employ have already probably seen these things and have worked on the technology."

Scott let Alex fume for a moment. "I don't want to argue with you, Alex. I know you are very passionate about that subject, and I have no right to sit here and berate your beliefs." He twisted the coffee mug in his hands. "I didn't come here tonight to talk to you about aliens and such."

"Then why?" Alex asked intrigued.

"I came here to talk you out of leaving."

"I'm sorry but I—"

"Please," Scott cut in, "listen to me for a moment." Alex nodded for him to continue.

"I've been offered another job," Scott said. "It will take me out of the field, but I will still be able to work with archaeologist and artifacts."

"What's the job?"

"The head curator of the London Museum of Natural History." Alex smiled. "Very prestigious position."

"I agree."

"What's the problem?"

"I need to find someone to take over the dig here in Egypt effective immediately." Scott looked at Alex. "You were my first choice."

Alex beamed. This was what she had been waiting for her entire life: to be the head of a funded archaeological dig in the Valley of the Kings. Alex's face quickly turned dark. "I appreciate the offer, but—"

"Why not, Alex?" Scott asked. "This is a position that most field archaeologists would die for. You would not only work on this dig, but every one the Museum funds."

Alex looked away from Scott. He was right and she knew it. Most people in her profession would jump at this. "There's something more at stake here, Professor Scott. I could find an answer to the question that has plagued mankind ever since we developed the ability to reason: 'Why are we here?' I want to prove that we are not products of this planet's evolution, or of an omnipotent god. I want to prove that we are the products of aliens."

"That's preposterous," Scott said in dismay. "Think of what you're throwing away to go on some damned fool crusade!"

That word again. "I will not sit here and listen to this. I have already made up my mind." Alex stood up out of the booth. "I am going to have to respectfully decline your offer." Alex turned and quickly walked out.

Scott jumped up from his seat and followed her out the door. "Alex!" Alex was already walking away. She made no effort to turn around, or even acknowledge Scott.

"Alex!" Scott screamed again, but it was useless. "Damned stubborn kids," he muttered to himself. "One day, she's going to get in way over her head." Scott turned to walk back into the coffee bar and pay his bill, when he noticed several men in black trench coats stepping out of the shadows. Scott stumbled back in fear, but the men walked right past him. He watched them move in the direction Alex was heading.

Chapter Ten

A knock on the door woke Faith from her sleep. Rolling over in bed, she glared at the red digital numbers of her alarm clock. "It's three forty in the morning," she muttered. Sitting up in bed, she tossed the covers off and adjusted her cream-colored silk nightgown. Pulling her feet over the edge of the bed, she groggily felt around with them for her slippers.

She heard another knock on the door. "I'm coming," she groaned. Faith stood and glanced over at Tyler. He was still sleeping soundly, wrapped up in his blankets. *Must be nice*, she thought. The knocking continued, this time, louder. "All right, all right! Hold on!" Faith walked through the bedroom and down the hall toward the front door. Grabbing the doorknob, she threw the door open, not even stopping to consider who would be standing there. Her eyes widened. "Oh my God!"

Durard stumbled in the door and collapsed. "Faith," he moaned. He had tied a temporary sling around his broken arm.

"Tyler!" Faith screamed. "Get out here!" She helped Durard off the floor and toward the couch. The front door was located on the left-hand side of the living room, with a couch and loveseat sitting in the middle of the floor. Faith slowly lowered Durard and looked at his arm. "What the hell did you do?"

Durard looked exhausted. His eyes were bloodshot. "Tried to get in the elevator, but the doors were closed."

Tyler ran out of the bedroom panicked. "What?" he shouted. He quickly spotted Durard on the couch. "What happened?"

Faith looked up at Tyler. "His arm's broken, and he could be in shock. Call 911!" Tyler nodded and quickly ran toward the phone. Faith looked at Durard. "How did you get here?"

"I drove," he responded calmly. "Tyler, hang up the phone, I'm fine."

"What are you talking about?" Faith argued. "Your arm is clearly broken!"

"Calm down, Faith," Durard said with a smile. "While I appreciate your concern, you're forgetting that I have medical training. I've already reset the fracture and immobilized it. I just look like hell because I've been driving non-stop to get here."

Tyler quickly hung up the phone and sat down on the loveseat. "What's going on?"

"The government is trying to bury it," Durard blurted out. "'Bury' what?" Faith asked.

"The Yellow Death," Durard said, sitting up on the couch. "They're trying to erase all records of it."

"How can they do that?" Tyler asked. "Practically the entire west coast of the United States was infected with TYD four years ago. Why do they want to cover that up?"

"Probably because of its extraterrestrial connection," Durard speculated. Rubbing his eyes, Durard stared at the ceiling. "You know how our government likes to hide things like that."

Faith shook her head. "How are they covering it up?"

"They've gone back and censored all the records and files containing any kind of reference to TYD," Durard paused, "and they're trying to eliminate anyone who has any knowledge of it.

That's how I ended up here. Two men smashed into my apartment and tried to kill me."

"Jesus!" Faith remarked. "Who were they?"

"I don't know," Durard thought, "but they looked like the boys from Area 51."

Faith suddenly became very afraid. "They're coming for everyone who knew about TYD?"

"I don't know that for sure," Durard said, "but that seems like their plan."

"That means they'll be coming for Tyler and me, doesn't it?"

Durard placed his hand on Faith's shoulder. "For all I know, they might just be pissed at me."

Faith tried to push the concern out of her mind. She always had the feeling this day would come. She had just hoped it wouldn't be this soon. She had just married Tyler, and they had just started to build their life together. "We need to make up the couch if you're planning on staying, Jim." Durard smiled. "That would be great. Thanks, Faith."

Tyler stood up and stretched. "I've got to get back to bed. I've got work tomorrow morning." He looked at Durard. "How long are you planning to stay?"

Durard shrugged. "I really don't know, Tyler. I can't go back to my apartment because they blew it up, and I can't go back to San Francisco because they're looking for me." Durard looked at Tyler. "If this is going to be a problem, I can stay somewhere else."

"Where would you go?" Tyler asked.

"I heard Jake's back up in Lake Tahoe," Durard offered.

"No," Tyler laughed. "It's no big deal. You can

stay here as long as you need."

Faith returned with a small stack of sheets and a pillow. Laying them gently on the couch, she stood next to Tyler. "If you need anything, you know where to find us."

Durard nodded. "Thanks."

"Anytime," Tyler said with a smile. "Now if you'll excuse us...."

"Oh, sure. I'm sorry I had to wake you up in the middle of the night," Durard apologized.

"It's no problem," Faith said while walking back to the bedroom. "Good night," she said and quickly shut the door. She watched Tyler begin to crawl back into bed. "What are you doing?" she asked in a whisper.

Tyler rolled over and looked at Faith. "Well, I was thinking about going back to bed."

"That's not what I meant," Faith snapped. "Why are we letting him stay here?"

"Because he's our friend, and he was almost killed!" Tyler retorted. "Please, keep your voice down," Faith warned him. "Did you hear what he said out there? He said they're killing everyone who knew about TYD! That includes us!"

"I am not going to send that man out into the cold just because you're worried about the government finding us." Tyler rolled onto his side and pulled up the covers. "He is my friend, and he deserves better than that." He closed his eyes. "Besides, if they haven't found us by now, then I don't think they will," Tyler tried to reassure her. "It's been four years since that incident in Las Vegas."

Faith shook her head as she climbed into bed.

"I hope you're right." Tyler looked at his wife as she lay there quietly. She was everything to him. He knew it sounded a bit cliché, but he was nothing without her. "So do I," he muttered under his breath.

***

Two days later, Alex and Griggs were in a small plane flying over the vast Pacific Ocean en route to Rapa Nui. They had taken a commercial flight from Egypt to Chile, then had to charter a plane to get them to Easter Island. Alex looked out her window. She could see the small triangular island floating quietly amidst a sea of blue. She wondered how the first settlers saw this island when they arrived. It must've been like a godsend with its lush green forest, but this small island was not without its perils. The island itself was formed when three volcanoes erupted, leaving the coastline a jagged mess of sheer volcanic rock the ocean waves endlessly pummeled.

The pilot had flown over the island, and then swung around to get access to the runway. Alex looked closer at the island as they began to descend. It was void of trees due to a mass deforestation by the natives. They had cut them down to use in the construction of their Moai. Researchers speculated the Rapa Nui natives used the logs to roll these mammoth ten ton rock sculptures into position over a thousand years ago.

Alex looked at Griggs across the aisle of the small plane. He had stretched out over two seats and was napping. Alex laughed. *How can men do that?*

We're on the verge of one of the biggest discoveries in man's history and I can't even eat, and he's fast asleep.

The pilot lowered the landing gear and eased the plane toward the small runway. Touching down, the pilot stepped on the brakes and brought them to a halt. This was not the smoothest landing Alex had ever been through, but not the worst either. Unbuckling herself, she glanced over at Griggs. He sat up and began to stretch.

"Okay, Alex," Griggs started. "We're here. Now how are we going to find this temple or whatever it is?"

Alex smiled. "The island's only sixty-four square miles. I don't think it'll be that hard."

The pilot, a rough looking Hispanic man of about forty, stood and looked at Alex. He ran his hands through his jet-black hair, and took off his dark sunglasses. "Everyone off," he announced with a thick South American accent.

Alex and Griggs stood up and walked toward the rear of the plane where their luggage was stowed. Undoing the two buckles of the brown restraining net that held them in place, Alex lifted her small green suitcase off the floor. Griggs reached down and snatched his black suitcase and a thick canvas bag filled with their equipment. He stood behind Alex at the hatch. The pilot squeezed by them. Grabbing the orange handle on the door, he twisted hard and opened the door. Stepping out of their way, the pilot motioned for them to exit.

Jumping the short distance onto the concrete runway, Alex stared at the tiny terminal of Mataveri Airport. For an island that survived entirely off tourism, they sure had a small airport. She turned to look at Griggs, who was walking next to her. He seemed amused by all this. "What are you smiling about?" Alex asked seriously.

"This island," Griggs replied. "It's supposed to be one of the most mysterious, remote places on Earth, and it has an airport. That just strikes me as funny."

Alex ignored the comment and looked up at the sky. The sun was beginning to set. It would be dark soon. "We need to get checked into our hotel."

Griggs laughed again. "They have hotels here, too! This is great! Where are we staying?"

Alex fished a small white piece of paper out of her pocket and unfolded it.

"It's called the 'Hotel Rano Raraku'. It's Rapa Nui's third largest hotel."

"How big is it?" Griggs asked.

"It has a total of thirty-eight rooms."

Griggs laughed again. "I love this place. The only thing it needs now is a fast-food restaurant." Griggs' face became very serious for a moment. "I can hear it already: would you like fries with that McMoai?" Griggs roared with laughter.

Alex sneered at Griggs. "Shut up."

Chapter Eleven

Jake slammed his fist against his desk in frustration. It had been two days since Samantha had been kidnapped, and there had been no word from the kidnappers. Being a former FBI agent, he knew the standard protocol of a hostage situation. The kidnappers never waited this long to make their demands known. Jake feared the worst. What if the kidnappers had no intention of keeping her alive for ransom? Jake shook his head. He couldn't let himself think that way. He couldn't allow himself to give up hope.

He flipped open the small yellow folder on his desk and began to read through the papers once again. He had read this same police report a hundred times since it had arrived, each time hoping the pages would reveal some new fact or clue that would point him toward the perpetrators of this heinous crime. Each time, he would find nothing but the facts presented there. The New York Police Department had no suspects in the case, only a five page report that verified Samantha had been abducted.

Jake closed the folder and carefully pushed it to the side. Resting his head on the wooden desk, he ran the facts through his mind again and again. It just didn't add up. Samantha had no discernable enemies. No one wanted to harm her in any way. Her friends and peers generally liked her. *How am I going to find my daughter when I have no leads?*

Jake lifted his head up and opened the top drawer of his desk. Reaching inside, he retrieved a small oval shaped glass bottle. He lifted the bottle and stared at its dark brown contents. Unscrewing the lid, he pressed the bottle to his lips and poured the thick alcohol down his throat. This was the only thing that made sense to Jake anymore. The stupor the alcohol caused made him forget, and forgetting was easier than dealing with his problems. Jake took another drink and set the bottle on his desk. It was almost empty, and he'd bought it this morning. Jake was about to finish the bottle when he heard a knock on his office door.

Standing up, he grabbed the edge of the desk to support himself. He quickly tried to get his balance to cooperate. Taking a deep breath, he walked carefully toward the door. He didn't want a potential client to see him in this condition. He tried to put on a sober face. Opening the door, he was greeted by a cool breeze and nothing else. He leaned out his door and looked around. There was no one on the sidewalk in front of his office, and no cars passing on the street. *Maybe I'm drunker than I thought.*

Jake began to pull his office door closed, when he noticed a small, brown box resting on his doorstep. He carefully leaned down and examined it. In big, black letters, it had his name written on it with a message below that said: "Open immediately". Carefully lifting the box, Jake felt the weight in his hands. *Not heavy or big enough to be a bomb,* he reasoned. Placing the parcel under his arm, he slowly closed the door and retreated back into his office.

Laying the box on his desk, he examined the plain brown wrapping paper. Pulling a small knife out of his pant pocket, he clicked open the blade and cut along the edge of the package. Once all the way around, he peeled off the paper and laid it neatly next to his desk. It was a plain brown box with no discernable markings on it. Using his knife, he cautiously slit open the packing tape. Opening the flaps, he saw two items inside: a videocassette with no label and a small white envelope.

Removing the contents, Jake pushed the box out of the way. Setting the videotape down, Jake opened the envelope with his fingers. He pulled out a letter and three photographs. Setting the letter down, he looked at the photos first.

His eyes widened and anger gripped his body. Each was a picture of Samantha lashed to a chair. Jake looked closely at the pictures. He could see no bruises or cuts on Samantha's face or arms, although her dress and shirt were torn and her hair was a mess. He scanned each photo in turn, finding only the same thing. Samantha tied to a metal chair in what looked to be a polished silver room. Each photo was taken from a slightly closer advantage point, showing more of Samantha's face.

Setting the photos aside, he grabbed the letter and unfolded it. Jake instantly recognized the handwriting as Samantha's. It was no longer than a single paragraph, and it appeared to be written very hastily. The usual care Samantha took in her handwriting wasn't present. Jake started at the top.

Dear Dad, I'm okay. The kidnappers say they won't hurt me, if you comply with the terms on the video. I can't say much, because they are standing over me as I write this. I don't know where I am, and I don't know who these people are, but I know they're serious. Please, do as they ask. I really want to come home.

Love, Samantha

Jake stopped and thought for a moment. He tried to push his rage away and examine this letter subjectively. It didn't sound like Samantha had written this of her own free will. It seemed very coerced, like her captors were telling her what to say. The biggest irregularity that stood out was her name. She never signed anything with "Samantha". She always signed her name as "Sam". Jake knew she didn't write this on her own.

Setting the letter down, he glared at the videotape. Turning around, he swiftly moved toward a large file cabinet on the far side of his office. Jake opened the doors and removed a small TV/VCR combo and set it on his desk. He always kept this handy, just in case one of his clients requested video. Plugging the power cord into a nearby outlet, he seated himself in his chair and turned on the TV. Sliding the tape into the VCR, he waited a moment before pressing the "play" button. He had to ready himself for whatever was on this tape. Taking a deep breath, he started the tape. His heart felt like it dropped into his feet when he saw the subject of the video.

"Hi, Jakey-poo!" Anne Carol stood smiling in front of the camera, wearing her Air Force blues like a badge. Her brown hair was streaked with shades of blonde, and hung almost to her shoulders, curling in at the bottom. Her deep green soulless eyes stared hauntingly at Jake. She was beautiful, but her black heart had twisted her soul into something grotesque. "Long time no see," she said with glee.

Jake stared in rage at the screen.

"I thought I would just send you a little tape to say 'hi'. Haven't seen you in about four years, and I've just been wondering what you've been up to." She smiled again and took a step closer to the camera. Lifting the collar of her jacket, she pointed to the three silver stars and smiled. "As you can see, I've been promoted to general."

Taking a step back, her smile faded as she stared into the camera. "I'm sorry this can't just be a social call, but, unfortunately, I have terms to discuss. By now, you've seen the pictures and read the letter and you're probably wondering what I have to do with all this." She smiled and pointed beside her. The camera slowly panned over to Samantha, sitting in the same chair she as in the photos. She was struggling frantically against the ropes, and her mouth was covered with duct tape. The camera quickly refocused on Anne. "We tried it once without the duct tape, but she was too noisy. Every time I yelled 'quiet on the set', she would just begin to scream and cry."

Anne smiled again, "But I digress. My purpose is to present you with your terms. I suggest you follow them to the letter, or you'll never see your daughter alive again. It's you I want, Jake, not your goofy little actress daughter, so I am willing to make a trade. I get you, and your daughter goes free to live a long, happy life. Unless, of course, you refuse," Anne's fierce green eyes hardened, "then I kill the little bitch."

Jake watched the remainder of the tape in

91

silence. As it finished, he quickly scribbled a few notes on a notepad and stood up. He knew he had no time to waste. Tearing the sheet of paper out of the notepad, he grabbed his worn leather jacket and was out the door and into his car in a flash. In his rush, he had left the photos and half of his note on the desk. The sun glared in through his office window on the torn piece of paper with two words written on it: Rapa Nui.

***

Anne Caroll was sitting quietly in her office at Area 51. Stacks of papers were beginning to pile up on the right-hand side of her large metal desk. Pulling one of the papers in front of her, she quickly scribbled her name on it and pushed it to the opposite side of her desk. Setting down her black pen, she leaned back in her black chair and glanced around her office. An evil grin spread across her face. All this was hers now. She didn't need to worry about the Pentagon sending some two-bit general to come in and take it away. She may not have gotten this promotion the traditional way, but she had it, nonetheless.

Anne glanced around her small, rectangular office. The walls were painted a drab white, and the floors were covered with a light green tile. It wasn't the most appealing thing to look at, but it was hers. Her large gray desk stood near the back of the room in front of the massive observation window, while two large metal file cabinets occupied the space next to the door on the front wall. A lone fern sat to the right of her desk, the leaves starting to wilt.

She had been working in this office for a full two years after she received her promotion before decorating it. She wanted to make sure her employer didn't find out she had helped kill the last man in command here, General Foster. Since then, though, she had hung numerous pictures and awards around her office.

Turning around to face the window, Anne reached up and removed the clip from her hair. Shaking her head, she let her brown hair fall around her face messily. She leaned back in her chair and crossed her legs. The sun was beginning to set in the Southern Nevada desert. Soon, the stars would be shining overhead. She actually enjoyed this time of day. The reds and oranges of the sunset melded effortlessly with the tans and browns of the desert, creating a seamless match between heaven and Earth. Anne ran her hand through her hair and began to relax.

Her mind wandered to the plan she had conceived over the past four years. Since the first day she walked into her office, still bleeding and bruised from their last battle, she had wanted revenge on Jake Silver. She had wanted him dead. It had taken a long time, but the pieces were finally starting to fall into place. Now that she had Jake's daughter, there was nothing that could stop it.

Reaching up, she dabbed a few beads of sweat off her forehead. Her body began to feel weak. The chemicals were beginning to wear off. Anne wondered when her scientists would come up with a complete cure. Reaching into the top desk drawer, she removed a small vial of red fluid and a syringe. Pulling the plastic cap off the needle, she pressed it into the cork top of the vial. Using both hands, she pulled up the plunger, filling the syringe with the liquid. Rolling up her sleeve, she tapped two fingers against her elbow. Lifting the needle, she pressed it slowly into her vein. Depressing the plunger, she felt the cold liquid run up her arm. Relief began to pass over her body as the drug began to work. Setting the needle back onto her desk, she pushed it and the vial back into her top drawer.

Spinning around in her chair, she ran her fingers over a small keypad that she had specially installed in her desk. It was a thin silver strip with twenty small black rubber keys arranged in two vertical rows on it. It also had a tiny speaker and microphone built into it. This instantly gave her communications with every part of the base. She wondered why no one had thought of this before. Pressing the second button from the top, she listened intently for a response.

"Yes, General Caroll?" a man's voice answered. "Is Colonel Jannis in Command?" Anne asked.

"Yes, General. I'll get him," the voice responded eagerly.

A few moments passed before Jannis came on the line. "Yes, General?"

"Jannis, I need to see you in my office immediately. We have a situation."

"Yes, General. I'm on my way."

Anne turned back around to face the window. She knew it would only take Jannis a few minutes to make the trip from Command to her office. This sprawling base was built almost entirely underground. The further down you went, the more secure you were. It was designed in the 1950's during the era of the Cuban Missile Crisis and the Red Scare. Fears about Communists launching ballistic missiles at America was a growing concern for the citizens. Thus, two secure bases were designed to withstand a direct nuclear assault, Area 51 in Nevada, and NORAD in Colorado.

In later years, unbeknownst to the public, the Pentagon was also taken underground. Miles and miles of storage facilities and connecting tunnels stretched out beneath Washington D.C. She knew the real reason why all the top military instillations in the country had gone underground, and it wasn't because of the Communist threat. The Government was scared of something else. Something they still had no defense against. Something they found in New Mexico in 1947.

Anne heard a knock on her door. "Come."

Jannis quickly opened Anne's office door and stepped inside. He snapped to attention and saluted. "You wanted to see me, General?"

"Cut the crap and close the door, Jannis. You don't have to salute me anymore."

Jannis relaxed and closed the door behind him. "What's the situation?" he asked. Anne had gotten very used to Jannis' familiar shaved head and scar over these past four years. He was a man of medium height, but large, muscular build. His black fatigues strained to hold in his massive chest and arms. He had a scar, from a battle still unknown to Anne, that ran down the left side of his face. It stretched from the bottom of his eye, to the corner of his mouth. It was extremely jagged and looked as if it could have been caused by a knife or broken bottle.

Once Anne had been promoted to general, she needed a competent, and faithful, first officer. She had quickly moved Jannis up the ranks from his position of captain to colonel in less than two years. Her superiors in Washington had questioned the move, but she had gone through with it anyway. She had never found anyone in her whole life whose evil rivaled her own like Jannis' did. She knew his heart had shriveled up and crumbled to dust many years ago.

Anne had a solemn look on her face. "I found out earlier this afternoon, the President put all branches of the military on alert. We've officially gone to DEFCON three."

Jannis looked surprised. "What prompted this action?"

"I haven't got all the details yet," Anne admitted, "but apparently, one of our boys over at NORAD spotted something on the radar just this side of Jupiter heading toward Earth."

Jannis laughed. "Something wicked this way comes."

"Probably not," Anne cautioned. "My guess is it's some huge chunk of space debris, or a meteor that's broken out of its orbit. It's got the suits in Washington all spooked, though."

"Well, you know the policy on noncatalogued objects in our solar system. Everything is viewed as hostile until it can be identified," Jannis reminded.

"I know," Anne slammed her fist on her desk. "This couldn't have come at a worse time, though. We've just set our plan into action."

"I realize this plan is very important to you," Jannis said hesitantly, "but maybe we should turn our resources toward finding out what's heading toward Earth. If it's alien, it falls under our jurisdiction."

Anne stood up and glared at Jannis. "Don't you dare try and tell me what my job is. I've worked a long time on this project, and I'm not going to let it slip away!" She took a step away from her desk and clasped her hands behind her back. "I'm going to finish this." She turned away from Jannis. "I can't believe that you are questioning the plan. You wanted this as bad as I did."

"Yes, but an approaching alien space craft is a lot more important than an old vendetta." Jannis was sure he was overstepping his boundaries, but he didn't care. Even he realized that work came before pleasure.

Anne stopped for a moment and tried to quell her anger. "It's too late. The wheels are already in motion. We have to continue with the plan. Anything else is secondary at this point."

Jannis knew he wasn't going to win this argument. "What's our course of action?"

Anne slowly returned to her seat. "A team has already been sent to Rapa Nui to see if they can validate this 'prophecy' discovered in Egypt. I want you to take a second squad of your best men and rendezvous with them there. I want you to take a chopper and leave tonight."

"What about you?" Jannis asked.

"I'll be joining you tomorrow morning with the girl. I want to be there personally to kill Jake Silver."

Jannis stood up and began to walk toward the door. "One question."

"Yes?"

"Who's the team leader of the other group?"

Anne smiled. "Greg Hollman."

Chapter Twelve

Alex looked out across the green landscape of Rapa Nui from the patio of the small cottage she and Griggs had rented. It was among ten other small one bedroom cottages at this particular hotel. The main building stood behind them. It was a squat and ugly building, only reaching one story into the sky. It was painted a drab brown, very common in South American influenced countries. After all, the country of Chile governed the island of Rapa Nui. They couldn't get too far from their roots.

Over the past thousand years, the original natives of Rapa Nui had cut down the lush tropical forest that once grew here, leaving only the grassy plains that occupy the island today. Tourists and immigrants from South America and Tahiti had brought with them palm trees. Even now, millennia later, only a few tall palms dotted the landscape. Archaeologists believed that shortly after the Rapa Nui culture reached its peak over six hundred years ago, wars started to erupt on the island. Warring tribes would smash each other's Moai, burn each other's villages, and salt the Earth so nothing could be grown. As quickly as the unique culture on Rapa Nui came into being, it crashed to the ground.

Still, little was known about these people. Scientists hadn't discovered a concrete reason why these people began sculpting and erecting these ten ton statues, or why they had the gaunt features they did. This type of sculpting differed from that of every other Polynesian civilization at the time.

Alex sipped a small bit of coffee out of the thick white mug she was holding in her hands. Even though it was summer in the States, it was winter here. A biting trade wind whipped around her, its stinging claws ripping into her skin. She had spent the past three years in Egypt, fighting through daytime temperatures of well over one hundred degrees. This cold and rainy winter day was too much for her.

Stepping back inside, she quickly set her coffee mug down and began to rub her hands together to try and warm them. The cottage was tiny. It was just as small as a normal hotel room, with one bathroom built-in. A queen-sized bed occupied the majority of the space, leaving only a small bit of area for a single wooden dresser and a table and two chairs. Everything in the room was trimmed with wood sculpted to resemble the bark of palm trees. The owners were apparently trying to give the room a tropical flavor.

"What are you doing?" Griggs asked while peeking his head around the bathroom door.

"Trying to warm up, what does it look like?" Alex snapped.

Griggs laughed. "It's sixty degrees outside, and you're cold? Must be a woman thing." He returned to his spot in the bathroom.

"You won't be laughing so hard when you get hit with the wind chill." She slowly sat down on the edge of the bed and looked down at her clothes. Without thinking, she had packed only shorts and t-shirts. She hadn't expected it to be this cold. She only had one of Griggs' shirts to wrap around her. Falling back on the bed, she stared at the ceiling. "Do you think I'm nuts?"

"Yeah," Griggs answered from the bathroom.

"No," Alex laughed. "Seriously. Do you think I'm crazy for coming here?" Griggs stepped out of the bathroom and leaned against the wall. He looked at Alex with amusement on his face. "Yeah, but what am I going to do?"

"What do you mean?" Alex asked.

"I didn't think I had much of a choice concerning coming here. You get these ideas, and it's best just to let you ride them out." Griggs laughed. "Hell, *I'm* just along for the ride most of the time."

Alex sat up on the bed. "I resent that."

"What?" Griggs said, still amused. "It's true, but I'm okay with that. I don't mind following you on your little adventures, as long as we're together." He walked over and sat next to Alex on the bed. He placed his hand on her leg.

Lifting Griggs' hand, Alex quickly stood up and walked to the opposite side of the room. "Is that what you think this is?" she asked angrily. "One of my 'little adventures'?"

"I didn't say that to start a fight, Alex." Griggs started to back off. "I was just making a joke."

"I don't think that's very funny. What I'm doing here is serious," Alex scolded him. "I'm here to solve the biggest riddle of all time!"

Griggs stood up and approached her. "I'm sorry. I didn't mean to upset you." He tried to put his hands on the side of her face, but Alex quickly pulled away. "What?" Griggs asked.

"I thought, out of everyone, that you would take this a little more seriously."

"I do."

"Then why don't you show it? You just tease

101

me."

"I tease you because I love you. If I didn't, then we'd be in real trouble," Griggs joked.

"See? There you go again! It's always a joke with you! Can't you be serious?"

"I'm sorry, I'm just having a hard time with this whole 'aliens influencing man's evolution' thing," Griggs shot back sarcastically. "I just don't believe," Griggs admitted with a sigh.

Alex's eyes widened. "How?" she asked in amazement. "After all you've seen, after all we've been through, how can you not believe?"

"It's not that I don't believe in aliens and UFOs, Alex. I've seen them with my own eyes! I just can't subscribe to the theory that an extraterrestrial entity came down and created us."

Alex began to quickly button up her shirt.

"What are you doing?" Griggs asked in frustration.

"I need to get out of here for a little while." She walked over and opened the door. "I'm going to walk over to the supermarket and see if I can get a pack of cigarettes."

She stepped out of the door and closed it behind her. She stood on the patio for a moment, looking up at the overcast sky. She heard a clap of thunder. A constant thumping noise began to fill the sky. She knew what it was, but couldn't place it. A sheet of lightning tore through the night sky, revealing the silhouettes of two black helicopters. The sky lit up again as another bolt of lightning crashed to the ground. She could see that the two helicopters were heading for Rano Raraku, Rapa Nui's biggest volcano. Her heart began to race. Terrified, she pulled the cottage's door open and ran inside. She quickly pressed herself against the wall.

Griggs stared at her with awe. The color had drained out of her face. She was as white as a sheet. "Did you see a ghost?"

Alex shook her head frantically and tried to catch her breath. Her heart felt like it was trying to push its way out of her mouth. "Something worse."

"What?" he asked. Griggs was starting to feel a little anxiety. He had never seen her this way before. "What happened?"

Alex swallowed hard. "The government," she finally mustered.

"What about them?" Griggs asked again, this time a little more frantic. "They're here!"

***

The makeshift base was built on the slope of Rano Raraku. Several large canvas tents had been erected around base camp. Many were for the personnel, but several were designed to house state-of-the-art research equipment. Giant spotlights had been raised, making the night almost as bright as the day. A large area, a few hundred feet from the camp, had been flattened while bright beacons surrounded it. They had created a small landing pad so that equipment and troops could be easily flown in and out without using the local airport.

The two black helicopters swung around the side of the volcano and headed toward the landing area. They quickly decreased their speed as they approached the camp. Circling over the landing pad, the helicopters began to slowly descend.

Five men stood on the outskirts of the landing pad, watching the helicopter's skids touch down. The men heard the helicopter's engines whine as their power was cut. The five men lowered themselves and began to approach the two choppers. The lead man waved off three of his companions toward the second helicopter, while he hobbled toward the first.

The side panels of the helicopters unlocked and slid open. Several soldiers began to pour out of the small cargo bay onto the landing pad. They assembled on the far side of the pad near one of the beacons and snapped to attention. As the mighty rotor blades finally ground to a halt, the two front doors popped open. The pilot and a second man slowly climbed out and began to walk toward their assembled team.

"Colonel Jannis?"

Jannis stopped and spun around. He smiled. "Dr. Hollman," he said. "Good to see you again," he added with a touch of sarcasm in his voice.

Hollman was dressed in the now standard Area 51 black fatigues. His brown hair was trimmed shorter than usual, and arranged in a stylishly messy way. He was walking with a severe limp and a cane at his side. "Colonel," he said acknowledging his senior officer. Hollman reached out and shook Jannis' hand.

"How's the limp?" Jannis asked. He knew it was a sore spot for Hollman, and he enjoyed rubbing it in. Hollman was also sensitive to the fact Jannis had been named first officer of Area 51 over him.

Hollman looked down at the brown wooden

104

cane that was helping to support his weight. "It's getting better, but Dr. Cisan doesn't think I'll ever be able to walk without it again. The bullet wound I received four years ago in Las Vegas did too much damage to my spine. Cisan thinks it's a miracle I can walk at all."

Jannis laughed. "Well, you can thank our little gray friends technology for that." Jannis turned and began to walk toward his men again. "What's the situation here, Doctor?"

Hollman was trying to catch up to Jannis. "Using an advanced sonar system, we've discovered there is a large null area under this entire island."

"This island is riddled with volcanic caves," Jannis pointed out. He had been studying this island and its culture during the flight here. He wanted to be prepared for whatever situation he ran into. "Could that be what your sonar is seeing?"

"I don't think so, Colonel," Hollman said. "You're right, this island is filled with volcanic caves, but if we were just seeing caves, the null areas would be a lot smaller and scattered around the island."

Jannis stopped in front of his men and quickly inspected them. "You men understand the task at hand?" he addressed the men. "Dismissed." He watched the men fall out, and begin to unload equipment from the helicopters.

"May I ask what this second team of men is for, Colonel?" Hollman asked while watching them go about their business.

"General Caroll wants them here for a special surprise she has planned."

"What 'surprise'?"

Jannis smiled. "I'm afraid I can't tell you. If I did, I'd have to kill you." Hollman laughed, then abruptly stopped. A long uncomfortable silence ensued between the two men. "You're kidding, right?" Jannis turned to Hollman and smiled.

Hollman cleared his throat to break the silence. "We think we've found what could be an entrance, or a connecting cave. Either way, we may have located our access tube."

"What do you expect to find here?" Jannis asked. "There's no proof aliens ever visited this site."

"We do have the one hieroglyph that was found in Egypt," Hollman countered.

"That's one symbol out of thousands," Jannis argued. "It could just be an incredible coincidence and nothing more."

"It's not my job to question the general," Hollman replied coolly. "I just go where she sends me and do what she says." He was lying.

"I know the feeling," Jannis added. "How long until we know if you've found the entrance or not?"

Hollman thought for a moment. "I've had two excavation teams working around the clock on it for a day and a half now. It could be anytime."

Jannis nodded. "In that case, I need to get some rest. General Caroll will be joining us here in the morning, and we expect our guest to arrive shortly after that."

"General Caroll is coming here?"

Chapter Thirteen

It turned out to be a beautiful morning. The night before had seen some rain, but as if on cue, the dark clouds had parted as the sun rose high into the sky. Small puddles still littered the streets and parking lots, but they would all be dry by afternoon.

Durard had been sitting in the shade on a small, wooden park bench for the past hour. He had been sipping coffee out of an insulated cup now resting next to him. He looked across this small, green area that stood in the middle of town. It was shaded entirely by a mass of oak trees that stretched from one side to the other. On the far side, he could see a family playing near a long metal swing set. The father was pushing his little girl higher and higher on the swing. Her laughter could be heard from every corner of the park. Turning his head to the left, he saw a group of teenagers playing volleyball. They were running and laughing as they bounced the small white ball back and forth over the net. The park was full of life.

Durard had made a trip to the department store this morning and purchased a new set of clothes. He had been careful not to use his credit cards, only the cash he had on hand to purchase a single pair of tan slacks, a pack of white t-shirts and a black button short sleeved shirt. Also, in an effort to disguise himself, he'd gone to the drug store and picked up a bottle of hair dye. His normally sandy blonde hair was now a dark shade of brown.

Durard looked down at the sling his arm was in. Unwrapping the bandage from around his shoulder, he carefully applied it to his broken arm. He knew that his forearm had been snapped cleanly, making resetting the wound very easy. His only concern now was to keep the limb as immobile as possible and allowing it time to heal. An arc of pain shot up his arm, then dissipated. He needed to pick up some kind of painkiller. Using a pin, he attached the bandage securely to the others, satisfied with the job he had done.

Durard looked down at the silver face of his wristwatch and shook his head. It was too nice of a morning to be inside, but that was exactly where he needed to be. He didn't want to be spotted. He knew the men who tried to kill him were probably still looking for him, although he wasn't sure why. Durard wondered if his stumbling on to the edited files was a factor. *Maybe the government was just doing a bit of "spring cleaning" and taking care of a few leftover problems.*

Standing, he tossed his cup in a nearby trash can. He walked steadily along the sidewalk that ran around the park, still enjoying the day. Faith and Tyler's house was less than a block from here, so he had opted not to drive. It was a huge risk walking in the open like this, but at the moment, he didn't care. His arm had stopped hurting, and it was a gorgeous day.

Durard stopped and looked to his left one last time to see the park full of life. He focused on the family near the swings again. They had spread out a blanket and were enjoying a picnic together. He wanted that. He had often wondered if he would have time for a family, or if he would ever meet the right woman. Always focused on his goals, he never allowed time to hang out with his friends or attend parties. He had always been the one sitting alone in his dorm room under the harsh light of a desk lamp wading through the pages of his chemistry and biology textbooks. Durard sometimes regretted that decision. He felt he'd missed out on a portion of his life he would never be able to get back. Durard shook his head and turned away. A professor he respected in college had told him once "Don't question the path you've taken. Make the best of it." Now in his thirtieth year, he was trying hard to make the best of it.

Durard took one last look at the park, and then continued on his way. He was about to pass by the final tree, when a man jumped out in front of him. Durard reacted instinctively. He threw a hard right hook into the man's face before he even knew who it was. The man tumbled to the ground holding his nose.

"What the hell are you doing?" Tulley asked.

"Jesus," Durard replied. He reached down to help the man off the sidewalk. He quickly began to dust him off. "I'm very sorry."

Tulley pulled his hand from his nose. He checked for blood, but found nothing. "You should be," Tulley added angrily.

"Why did you jump out at me?" Durard shot back.

"I was just coming around the corner to talk to you," Tulley insisted.

A spark of recognition crossed Durard's face. "Hey, wait a minute, you're that reporter that came to talk to me a few days ago. Have you been following me?"

Tulley nodded. "I saw what those goons did to

your apartment back in San Francisco, so I followed you here."

"Why?" Durard asked. "What kind of story could you be doing on me?" Tulley smiled. "It's not entirely about you, at least not anymore. I originally wanted to find out about TYD and your involvement with it, but since then, I've been doing some digging and it appears your path has crossed Area 51's. That would make a much more interesting story."

Durard turned and began to walk away. "I'm afraid I don't know anything about that. Now if you'll excuse me."

"That's bullshit and you know it," Tulley said as he grabbed Durard's arm. Durard turned around to face Tulley. He was taller than Tulley by at least four inches. "Look, Mr. Tulley, even if I did know something about that damned base in Nevada, why would I tell you? You'll just go print it in your newspaper and end up getting me killed."

"Not a good excuse," Tulley argued.

Durard had to stifle an uneasy laugh. "That's about as good a reason as there is, Mr. Tulley."

Tulley shook his head. "The American people need to know the truth about that place and what it's doing."

"Let's pretend just for a moment that I *do* know something about Area 51 and TYD. Let's also pretend that after everything was all said and done, and I accepted my promotion at FEMA, that I had to sign certain confidentiality forms."

Tulley's eyes widened. "You mean in order to get your promotion, they made you sign confidentiality forms?"

110

"We were just pretending, remember?"

"This is incredible! Do you realize what that means?" Tulley waited for Durard to answer. When he didn't, Tulley jumped back in. "The government bought your silence!"

"What?" Durard asked with disbelief.

"Don't you see?" Tulley asked again. "In order to keep you quiet, they gave you a raise and a promotion."

"That's...." Durard let his words trail off. He felt his heart sink in his chest. Tulley was telling the truth. This new epiphany enraged him. He had actually become a puppet of the very same government that had released TYD and killed millions of innocent people. He turned to look at Tulley. "I'll tell you everything you want to know, and more."

***

Jake stood alone in the middle of Santiago Airport in Chile. It was, in his opinion, controlled chaos. Nationals were dragging huge suitcases behind them as they neared the ticket counters, and tourists just off their planes were already taking pictures of everything they saw. It was winter in South America, but not to a perceivable degree. One of the flight attendants on his previous flight had informed him that it never dropped below sixty degrees in the winter. Most of the travelers, he noticed, were still wearing short sleeved shirts or tank tops.

The airport was colored a dingy white. It had a high ceiling throughout the terminal with ventilation vents about every twenty feet. Large glass windows looked out onto the tarmac, allowing the passengers to watch planes arrive and depart. Ferns and palm trees littered every free corner of the terminal, making it look more like a jungle than an airport.

Jake was pacing back and forth in the small glass booth they had designated the "smoking area", anxious to finish this trip. Samantha was the only thing he had been able to think about since he had received the videotape and photographs. Jake had almost an hour to waste while he waited on the connecting flight to Rapa Nui. He walked around the two rows of chairs in the booth and sat down on the far side of the room. There were about ten people in this tiny booth, all smoking at the same time. Apparently, the fans in the ceiling were broke, because the smoke was billowing out of the door and into the main terminal.

Jake pulled a cigar out of his small black travel bag and placed it in his mouth. He hadn't had one since he left his house on the way to the Reno airport. They didn't have a smoking area there, and he didn't want to chance missing his flight. This was too important. Digging into the bag, Jake rooted around for a second before finding his lighter. Pulling out the silver device, he flipped the lid open and flicked it. Lifting it to the end of the cigar, Jake took in a few long puffs until he was satisfied it was fully lit. He dropped the lighter back into the bag and leaned back in the chair.

Sitting straight up, Jake realized he hadn't told anyone where he was going. He hadn't even had the foresight to call his ex-wife to let her know he had found Samantha. *Maybe it's better this way. My life's a disaster.* Jake took a drag off his cigar and slowly exhaled it. His mind slowly shifted to Alex. He realized fate must have been playing a cruel joke with his life. *For the first time in four years she calls,* Jake complained, *and it's to ask me to go on another insane adventure, and now this!*

Jake heard an announcement over the loudspeaker in Spanish, then in English. "Flight three-zero-nine to Rapa Nui and Tahiti is now boarding at gate four. Flight three-zero-nine to Rapa Nui and Tahiti is now boarding at gate four."

Leaning over, Jake crushed his cigar out in the metal ashtray sitting next to him. He stood up and grabbed his black duffel off the ground. Slinging it over his shoulder, he quickly left the smoking area and began to head toward gate four. He was weaving his way through the crowds, when he saw a tall man approaching him.

The man, of Hispanic descent, looked about thirty years old. He was wearing a pair of black pants, a white t-shirt and a long black trench coat and had a goatee and a shaved head,. He had a handful of what looked like colorful pamphlets. "Would you like to learn more about the Brotherhood of the Divine Sanctuary, sir?" he asked in choppy English.

Jake shook his head and tried to walk around the man. "I'm sorry, but I don't have a lot of time."

The man quickly stepped in front of Jake. His movements were very controlled and concise. "You should make time for this."

Jake was about to reply when the man dropped his pamphlets and pulled a pistol. He quickly shoved it into Jake's midsection.

113

"What the hell are you doing?" Jake asked in horror. "We're in the middle of a crowded airport."

"I need you to come with me, Mr. Silver," the man in the dark coat replied calmly. He was hiding the weapon with the flap of his jacket.

Jake was startled the man knew his name. "How...?"

"That's not important now," the man replied. "You need to come with me, or I'll shoot you right here."

"What if I kick your ass?"

The man in the dark coat smiled. "Then my associates will kill you." He nodded toward several more men dressed in similar fashion standing nonchalantly around the terminal.

"You don't understand. I'm going to get my daughter back."

"We know all about you, Mr. Silver," the man glanced around the busy terminal. "We need to go now. We're beginning to arouse suspicion." He jabbed the gun harder into Jake's gut. "Now turn around slowly and walk toward the exit."

Jake complied and started to move. "What are you guys? The Chilean Mafia or something?"

The man in the dark coat laughed. "Don't be ignorant," the man said. "What you've stumbled into is much more important that some two-bit drug running operation."

Jake looked at the exit looming ahead of him and quickly started to form a plan in his mind. "So what is this?"

"As I told you, we are the Brotherhood of the Divine Sanctuary."

"I've never been really big on religion," Jake

114

admitted. *That's good. Keep him talking,* he thought as a plan began to take shape.

"I'm sorry you feel that way," the man said. "We are a religious organization, but we're more like," the man in the dark coat searched for the proper English translation, "protectors than anything else."

Jake slowly slipped his black duffel off his shoulder. Above him, he heard the announcement for the departure of his flight again. He had to act now. "Protectors of what?"

"Of—"

Jake slung his black duffel around hitting the man squarely in the head. He fell to the floor dazed while his weapon went skittering away. Tossing his black bag over his shoulder again, Jake took off in a dead sprint into the terminal. He glanced behind him to see the other men dressed in black coats chasing after him, and beginning to gain ground. Jake whipped his head back around and cursed under his breath. A group of tourists were standing in front of him. "Get out of the way!" Jake yelled as he plunged headlong into the group. Tourists fell to the ground as they scattered. Pushing off an elderly man, Jake spun out of the path of an oncoming attacker.

Jake saw his gate ahead of him. The flight attendant was starting to pull a rope across the gate. "Wait!" Jake yelled. Tossing his ticket at the attendant, Jake sprinted down the skyway toward the plane. He turned around to see the men being stopped by the attendant and airport security. Jake laughed as he walked through the plane's waiting hatch.

Moving to the rear of the plane, Jake stowed his duffel in the overhead compartment, then slumped down into his coach seat. He noticed the passenger sitting next to him was reading a local newspaper. Jake looked over at the passenger's newspaper and smiled when he saw it was written in English. "Hey, buddy," Jake started. "Are you reading the sports section?" The passenger slowly lowered the paper and looked over. Startled, Jake jumped up out of his seat. "How did you get here?"

The man in the dark coat smiled through his goatee. "I told you it was important we talk."

Chapter Fourteen

Morning couldn't come soon enough for Alex and Griggs. They both sat quietly staring at the doors and windows of the small cottage. They hadn't slept at all, let alone closed their eyes other than to blink. They were both exhausted.

Griggs was sitting in one of the wooden chairs with a small black revolver cradled tightly in his hands. Alex, meanwhile, had taken a central position on the bed and was staring at one of the two windows in the cottage. Griggs had tried to tell her he would stand guard while she slept, but she couldn't force herself to close her eyes.

Griggs stood up and stretched. "I don't think they're coming, Alex."

"How do you know?" Alex asked quietly. She still had her eyes trained on the window.

"They would've been here by now." Griggs set the revolver on the table and walked toward Alex. He slowly sat next to her on the bed. "The government doesn't fuck around when it comes to things like this. They would've killed us both as soon as they set foot on this island."

Alex still had her eyes fixed on the window.

"I don't think they know we're here," Griggs speculated.

For the first time all night, Alex closed her eyes and slumped down on the bed. She grabbed a pillow and held it tightly to her face as she started to sob. "I don't want to go through this again," she moaned.

"I know," Griggs comforted her. Reaching over, he removed the pillow from her face. "Come here." He lifted her up and held her next to him.

117

Alex wrapped her arms around his chest and buried her face. She allowed herself to cry. "I'm so sorry, Jason."

"Why?" Griggs asked caringly while he ran his hand through her hair. "If it weren't for me, none of this would be happening."

"How can you say that?"

"If I hadn't been snooping around in Egypt six years ago and found the alien device, you and Jake wouldn't have had to come and rescue me."

Griggs suddenly felt a stabbing pain in his chest. He tried to ignore it. "You were just doing what you thought was right." The pain was steadily growing worse.

"Maybe I am on some kind of damned crusade," she said with a sigh. "I keep looking for these little green men, no matter what the cost." Alex felt Griggs stop rubbing her back and looked up. His face had twisted into a horrible grimace of pain. "Jason!" She jumped up and laid him flat on the bed. "What's the matter?"

"I don't know," Griggs gasped. He grabbed his chest with his hands. "It feels like my heart," he stated gravely.

Alex started to panic. There was no hospital on this island. Emergencies were all flown back nearly two thousand miles to Chile. She quickly leaned over and listened to his chest. His heart was beating irregularly. She didn't know what to do. "Jason, stay with me."

Griggs moaned in agony. "It feels like someone's stabbing me in the chest with a knife!" He twisted over onto his side and curled up in an effort to make the pain subside. "It's getting worse," he said while gritting his teeth.

Alex jumped up and ran to the bathroom. Grabbing a washcloth off the counter, she quickly held it under the tap and turned on the cold water. After wringing out the rag, she ran back to Griggs and laid it on his forehead. "Don't you die on me," she warned him. "I'm going to try and get some help."

Alex sprinted for the door. Grabbing the handle, she threw the door open and came face to face with her worst fears. A man dressed in black fatigues was standing at the ready with his weapon drawn. His face was entirely covered by a black mask, while a pair of dark goggles covered his eyes. Alex couldn't even scream. She stumbled back and fell to the floor. She frantically tried to pull herself away from the man, but it was no use.

Two more men dressed in black moved into the room, while a fourth was using the butt of his rifle to break through the window. Alex pushed off the floor and ran for Griggs. His body had started to convulse. Tears were streaming from Alex's eyes as she watched the three men approach. The first one grabbed her by the hair and pulled her off of the bed, while the other two lifted Griggs. Alex was kicking and screaming as the man pinned her to the floor. Pressing his right hand to her throat, he used the other to pull a small silver device off this belt. It was long and silver with a tapered end and a blue button on the side. The man held it to Alex's neck and depressed the blue button. Alex heard a hiss as a cold sensation began to pass down her neck into her shoulders. She looked up at the man one final time before everything went dark.

***

"You mean to tell me The Yellow Death was an extraterrestrial virus?" Tulley asked in disbelief.

Durard nodded. The two had made their way back to Faith and Tyler's house and were sitting on opposite sides of the small living room. Durard had taken up position on a small tan loveseat, while Tulley had spread his notes over a similarly colored couch. A long dark wooden coffee table ran the length of the couch and stood between them. Faith had decorated it with several photos of her wedding, while Tyler had the latest issue of a UFO magazine sitting prominently next to the photos. All in all, Faith had done a wonderful job decorating this small house. It truly felt cozy; like a home.

Tulley had been writing notes vigorously in his small black notepad, while Durard had been telling him everything he knew. "How did you discover this?" Durard thought for a moment. "I didn't discover anything," Durard admitted dryly. "A former colleague of mine, a man named Greg Hollman, confessed before he died."

"How did he die?"

"He was shot in the back by a co-conspirator."

"Dear God," Tulley muttered while writing. "So these conspirators had actually intended to use TYD as a biological weapon they would sell to the highest bidder?"

Durard nodded again. "The strange part is they didn't even have a cure or vaccine prepared when they released it."

"Incredible," Tulley said while still writing.

120

"About the vaccine," he said. "How did you create one?"

"That was actually the easy part," Durard said while leaning forward. "We discovered that, somehow, Tyler had a natural immunity to TYD. We used antibody samples from his body to synthesize a very powerful vaccine that effectively wiped out all cases of TYD."

"This doesn't add up," Tulley admitted. "If TYD was extraterrestrial, then how did this young man have a 'natural immunity' to it?"

"We're still not entirely sure. Tyler, to this day, claims that aliens abducted him and altered his DNA." Durard rubbed his hand through his now dark brown hair. "It's funny though," Durard laughed, "his explanation is really the only one that makes any sense."

"I see," Tulley said thoughtfully. "You do realize if I print this story, they'll label me a 'nut'."

Durard smiled. "That's why none of us have readily stepped forward to tell it."

Tully was surprised by the comment. "Then why are you telling me?"

"I've had it," Durard admitted. "I'm not taking any more of this government's Nazi tactics. I have officially drawn a line in the sand."

"That's very brave."

"Or foolhardy," Durard countered.

The two were interrupted by the sound of the door handle being jiggled. Durard instantly scrambled. He leapt over the back of the couch and quickly crouched down in the kitchen. Tulley, meanwhile, was hastily trying to round up his papers and notes and stuff them back into his satchel. Both men heard the door handle twist and the door creak open. Peeking over the couch, Durard was relieved to see Faith standing in the doorway.

"What the hell is going on here?" Faith asked angrily.

Durard stood up in the kitchen. "I'm sorry, Faith, we thought you were a killer."

She pointed at two glasses sitting on her coffee table. "I will be if you don't start using coasters!"

Durard ran back into the living room and inserted a small doily under each glass. "Sorry, Faith."

Faith carefully navigated through the living room toward the kitchen holding two large brown bags in her arms. Setting them down, she dropped her keys and purse on their small kitchen table. Spinning around, she sized up the two men standing in her living room. "Jim," she said in a very pleasant tone, "who's this?"

Durard looked to Tulley. "This is Jeff Tulley, a reporter with the *High Desert Reporter*."

"What's he doing in my house?" Faith asked angrily. Her usually calm brown eyes looked as if the very flames of perdition were licking them.

"He wants to know our story."

Faith's eyes widened. "You didn't use my name, did you?" She marched toward Tulley. "If you use my name in your article, I will make sure you are promptly fired, then I will sue you for public slander!"

Tulley took a step back. "Whoa, lady," he said, holding his hands up. "I'm not the bad guy here."

"The hell you're not. I've spent the better part

of the last four years hiding from the government. I'm not going to throw that all away just because you want to do a story on aliens and UFOs." Faith turned and walked back into the kitchen. She haphazardly began to pull her groceries out of the bags and toss them on the counter. "Besides," she started, trying to regain control of her anger, "aren't aliens and UFOs out?"

"What do you mean 'out'?" Tulley asked.

"I mean they aren't in style anymore," Faith corrected. "Heck, even 'The X-Files' aren't as good as they used to be." Durard laughed. "I agree."

Tulley shook his head. "Aliens may be out of fashion, but the truth isn't. I don't care if this story dealt with 'Plan nine from outer space', it's still the truth."

Durard smiled at Tulley's obscure movie reference. "He's right, Faith. We have an obligation to tell our story. To inform the citizens of America that the government is really doing these horrible things."

"I don't care," Faith said, slamming a head of lettuce down on the counter. She quickly tried to calm her temper as she walked into the living room. She stood facing the two men. "I'm married now. I'm happy. I have a wonderful home and a good life. I'm not going to throw that all away." Her attitude quickly changed as she looked at the two men with fear in her eyes. "I don't want to lose Tyler."

Durard suddenly realized the ramifications of Faith's statement. He was single. He didn't have anyone to lose because of this. Faith, however, had everything to lose. "I understand," he said

123

sympathetically, "and I respect your decision."

Faith quickly stepped toward Durard and wrapped her arms around him in an embrace. "Thank you. I knew you would."

Chapter Fifteen

The man in the dark coat smiled as the plane began to descend toward Rapa Nui. He leaned over and tapped Jake on the shoulder. "Take a look at this," the man said, pointing out the window.

Jake slowly leaned over toward the cabin window and looked down at the small triangle shaped island. He was still very leery of the man sitting next to him. Jake kept glancing back at the man's hands. "What am I looking at?"

"You see the airport down there?" the man asked quietly. Jake nodded.

"A few years ago, the U.S. Government came in and extended the runway at Mataveri Airport," the man said with a hint of pride in his voice.

"Why?" Jake asked.

"To accommodate the Space Shuttle, in case of an emergency landing," the man noted. "They completely funded the project themselves without the help of the Rapa Nui, or the Chilean government."

"Why would they do that?"

The man in the dark coat laughed. "Look around, Mr. Silver. There's nothing but the Pacific Ocean for two thousand miles in every direction. This is one of the most remote corners of the world. NASA didn't really want to have to ditch a multi-billion dollar vehicle in the ocean if they didn't have to."

Jake quickly leaned back in his seat. "That's very interesting, but—"

"You're wondering when I'm going to tell you why I'm here," the man in the dark coat cut in.

"We've been on this flight a long time and you've said nothing. All you've done is sit there quietly and read your newspaper." Jake looked at the man for a long moment. "It's driving me insane!"

"Patience, Mr. Silver," the man said with a gentle smile. "All in good time." Jake was starting to get the feeling he was never going to see his daughter again.

***

Alex slowly came to strapped to a small, wooden chair. Her mind was groggy at first, but she quickly remembered what had happened. She glanced around, trying to make sense of where she was. All she could see where the bland, tan interior walls of the tent. A small green footlocker sat near the rear, while she was positioned in the direct center.

Her hands were bound with rope behind the chair, and her feet, legs and body were lashed to it. Alex began to struggle, but it was to no avail. The ropes were tied securely. She suddenly became very weak and woozy, probably an aftereffect of the drug she was injected with.

From the shadows on the tent's sides, she could tell night had fallen. She wondered how many hours, or days for that matter, had gone by since she had been brought here. Her mind instantly flashed to Griggs. A sick feeling in the pit of her stomach began to grow. *Is he okay?*

The tent flaps were suddenly thrown open and a familiar figure entered. "You son of a bitch!" Alex

126

shouted while trying to break free of her bonds. She knew if she could, she would kill him with her bare hands.

"Well," Hollman said with a smile. "Is that any way to treat an old friend?" Hollman quickly staggered inside the tent. Two men in black garb accompanied him. He pointed toward the green footlocker. "Bring that over here," he said to one of the men. The soldier quickly complied and scooted the box in front of Alex.

"What the hell are you doing here?" Alex asked spitefully.

The second soldier removed a bottle of champagne and two glasses from a bag that he had slung over his shoulder and set them on the footlocker. "Will that be all, sir?"

Hollman nodded. "Don't go far, though. I may need you again."

"Understood." The two soldiers spun on their heels and exited the tent. Hollman gently laid his cane against the side of the footlocker and lifted the bottle of champagne. "The trick is," he said while tearing the wrapping off the bottle, "to apply equal pressure on both sides of the cork with your thumbs." He pressed hard, sending the cork shooting off.

"You never answered my question," Alex said spitefully. "What are you doing here, Dr. Hollman?"

Hollman filled the two glasses with the bubbly liquid. He lifted one in front of him. "To our success," he said and then took a sip of the alcohol. Hollman smiled. "You can never have enough champagne in your life," he said half to himself.

127

"Don't you agree, Dr. Robinson?"

Alex turned away from Hollman. "Fuck off."

Hollman laughed out loud. "Such anger from you, and on this, the eve of the biggest discovery in human history."

"What the hell are you talking about?"

"We've discovered something," Hollman searched for the most appropriate adjective to describe the situation, "extraordinary."

"What?" Alex was getting sick of Hollman's games.

"The entrance to what we believe is an ancient alien stronghold on this island."

"What are you talking about?" Alex asked, feigning ignorance.

"The prophecy you discovered in Egypt led us here," Hollman admitted. "How did you know about that?" Alex screamed.

Hollman's face was smug with glee. "We have spies everywhere."

"You bastard, that was my discovery!"

"Bah!" Hollman dismissed her claim outright. "It doesn't make a difference who discovered it, all that matters is that we got here first."

"It does matter who discovers it," Alex argued. "If we found it first, we would share the knowledge with the entire world, but since you found it, you'll probably go and hoard it in one of your little secret bases. No one will benefit from this now!"

"I beg to differ," Hollman said, after taking another sip of his champagne. "The United States of America will benefit from this." Hollman pushed the bottle aside on the footlocker and sat down. He

128

leaned toward Alex. "Since the 1950's, we've been using recovered alien technology to develop faster and better war craft. The U.S. will be virtually unstoppable if another world war breaks out." Hollman finished his glass and tossed it aside. "Imagine this: wave after wave of stealth aircraft bomb our enemies into submission without any fear of being shot down. Their radar won't be able to see us. Then, if there's any resistance left, we send in the ground troops with advanced weaponry. It will be a glorious sight."

"You're insane," Alex growled.

"Possibly," Hollman agreed, "but I'm going to be the first human to ever set foot inside the alien stronghold, while you're tied up here in this tent."

Alex stared angrily at Hollman. "When I get free...."

Hollman stood up and smiled. "I have posted guards outside this tent, just to make sure that doesn't happen." Reaching down, he retrieved his cane. "I'm afraid it's time for me to bid you adieu." He pointed to the bottle of champagne still sitting on the footlocker. "I'll leave this here, just in case you get thirsty." Hollman laughed loudly as he limped out of the tent.

"Damn," Alex muttered. She stared around the tent. *I have to get free,* she thought, *I've got to find Jason.*

***

Two figures stepped out of the Aurora and began to walk toward the base camp. The Aurora had approached silently from the northeast and landed vertically on the pad next to the two black helicopters. The strange black triangle shaped craft towered over the two small choppers like they were insects.

Jannis was standing at the mouth of the access platform awaiting his guests. He had snapped to attention the moment the Aurora landed. "It's good to see you, General."

Anne sneered as she emerged from the landing platform. "I've brought you a little present." Reaching behind her, she grabbed the chain between the prisoner's handcuffs and pulled her into the light. Samantha Silver stumbled to the ground at Jannis' feet. "See that she's taken care of."

"Yes, General," Jannis replied with no emotion in his voice. After years of military training, he knew to follow orders without any personal feelings on the matter.

Jannis reached down and lifted the frightened girl off the ground. Her brown hair was matted to her bruised face and her clothes were tattered. Her eyes were red and dark bags had developed because she had been crying. Samantha looked up at him. He could see the terror in her eyes. Jannis had a sudden flash of the young girl curled up alone in her hotel room in Las Vegas, crying over the dead bodies of her parents. He'd found her four years ago when Hollman needed a new test subject for TYD. He'd pretended to be her savior, but ultimately, he had been the angel of death. He didn't want history to repeat itself.

The three began to walk down the adjoining ramp toward camp. Anne had taken the lead, while Jannis attended to Samantha. "How's the project progressing, Colonel?"

"Everything's going according to plan, General, and we have a little added bonus for you."

Anne stopped and turned to face Jannis. "What?"

"It turns out that Alex Robinson and Jason Griggs arrived on Rapa Nui right after we did," Jannis explained.

"What action was taken?" Anne asked.

"We easily identified Dr. Robinson when we were flying in. As soon as I arrived, I assigned five members of my team to recover them."

"How did it go?" Anne asked delightedly.

"Flawlessly," Jannis said with pride in his voice. "There's one problem though."

Anne's smile quickly faded. "What's the problem, Colonel?"

"When we found Major Griggs, he was suffering from some kind of seizure."

"Prognosis?"

"We're not sure yet, but we do know one thing for sure."

"What's that, Colonel?"

Jannis paused for a moment. He wasn't sure how Anne would take the news. "According to Dr. Hollman and Dr. Cisan, his clone body is apparently beginning to break down."

Anne frowned. "Did any of our researchers know this would happen?" Jannis shook his head, "No. This is a completely unexpected effect of the project."

Anne ran her hand down her chest to her stomach, then stopped. "I want to know why and how this is happening, and I want to know quickly."

131

Chapter Sixteen

Jake dropped his duffel bag on the floor and immediately spun around to face the man in the dark coat. "If you're planning on killing me, now would be a good time."

The man laughed out loud as he closed the door to the hotel room behind him. He had taken Jake to one of the larger hotels on the island, Hotel Rano Raraku. The man in the dark coat had insisted they take one of the smaller rooms in the hotel, instead of one of the stand-alone cottages. He explained he felt more secure this way. "Mr. Silver, if everything goes well, no one will be dying. Especially you." The man quickly moved to the window and looked outside. Scanning the landscape, he looked for strategic advantage points. "This island is hell for military operations," he declared to himself. "This will be a very difficult operation."

"What are you talking about?" Jake asked angrily, still standing just inside the door. "I demand an explanation!"

The man wrapped his long fingers around the window shades and drew them tightly closed. Spinning around, his black trench coat billowed around him like a cape, giving him an almost mythical appearance. "Then your demands will be met," he answered quietly. "Please," he said, motioning to a table and chairs on the far side of the room, "sit down."

Jake cautiously moved toward a chair and sank into it. He kept his unblinking eyes focused on the man in the dark coat. "What's your name?"

The man shook his head. "We have no use for

names. Our cause negates the affectations of personal identification," he said. Whipping his coat aside, he sat down eerily in the chair and folded his hands in his lap.

Jake had been observing his movements ever since he had first seen him in the airport. The man in the dark coat moved with a very languid motion, almost seamlessly. He had the grace of a dancer and looked as if every tiny gesture was coldly calculated for maximum efficiency. "So what do I call you?" Jake asked. "How about 'The Man in the Dark Coat'?"

The man shook his head slowly. "If you truly desire to refer to me as something, you may call me One."

"Why One?"

"Because I am only one of many."

"Many what?"

One smiled. "We can't begin this way. We have to start from the beginning."

Jake leaned over and rested his elbows on the table. He looked directly into One's eyes. He scanned them for any trace of what he was about to say, but found nothing. No trace of personality, no evidence of individuality. "Okay," Jake announced uneasily, "from the top."

"We are the Brotherhood of the Divine Sanctuary," One said as he spread his arms wide. "We are the sworn protectors of the refuge of God here on Rapa Nui."

"What?" Jake said in disbelief as he sat up. "You can't be serious!" One's facial expression didn't waver. He remained calm and collected.

"We are very serious, Mr. Silver. Father

133

Santiago Andres founded our order in the eighth century A.D. He was assigned by the Catholic Church in Mexico to be a missionary to the people of Rapa Nui. The Catholic Church wanted to bring Christianity to the heathens, but when Father Andres arrived, the heathens brought God to him."

"I don't understand," Jake admitted. "I didn't think the Catholic church ever sent missionaries to Easter Island."

One nodded. "You are historically correct. There are no records of missionaries ever being assigned to Rapa Nui, because Father Andres destroyed them upon his return to Mexico."

"Why would he do that?"

"He wanted no one to discover the secret he had found here on Rapa Nui."

"What secret?" Jake asked quietly.

"That God himself had once set foot upon this small island in the middle of the South Pacific." One sat forward. Even though his face was still expressionless, Jake could tell he enjoyed telling this tale. "Upon his arrival, Father Andres discovered the natives carving these huge stone monoliths and erecting them around the island. He asked why they would build these huge ten ton statues. The natives replied they were honoring God. This perplexed Father Andres. No other known civilization at the time was carving statues like this, or representing any god in this fashion."

"So how did they know that's what God looks like?" Jake asked. His mind was swimming with disbelief. Lessons he learned in Sunday school as a child began to resurface. He remembered a quote from his teacher: *No one can look upon the face of*

God and survive....

"One day, Father Andres asked the natives to explain why they thought God looked this way. They informed him that they couldn't explain, rather they would have to show him. The natives took him across the island to the slopes of the volcano Rano Raraku. Once there, the natives showed Father Andres an entrance they had uncovered while mining the volcanic rock there. This was unlike anything he had ever seen before. When the natives refused to enter with him, Father Andres entered the darkness. Using only a small candle to light his way, he followed the shaft down for miles, until he came upon the Divine Sanctuary."

"What did it look like?" Jake asked, actually surprised he had become wrapped up in One's tale.

One shrugged gracefully. "No one knows."

Jake was astonished. "Let me get this straight," he said as he leaned back in his chair. "Father Andres never told a single soul what he found at the end of that shaft, and yet he felt it was so important, that he destroyed all records of his ever visiting there?"

"And created the Brotherhood to protect it."

Jake scoffed. "Seems a little far-fetched to me, One."

"That is why you are not a member of the Brotherhood," One reassured him. "We are hand-picked and raised from childhood believing in only one thing: the sanctity of the Divine Sanctuary. It is my sworn duty to protect it. The priests who raise us do not give us names, or allow us to blossom creatively. They teach us the way of God, and

135

instruct us on how to protect Him." One smiled, "I could kill you right now without leaving this chair, Mr. Silver. We are God's archangels on Earth," One said while looking at his hands. "Our faces turned toward Heaven's glorious light, while our wingtips are dipped in blood."

Jake's anxiety quickly returned. He knew he was dealing with a religious fanatic. "So why me?"

"You're fated to walk this path," One said cryptically. "I don't believe in fate," Jake shot back.

One leaned forward. "You don't have to." He slowly sat back and let the words sink in. "You were destined to come to this place." One stopped for a moment. "I have never seen the Divine Sanctuary," One said with regret, "but you are meant to."

Jake was dumbfounded. He couldn't find any words.

"Your daughter is here on the island right now, and she is unharmed." Jake's eyes widened. "How do you know that?"

"God wills me to."

"Then why are you here?"

"As I said before, I am here to protect the sanctity of the Divine Sanctuary. Nothing more." One ran his hand carefully over his forehead, stopping a bead of sweat that had rolled down his scalp. "Helping you and your daughter is inconsequential to our mission, but we will help anyway."

"Why?" Jake asked softly.

"Over the years, I have done things in the name of God I have grown to regret," One said, for the first time, allowing emotion to betray his cool exterior. He turned his eyes away from Jake in shame. "It is time I found some redemption."

Jake's fears and anxiety quickly melted away. He suddenly felt connected to this man on a very personal level. He actually felt sorry for One. "Thank you. I can use any help I can get."

One looked up at Jake. "Thank *you*, Mr. Silver."

***

The stars were shining brightly overhead as Tyler and Faith sat quietly on their deck. Wooden railings ran the length of it, with only a gap for stairs running down to the ground. A tall, square, black barbecue occupied a far corner, while three large potted plants lived in the other corners. A round table sat in the center with a collapsible umbrella jutting out of the middle as if it were reaching for the very same stars Tyler was looking at. They had turned off all the lights in the house so they could more clearly look at the sky.

It was a beautiful summer night. A cool breeze was blowing across the two lovers, giving them some relief from the extraordinarily hot Nevada days. In front of them, they could see the entire town of Elko stretched out before them in the valley. The lights of the town twinkled in the distance offset by the bright blues and reds of the downtown casinos. Behind the town, a long range of mountains, which made up one side of the valley, endlessly stretched off into the distance. On one of the far ridges, the two could see the flames of a brush fire licking the sky and casting an orange glow around the peak.

Neither liked to admit it, but they both loved it here. They both enjoyed complaining about life in a small town, but enjoyed it at the same time. The town was big enough to grant them some anonymity, yet small enough to keep them connected.

Lifting a glass of water off the table, Tyler lifted it to his mouth and took a long sip. Setting it down, he heard the unmistakable sound of an approaching aircraft. Looking up, he saw the collision lights of a private casino jet streaking across the sky toward the local airport. He watched it pass until it disappeared behind a neighboring house.

Tyler had pulled off his shoes and socks and had his feet propped up on the table. He reached down and flicked a small bit of dirt off his worn jeans. Adjusting his green t-shirt, he settled back into the chair and folded his hands behind his head. He turned to look at his wife of two years. She was every bit as beautiful now as when he first met her that day on a North Carolina road.

Faith glanced over and caught Tyler staring at her. She had pulled her long dark hair up into a ponytail. Faith knew Tyler always liked it when she did that; he liked how it accentuated her well-defined cheekbones. She was wearing a pair of his blue boxers and a tight fitting, white tank top. "What?" she asked softly with a smile on her face.

"Nothing," Tyler answered coyly.

"Why were you staring at me?" Faith asked again.

Tyler smiled, "I was just wondering how a guy

like me got so lucky."

Faith blushed. "You know," she said as she turned her chair toward Tyler, "I was just wondering how a girl like me got so lucky."

Tyler laughed. "Great minds think alike, I guess."

Faith ran her hands over his naked feet. Her smile quickly faded as uncertainties gripped her mind. "Tyler?"

"Yeah?" Tyler replied. "I'm worried."

Tyler pulled his feet off of the table and sat up. He quickly moved closer to his wife. "Why?"

"No, never mind," she dismissed her worries with a shake of her head. Faith didn't want to tell Tyler.

"You can tell me," Tyler pressed. He wanted to know what was bothering her.

Faith paused, then decided to talk. "Jim was almost killed back in San Francisco, and now he's here."

"That's good news," Tyler said with a smile. "He's safe here."

"That's what I'm worried about," Faith replied.

"I don't understand."

Faith sighed. "I know Jim is one of our friends," she didn't want to finish the sentence. She knew it was something Tyler didn't want to hear, "But I really think he needs to leave."

"What?" Tyler stood up. "After all he's done for us?" He turned and walked toward the railing. Leaning over on it, he again began to look at the twinkling lights of the city below. "He, Jake and Alex helped save our lives. We owe them everything."

139

"I know, and I'm truly grateful for that but...." Faith allowed her words to trail off.

"But what?" Tyler asked turning around.

"But," Faith accentuated, "it's dangerous." She stood up and walked toward Tyler. "What if those men come looking for him again and find him here? They'll kill us all."

Tyler turned and took a step away from Faith. "That's a risk we take every single day of our lives. At any moment, the government could find us and whack us. That's just something we have to live with. I don't think that's a fair reason to kick Durard out."

"Dammit, Tyler!" Faith screamed. "I am not going to lose you!" She tried to choke back the tears, but they had already started to run.

Tyler turned around and pulled Faith into his arms. "Everything's going to be all right." He ran his hand down her back, "I promise."

Faith looked up at her husband with tears in her eyes. She loved him more than words could explain. He was her world, and she knew she couldn't survive without him. "I love you."

"I love you, too," Tyler echoed.

Faith slowly pulled out of his arms and began to wipe the tears off his cheek. "Hey, how about I go get that chicken I have in the fridge, and we can barbecue it for dinner tonight?" Faith looked up to see Tyler holding the sides of his head in pain. Before she could reach out, he collapsed to the ground. Kneeling down, she became frantic. "Tyler! What's the matter?"

Tyler was curled up in the fetal position with his hands still pressed against the sides of his head.

140

His face was contorted into an awful expression of pain. His lips were peeled back allowing Faith to see him grinding his teeth together. Then, as quickly as it began, the pain was gone. Tyler slowly sat up and leaned against the railing.

"What happened?" Faith asked with fear in her voice.

"I don't know," Tyler replied groggily. "Suddenly, it felt like my head was about to explode and," Tyler looked up at Faith with a worried look on his face, "I heard a voice."

Faith was taken aback. "What did it say?"

Tyler shook his head, "I couldn't understand most of it, but I do know it said 'come'."

"'Come'?" Faith asked. "What does that mean?"

Tyler stood up and looked up into the sky. "Something's wrong," he said eerily. "Something's wrong with the Keeper."

***

Anne sat up on her cot and looked around her small tent. Her heart was beating wildly in her chest and she felt short of breath. Standing up, she pressed her bare feet to the wooden floor. She was wearing only a long t-shirt as she crossed the floor toward her footlocker. Kneeling down, she flipped the lid open and began to dig inside. She quickly came to a small, black canvas bag. Lifting it out of the locker, she set it on the floor and unzipped it.

Reaching inside, she removed a syringe and a small glass vial. Lifting the vial, she stared into it. Her eyes widened at the sight. "Empty," she

141

moaned.

Tossing the bottle aside, she frantically rummaged through the bag. Her fear began to grow as the seconds ticked past. Lifting the bag, she dumped the remaining contents on the floor. "I know I packed an extra bottle," she assured herself.

Pushing the bag and contents away, she leaned over and dug into her footlocker. Sweat was rolling down her face and she was beginning to lose control of her hands. Her fingers felt numb as they dug through the clothes. Tossing everything she came across out of the locker, she finally reached the bottom. There was a small, brown paper bag there. Lifting the bag, she fearfully tore it open. Its precious contents came spilling out onto the floor. Grabbing one of the bottles, she lifted it into a shaft of moonlight that was spilling into her tent. The red fluid shone in the light as she pulled off the cap.

Grabbing a needle off the ground, she pushed it into the top of the bottle and filled it with the red liquid. Dropping the vial, she watched the red liquid spill out onto the floor. She couldn't be concerned with that now though, she had to administer the drug. Pressing the needle into her neck, she pushed firmly on the plunger. Her body was too weak to hold itself up. She fell to the floor hoping the drug would kick in.

**

A warning claxon began to sound inside NORAD. The night shift instantly snapped to attention. Men began to punch controls on their consoles to try and verify the alarms. The room, quiet and almost dark just moments ago, was now alive with chatter and men running to and fro.

From the back, General Summers entered the box through a set of double glass doors. Pulling on his dark blue uniform jacket, he quickly made his way down a flight of stairs toward the center console. Narrowly avoiding men rushing papers and data sheets to the appropriate stations, he finally arrived at the command console. Lifting a small black headset, he quickly slipped it on and keyed the mic. "Report!" His deep Texas accent reverberated off the walls of the box.

Lieutenant Stewart jumped up from his board and ran toward Summers. "General, I've got bad news."

Summers turned off the microphone on his headset and addressed the young officer. "Then spill it!"

Stewart pressed a sequence of keys on the command console and pointed toward the three main view screens at the front of the room. A computer generated graphic of the solar system blinked on. "You see that orange dot?" Stewart asked.

Summers nodded. "Dear God, is that the intruder?"

Stewart nodded. "It's just beyond the orbit of Mars, General. It activated our early alert system, setting off all our alarms."

"You mean that hunk of shit Star Wars satellite system we sent up there during Reagan's administration is still operational?" Summers asked.

"Apparently, sir, and if I might add, working well."

"Jesus Christ," Summers said. "As soon as the boys in Washington hear about this, they're never going to let us live down the fact we convinced the President to scrub that project." He rubbed his hand over his face. Moments before the alarms sounded, he had been trying to catch a quick nap on the sofa in his office. He was still a bit groggy. "What else have you got? Any information on the intruder itself yet?"

The Lieutenant nodded and punched several more keys on the command console. The image shifted to a clear color photo of the stars. "We requisitioned some time on Hubble earlier this afternoon and tried to get some images of the intruder. This is what we got." He pressed a key and the image dissolved. It was quickly replaced with a shot of a star field and a great gray mass in the center. "This is the intruder."

"It just looks like a big blob on the photo," Summers admitted.

"That was the photo before we sent it through the image translators and cleaned it up." Stewart hit another key. The blurry image quickly came into focus.

"Jesus H tap dancing Christ!" Summers blurted out.

"That was roughly our response, too," Stewart commented. "We found that the mass is actually comprised of over fifty saucer shaped spacecraft."

"It's a Goddamned invasion armada," Summers said in awe. "How big are they?"

"It was hard to tell in this photo with no celestial body as a point of reference," Stewart replied, "but we estimate that each one is about the

144

size of two football fields."

Summers straightened up and adjusted his uniform. He began to walk down the steps toward the three large monitors. Transfixed by the image, he finally pulled himself away. Turning around, he looked up at Stewart. "Has the President seen this yet?"

"No, General."

"Good. Arrange a transport. I want to take it to him personally."

"Yes, General." Stewart turned and began to walk back toward his console. "Lieutenant?"

Stewart perked up. "Yes, General Summers?"

"How long until the armada reaches Earth?"

"Checking." Stewart leaned over and began to work feverishly at his console. Almost instantly, a figure appeared on his screen. "At current velocity," Stewart began to read the answer, "the armada will arrive in two days."

"Shit," Summers muttered under his breath. "Cancel that transport, Lieutenant. I'm just going to have to stay here."

"Understood, sir."

Chapter Seventeen

Crews were working diligently on the slopes of Rano Raraku. This was the largest volcanic crater on the island, located on the southern tip of Rapa Nui, just below the landing strip of Mataveri Airport. Hollman, Jannis and Anne were standing on a small outcropping supervising the operation.

"We identified the entrance easily," Hollman said with pride. He pointed to a section a few men were working on with jackhammers. "Apparently, this whole island is hollow underneath."

"How long until we gain access to the entrance?" Anne asked impatiently. "I would estimate in about a day's time," Hollman answered.

"What about Silver?" Jannis asked.

"He will be dealt with tomorrow," Anne reassured him. The three began to walk down the slope toward the camp. "I want the girl ready for the exchange first thing in the morning."

"How can you be sure he's on the island?" Jannis asked.

"One of our operatives in the Chilean Airport saw him board a plane bound for here. He's here," Anne answered coolly.

"What about the girl?" Jannis wondered. "What about her?" Anne shot back. "What's to happen to her?"

"As soon as Jake is dead, I want you to kill her," Anne instructed him without emotion.

Jannis tried to hide his horror. "General, if you don't mind me saying, the girl's done nothing to you. She's just an innocent bystander."

"There are always casualties in war," Anne

announced.

"General, I don't think we should kill her. You will have your revenge against Jake, why not just let her go?"

Anne stopped and spun around to face Jannis. He could see the fire burning in her eyes. "So, you've finally developed a conscience," she said angrily.

"No, General, that's not it." Jannis refuted the accusation.

"Then what? Do you have a special place in your heart for that little bitch?" Anne asked with hatred oozing from her words. "Oh, I get it," she said. "You've got a thing for her. You want her for yourself."

"No, General, I—"

"Then what, Colonel?"

"I've just had my fill of killing children."

Anne took a step back and looked over Jannis. "Fine," she finally said. "I won't kill the girl. She's your problem now. After Jake's dead, I want you to personally put her on a plane back to New York."

"Thank you, General. I appreciate your kindness in this matter," Jannis replied. He quickly walked past Anne and continued down the slope toward the camp.

Anne turned to Hollman. "Assign one of the members of your team to kill the Silver girl after Jake's dead," she said quietly. "If Colonel Jannis gets in your way, you have the authority to kill him too."

Hollman smiled. "Understood, General. I'll see to it personally."

The three arrived at the camp. Moving through

147

the tents, they came upon the one set aside for medical purposes. It was far larger than the rest of the tents, and at least three feet taller. Like the others, it had no markings on it anywhere. Jannis lifted the flap out of the way, allowing Hollman and Anne to enter. The inside, for the most part, was empty. A few cots stood in the front, just in case workers injured themselves, and four large storage lockers sat in the rear. Anne could see a lone man lying on a cot near the rear and a woman attending to him. The three began to quickly make their way toward the back of the tent.

Dr. Heidi Cisan turned to see Anne and Jannis and saluted. "Good evening, General." Cisan was a tall and beautiful woman. Her blonde hair hung around the shoulders of her white lab coat. She was swathed in blue medical scrubs beneath the coat that did nothing for her figure. Cisan had been working with Anne at Area 51 since before the TYD epidemic. She had been Hollman's lab assistant while they tried to find a cure. She had been in the middle of changing her patient's IV.

"Dr. Cisan, it's good to see you again," Anne replied cordially. "What's the status of our patient?"

Cisan looked down at Griggs on the cot. He had an IV needle inserted into his hand, an oxygen tube in his nose and several sensors placed at various points on his body. The sensors were connected by cable to a small laptop computer sitting on a nearby table, displaying Griggs' vital signs. "I just can't understand it, General. His vitals are strong, but he's been in and out of consciousness ever since he arrived here."

Anne nodded. "Dr. Hollman informed me that

his body is beginning to breakdown. What does that mean?"

"It's strange," Cisan replied. "From the tests we could perform here on the island, we found that the cellular mitosis has stopped in his body. The cells are no longer taking nutrients and dividing, but rather, dying."

"Why is this happening?" Anne asked. She stared at the man on the table she had created four years ago.

"As far as we can tell, General, it appears the 'Uber-Soldier Project' was a failure. It just looks like there's no cohesion in his cells anymore. His body appears to be dying from the inside."

"Well," Anne said with a sigh. "These soldiers were created to be disposable. That they would have a limited life span doesn't surprise me."

"You don't know this for sure?" Hollman asked.

"Most of our original project researchers were killed when Area 51 was destroyed five years ago," Anne admitted. "Dr. Yokama and Dr. Anderson were the top minds in their field, but they are dead and most of their data was lost."

"So you cloned this man without the use of their data?" Cisan asked.

"We had to." Anne ran her hand along Griggs' chest affectionately, like an artist admiring their sculpture. "He was created not only with the DNA samples from Jason Griggs, but those that had been harvested during the original project."

"So this man isn't entirely Jason Griggs?" Hollman asked.

"No," Anne said, shaking her head. "He has the

149

memory and body of Griggs, but he also has the genetic code of about twenty other specimens."

"Why was this done?" Cisan wondered.

"He was designed to be the perfect weapon: faster, stronger, more intelligent than an average soldier, and disposable. We could make thousands of clones we could send into battle to die without losing the life of a single American soldier."

"The plan was just," Hollman added, "but I don't think the technology was quite there yet."

Anne agreed. "I'm not sure our scientists had a complete grasp of the alien technology they were using."

"So why was he created?" Jannis asked. He had worked with Griggs on a few missions and never knew he was a clone until now.

"He was to be my revenge on Jake Silver and Alex Robinson," Anne smiled. "I couldn't think of a more poetic way for them to die than at the hands of their friend."

"The plan backfired, though," Cisan interjected.

Anne shot an icy glance at Cisan. "*That* plan did, but of the whole, it was only a piece." Anne looked at Griggs' silent face. "Ultimately, it all worked in my favor."

"How do you mean, General?" Jannis inquired.

"If Griggs had never been returned to Alex, she would've never had to protect him, and she would've never shot the former head of Area 51, General Foster." Anne took a step back from Griggs. "With him out of the way, I was promoted to General with full control over Area 51."

Hollman laughed out loud. "So they did your dirty work for you, and you received a promotion."

"Right," Anne said with a smile.

"So why are we here?" Cisan asked.

Anne looked at Cisan. "We, my dear, are rebuilding the former glory of Area 51."

"Most of the test flights and newly engineered craft were moved from Area 51 to Blue 9 after our little incident five years ago," Jannis interjected. "We want those back."

"'Blue 9'?" Hollman asked.

"It's a top secret base in Southern Utah." Anne explained. "It was formerly a civilian engineering plant, but the U.S. Government bought it and converted it."

"Then why was Area 51 rebuilt after its destruction?" Cisan asked. She had transferred in after the base had been repaired. She knew nothing of the former General, or Area 51's politics.

"Mostly as a ruse," Anne answered. "The base has developed such a distinct place in American pop culture, that to abandon it would do too much harm. While the focus of all the UFO enthusiasts and conspiracy theorists is still squarely on Area 51, the government can conduct its research in secret. Hell, even the Russians still have spy satellites that photograph the base every day. To abandon the base would also arouse suspicion from neighboring governments."

"Incredible," remarked Cisan. "The U.S. Government was willing to spend over a billion dollars to repair a useless base, just to keep the public and neighboring governments happy?"

"Counterintelligence is a beautiful thing," Jannis laughed.

Anne turned and began to walk away from

Cisan. "Keep me appraised, Doctor."

"General?" Cisan asked. "What's going to happen to Griggs?"

Anne spun around and looked at Griggs lying helplessly on the cot. His eyes were closed tightly, and his body at rest. "Tomorrow morning, I am going to kill Jake Silver and Alex Robinson." She thought for a moment. "I want you to put him down tomorrow, no matter what his condition is."

"But, General," Cisan jumped in, "he's valuable to us for research material. If we can find out why his body is beginning to breakdown, we can salvage the 'Uber-Soldier Project'."

Anne considered it for a moment. "My order stands. I want Griggs dead."

Cisan nodded. "Yes, General."

Jannis and Hollman turned and accompanied Anne out of the tent. Cisan looked down at the man lying on the cot before her. He was a pawn in her sadistic game, and now he was going to have to die a second time.

***

The moonlight was casting a bluish haze over Jake's body. He was lying in the small bed with the covers around his waist. He had crossed his arms behind his head and propped himself up against the headboard. Turning his head, he stared out the small window across from the bed.

A brief rainstorm had passed over the island during the evening. Sheets of rain pounded down on the window and roof of Jake's hotel room. He wasn't sure why, but the rain had a calming effect on him. For the first time since Samantha's abduction, he found a moment of peace during the storm. Looking out the window now, though, the brisk trade winds had blown the storm east into the Pacific Ocean. The stars and moon had broken through the clouds and were shining brightly. Jake marveled at their simple beauty and began to lose himself. Suddenly, the emotions he had been trying to bury gripped him. The twinkle of the stars reminded him of the sparkle in Samantha's eyes when she was a child.

She was always so full of wonder, he remembered. Always questioning everything. Jake had taught her that. He knew that to truly learn in this world, you must not only ingest knowledge, but to question it. He could see her small round face when she was eight years old. One Saturday morning, she had decided she was actually going to try and dig a hole to China in the backyard. Jake had watched her from their kitchen window trying to maneuver a shovel bigger than she was into a small dirt hole. After about half an hour of digging, she had only produced a hole no more than six inches deep. She dropped the shovel to the ground and sat down, defeated. Opening the back door, Jake walked slowly toward Samantha. She instantly had a look of guilt on her face for digging a hole in the backyard. Jake sat down next to her and smiled. "What are you doing?" he asked.

Samantha thought for a moment. "I learned in school today that there are other people on Earth and that they live below us."

"That's right," Jake said with a look of amusement on his face, "but why are you digging the hole?"

"I want to see them, Daddy." Samantha looked down at the hole with her dirty face.

"I see," Jake said with a smile. He ran his hand through her brown hair. Her face was so sad. She hated to fail at anything she tried. "I promise that one day, you will meet those people, Sam."

"Why not today?" she asked innocently. "Because I'm taking you to lunch."

Samantha jumped up and wrapped her tiny arms around Jake's neck. "I love you, Daddy."

"I love you too, Sam. Now go get cleaned up."

Jake watched Samantha run across the backyard toward their yellow house in New Orleans. She moved up the back steps and disappeared inside the house. Standing up, Jake snatched his shovel off the ground and carried it back to its home in the tool shed. Stepping out of the shed, he looked up at the blue sky above him. He secretly made a wish to God. *Please don't ever let her grow up....*

Jake lifted the covers of his bed and wiped a tear off his face. He loved her and would do anything for her. Tomorrow would bring the exchange. Jake steeled his nerves. He knew he was going to die tomorrow at the hands of Anne, but he knew his daughter would live. That was all that mattered to him.

Chapter Eighteen

Durard and Tulley were sitting alone in a downtown restaurant. It was a greasy spoon only locals knew even existed. The building was longer than it was wide, only accommodating two rows of booths and a bar that ran the length of the room. The place had been decorated in blue with silver highlights and trim. It had a real '50's retro feel. The air was thick in here. Three ceiling fans were trying to circulate it, but weren't doing much good. They could both smell the day's special burning in the back. A lone waitress dressed in jeans and a t-shirt was patrolling the area. A row of large windows ran down the length of the building that faced the street.

The two were enjoying a cup of coffee and two orders of mozzarella sticks. Durard glanced up at the neon clock above the bar. It was approaching midnight, but he wasn't tired. He attributed that to either the exhilaration of finally being able to relay his story, or the caffeine. Tulley had just pulled another cigarette from his pack and had it dangling from his mouth as he scribbled notes on his small black notepad. Stopping, he scooped his lighter off the table and flicked it. He sucked on the cigarette until it was lit.

"You know, for each one of those you smoke, you take a year off your life," Durard commented, tiring of inhaling second-hand smoke.

"Well, in that case," Tulley said, exhaling the gray smoke, "I should already be dead." He took another drag and sat the cigarette down in the already overflowing ashtray. "I've been inhaling these damn 'coffin nails' since I was fifteen. Now look, I'm almost forty years old and—"

"You don't look at day over a hundred," Durard joked.

Tulley smiled. "Hell, even if these things do take a year off your life every time you smoke one, they're the crappy years at the end. I think I can miss that," he smiled.

Durard waved some of the smoke out of his face. "Mr. Tulley, do you mind if I ask you a question?"

"Please, Mr. Tulley sounds so formal. Call me Jeff."

"Sure, Jeff."

"What do you want to know?" Tulley asked while flicking his ashes into the ashtray.

"Do you believe in UFOs?" Durard asked seriously.

Tulley was taken aback by the question. He had never heard someone ask it so directly. "Why?"

Durard allowed his hands to fumble around the table aimlessly. "I've been telling you my story for the past several hours. I just want to know if I'm wasting my time. I mean, you've been taking copious notes, but are you going to put them in the 'weirdo column' when you're done?"

"No," Tulley reassured. "Of course not."

"Then what are you going to do with my story?" Durard asked with apprehension in his voice.

"I'm not entirely sure yet," Tulley admitted. "I know the paper I work for won't print any of this, but maybe I can write a book or something." Tulley crushed out his cigarette in the ashtray. "Either way,

I will present this story to the public."

Durard nodded. "I've read a few books in my life labeled non-fiction that I dismissed outright. You're going to have to try very hard to present this in the best possible light, or come off making everyone involved sound like terrorists."

"Trust me," Tulley said with a smile, "that's the last thing I want." Tulley took a sip of his coffee and quickly set the mug down on the table. "Now about Christina Anderson, what do you know about her?"

Durard lifted his warm cup of coffee. "I really don't know—"

Durard's coffee mug shattered in his hand, sending fragments of the porcelain cup and the dark liquid everywhere. Durard and Tulley immediately leapt out of the booth and pressed themselves to the floor. "What the hell?" Durard yelled.

A hail of bullets shattered two of the restaurant's windows. The sound of the glass and the gunshots were deafening. Durard looked to his right to see the waitress lying on the ground. One of the shots had hit her in the chest and her blood was beginning to pool on the ground around her. Small fragments of debris began to rain down on the two as the bullets tore into the countertop and seats of the booth. Durard glanced over at Tulley. He had flattened himself to the floor with his arms covering his head. "Shit," Durard muttered.

As suddenly as it began, the gunfire stopped. An eerie silence fell over the restaurant. Only the throbbing sound of the fan motors overhead could be heard. Durard lifted himself to his knees and skittered across the floor toward the waitress.

Reaching down, he pressed his fingers against her neck. "No pulse," he said quietly to Tulley. He looked at the expression of terror frozen on the woman's face. Her eyes were still wide open. Reaching up, Durard slowly closed her eyelids. "I'm sorry," he whispered. Moving back over to Tulley, Durard tapped him on the shoulder. Tulley jumped back in terror. "It's just me, Jeff."

"Christ!" Tulley moaned. "What the hell is going on here?"

"We need to get out of here right now!" Durard announced. "Give me the keys to your car."

Tulley dug into his jacket pocket and retrieved the jingling mess of keys. "I don't understand—" Another salvo of bullets stopped Tulley in mid-thought. The two pressed themselves to the floor again.

Durard looked at Tulley. Fear had paralyzed him. "When I give the signal, run like hell for your car!" Tulley was too frightened to even acknowledge him. "Dammit, Tulley!" Durard grabbed the reporter by the shoulder. "Are you listening to me? We need to move or we're going to die! Tulley!"

Tulley slowly turned his head toward Durard. "I can't. I'm too scared," he said meekly.

"On the count of three, we go."

Tulley shook his head frantically. "I can't!"

"One...." Durard started.

"Just leave me!" Tulley cried. "Two...."

"I...!"

"Three!"

The two men jumped up from their positions and charged toward the door. Bullets began to tear through everything behind them. Durard dove for the front door and crashed through it. Tulley scrambled over to Durard and picked him up off the ground.

Stopping for a moment, the two men pressed themselves against the brick wall just outside the door. A lone gunshot ricocheted off the wall, sending a cloud of dust into the air. Durard snapped his head toward Tulley and nodded once. They could see Tulley's car from here. It was only about ten feet away, but that entire area was uncovered. They would be wide open. Tulley nodded back at Durard.

Pushing off the wall, Durard sprinted hard for the car. Diving over the trunk, he dropped down in front of the door and popped the latch. Sliding into the driver's seat, he jammed the keys into the ignition and started the sedan. Not even waiting for Tulley to close his door, Durard cranked the gear shifter down into drive and smashed the gas pedal to the floor. The back tires began to spin, sending white smoke barreling off the tires. Durard and Tulley were thrown back into their seats as the tires finally began to grip. The beat up sedan went careening away from the curve wildly into the street amidst a barrage of bullets.

"Are you hurt?" Durard asked.

Tulley patted his hands quickly over his chest. "I don't think so."

"Good. I think we got away."

The back window of the car shattered inward as a bullet grazed Tulley's head. "Shit!" Tulley yelled. He pressed his hand against his head trying to stop the blood.

"Get down!" Durard instructed him. Looking in the rear-view mirror, Durard caught sight of a white jeep barreling down on them. A man dressed in black was leaning out the window with a machine gun in his hands. "Fuck," Durard swore under his breath.

The streets were littered with vehicles on this Saturday night. Most of the teenagers had come out to "Drag the strip", and others were just looking for a good party. Durard swerved the older car in and out of traffic trying to lose his pursuers. Gunning the engine, Durard cranked the steering wheel to the left, just narrowly missing two vehicles stopped at an intersection. Twisting his head back, Durard watched the white jeep do the same. Immediately, the passenger in the jeep began to fire again. The rat-a-tat-tat of the machine gun echoed loudly in his ears. He could hear the bullets impacting the trunk.

Snapping his back around, he saw a traffic jam in the lane ahead of him. Using both feet, he smashed the brake pedal to the floor. The car began to skid uncontrollably toward the other vehicles. Durard held his breath. "Brace yourself, Jeff," he warned him. The sedan twisted sideways and smashed the passenger side into the rear of a stopped truck. The passenger side crumpled like a piece of flimsy tinfoil sending shards of glass from the window raining down on Tulley. Turning his head to the left, Durard saw the jeep screech to a halt next to them. "Get down now!" Durard yelled.

The passenger of the jeep pressed the trigger down on his weapon and began to fire point blank into the sedan. The man driving the truck that Durard had careened into saw the attack behind him and panicked. Throwing his truck into first, he popped the clutch and pulled away from Tulley's car. Not watching where he was going, the man viciously rear-ended the small automobile in front of him. People were foolishly leaving their vehicles and scattering in all directions. Looking to his left, Durard saw they were free of the truck. Pressing the gas pedal down, he peeled away from the jeep and straight into oncoming traffic.

Durard swerved madly trying to avoid the vehicles. Turning left, Durard sent Tulley's car up onto the sidewalk. Glancing behind him, he watched the white jeep pull into traffic and begin to pursue him again. "These guys are relentless," he said to himself. He gunned the engine again. A group of pedestrians in front of him tried to scatter out of the way.

Tulley peeked over the back of his seat. "They're still coming!"

"I know," Durard said unemotionally. "Stay down."

Durard pulled the sedan back onto the street and crossed traffic. He twisted the steering wheel hard and pulled back into the flow of traffic. Another spray of bullets tore through the sedan as he screamed around a car slowing down to make a turn. He looked ahead of him. The light at the next intersection was about to turn red.

Jumping out of traffic, he sent the car twisting into the intersection, narrowly avoiding several vehicles. Pressing the gas again, he turned left and flew down a connecting street. Turning around, he watched the white jeep slam into two cars in the intersection and begin to roll. Durard allowed himself to breathe a sigh of relief. He looked over at his passenger huddled on the seat. "Are you okay?"

Tulley slowly sat up and looked behind them. Facing forward, he ran his hand across the gash on his head. Blood was flowing from the open wound. "I think I'm going to be okay," he admitted. Tulley looked at his battered and broken vehicle. "Oh, man," he sighed.

"What?" Durard asked.

"One more payment and this baby was mine."

***

Samantha was cold and alone. She had curled herself up in the corner of the tent she was being held in and was softly weeping. Her clothes were in tatters and her body was bruised. She still didn't know why she was here, but she did know it had something to do with her father. She had heard the woman who beat her refer to him many times.

Wiping a few errant locks of hair out of her face, she sat up and looked around. There was nothing in this tent but a wooden floor. Reaching behind her, she tried to lift one of the flaps of the tent, but found they had been bolted to the floorboards. Using her sleeves, she wiped the tears from her eyes. Her mascara had long since run down her face, leaving faint black tear trails on her cheeks from the dark rings beneath her eyes. She was a wreck.

Finding the courage to stand up, she unintentionally began to pace back and forth along the wooden floors. Samantha's shoes made a dull hollow thump every time she took a step. She stopped and thought for a moment. Looking down at the floor, she noticed that the individual planks of wood hadn't been joined in any way. Crouching down, she slid her tired hands between two of the boards and lifted them up. There was dirt underneath. Loud voices suddenly startled her. Dropping the board, she pressed it back into place with her foot and leapt back into the corner. Looking down at the end of the tent, Samantha could see the silhouettes of several figures standing there. To her dismay, one of the figures reached down and began to lift the tent flap. Samantha pulled her knees in close to her chest in a defensive posture.

"How's our prisoner tonight?" a man's voice asked.

Samantha had buried her face in her body and would not acknowledge the question.

"How are you tonight?" the man asked again. Samantha could hear the thump of his boots getting closer.

Finally, she heard the man stop in front of her. Summoning her courage, she balled her fists and leapt up from her position. Samantha threw a punch that connected with the man's chin. The man stumbled backwards and fell to the floor. Diving on top of him, Samantha began to claw wildly at his face and chest. She was determined to live.

"Stop!" Jannis yelled. Grabbing Samantha's arms, he easily tossed her off him. "What the hell do you think you're doing?" the man asked as he pulled himself back to his feet. Using the back of his hand, he rubbed across a bleeding scratch on his face.

Samantha crouched in the corner like a cornered animal. Her brown eyes were brimming with hatred and exhaustion. "Let me go," she hissed.

Jannis wiped the blood on his black shirt as he took a step back from Samantha. "Whoa," he said in a calm voice. "I don't want any trouble here." Samantha lifted herself onto the balls of her feet and stood ready to pounce again. "You have no right to hold me like this!"

"I know," Jannis replied sympathetically. "You just have to endure one more night and then you'll be released."

The comment caught her off-guard. She stood straight up and looked at the bald man before her. "What did you say?"

"I came here tonight to tell you that it would be all over soon."

"I don't understand," Samantha admitted. "Why am I being held here?"

"It's a long story, and I don't have much time," Jannis replied. Turning to look behind him at the tent flap, he quickly pulled a small cantina off his belt. Jannis tossed it to Samantha and smiled. "It's only water, but it's the best I could do."

Samantha's eyes lit up with excitement. She hadn't had any food or water in at least two days. Unscrewing the lid, she lifted the bottle to her lips and guzzled the liquid down. Without even stopping to take a breath, she drank the whole cantina. Pulling the bottle away, she wiped her mouth with her arm. "Thank you," she said as she tossed the bottle back to Jannis. "What's your name?"

"My name's Andrew, but everyone calls me

Jannis," he said with a smile. "Thank you, Andrew."

Jannis nodded. Turning around, he quickly made his way out of the tent.

Chapter Nineteen

"General Caroll?" a young man asked.

Anne rolled over on her cot and looked at her open tent flap. "What?" she asked, still half asleep.

"Sir, we've broken through."

Anne sat up and looked directly at the man. "What did you say?"

"We've broken through the rock, General. Dr. Hollman has located the entrance."

Anne jumped out of bed and began to pull on her uniform. "Inform Dr. Hollman that I'm on my way."

"Yes, General Caroll."

***

Hollman was standing at the mouth of the cave as the last bits of rubble were being cleared away. Immense spotlights had been hauled into position in front of the cave and were shining directly down its throat. Hollman tried to see around the workers into the hollow, but saw only darkness.

"Report," Anne yelled while she was still walking up the slope of the volcano.

Hollman spun around to face Anne. "We had to dig out several layers of volcanic rock that were covering the entrance. I had two teams working non-stop since we found it."

"Very good, Dr. Hollman," Anne said with a smile. "Let's go."

"Go?" Hollman asked with trepidation.

"Into the cave, Doctor."

General, we have no idea what's down there."

Hollman turned to look at the mouth of the cave. "We need to assign a full research team, and even then, it may take weeks to venture through the cave."

"I don't want to hear that," Anne scolded him.

"I'm sorry, General," Hollman said, "but who knows what kinds of traps are hidden in there. We could be walking into a potentially deadly situation."

Anne shook her head and smiled. "Then send in a member of the team instead."

Hollman returned Anne's smile. "Officer thinking." Hollman quickly scanned the group of workers who were standing around the cave. "Allen! Get over here!"

One of the workers, a tall and well-built man in his twenties, quickly began to trot over to Hollman's position. He stopped and saluted Anne. "Yes, sir?" He asked in a deep, rich voice. He had pulled off his black shirt and was wearing only a tight, white tank top over his rippling chest. His dark hair was slicked back with sweat showing off his deep brown eyes.

"We need a volunteer to go into the cave," Hollman said. "I don't think I'm qualified, sir," Allen responded.

"Thanks for volunteering, Private Allen," Anne said. "Yes, General." Allen snapped to attention.

"Grab a flashlight and a radio, Private," Hollman instructed him. "I want you in that cave in five minutes."

Allen quickly saluted, then left to follow his orders.

Hollman leaned closer to Anne. "He's going to

die, you know."

"Such a shame," Anne purred. "He's such a lovely young thing." Hollman shook his head and retook his position. He looked over at the cave again. He knew its inky blackness was hiding a secret, but he wasn't sure of what kind. The wind suddenly began to pick up around the excavation site sending a chill down Hollman's spine. All at once, a deep howl echoed from the cave startling the men. The workers quickly scattered like rats.

"What the hell was that?" Anne asked.

"Probably just the wind blowing over the cave's mouth," Hollman speculated. He didn't want to admit it, but the howl unnerved him. He felt like the cave was crying out a warning to those standing around it.

"General Caroll?"

Anne jumped. "Don't you ever do that again, Private," she warned the young man. Her nerves were on end after the howl.

"Sorry, General," Allen said. He was holding a large black flashlight and had strapped a radio to his belt. "I just wanted to inform you that I was ready."

"Good," Anne said, "let's get this little party started. I want you to stay in constant radio contact with Dr. Hollman. You need to describe everything you see while in the cave. Do you understand?"

Allen nodded. "Yes, General."

Anne pointed at the cave. "In the hole."

Allen turned around and walked briskly toward the cave's mouth. It was a large half circle carved directly into the volcano. The rock around it was black, giving it an even more oppressive look. Stopping at the entrance, Allen switched on his flashlight and keyed his radio. "Quick radio check," he announced into the long rectangular box.

Hollman lifted his radio. "We've gotcha, Private."

Allen stood looking into the blackness of the cave. The entrance, from what he could see, sloped down immediately. Even with the spotlights behind him, he still couldn't see very far inside. Allen thought he was looking at the surface of a lake when he'd shine a flashlight into it. It quickly begins to defuse and bend the light as it enters. It looked very murky in there.

Forcing himself to continue, Allen shuffled his feet as he made his way into the cave. Glancing behind him, he watched his fellow soldiers watching in awe as he moved further inside. He was several meters into the cave when he lost sight of the entrance. The only visible light was that of his flashlight, and it wasn't doing a whole lot of good at the moment. Allen keyed his radio with his powerful hands. "Do you read me, Dr. Hollman?"

His radio cracked for a moment. "We've still got you, Private. What do you see?"

"A whole lot of nothing," Allen said with a bit of fear in his voice. "The darkness is so thick in here, you could cut it with a knife." Allen shone his light on the walls of the cave. "The walls appear to be made of the same stone as the mouth is, a black rock with thousands of air pockets carved into them." Allen shifted his flashlight forward and began to traverse further into the cave. "It's the same thing the further I go: black rock all around." Allen spun around and shone his flashlight back the way he came. There was nothing except blackness in all directions. Returning forward, his light bounced off something shiny on the wall. "Wait, I may have found something."

"What do you see, Private?" Hollman asked. His signal filled with static. Allen walked toward the wall on his right. There was a small glistening object. "It appears to be made of some type of alloy," he said into the radio. "I can't tell what kind, but it looks like one of the statues."

"What statues?" Hollman asked.

Allen hit the talk button. "The one's here on the island. It looks like one of those faces."

"You mean the Moai?" Hollman asked.

"Yeah," Allen replied. He ran his fingers over the shiny silver surface of the face. Immediately, the two rectangular eyes began to glow red. "Uh-oh," Allen muttered. He stumbled away from the shiny silver face, tripping over a large rock. His flashlight fell to the floor and snapped off, while he kept hold of the radio.

"What's happening down there?" Hollman yelled over the radio.

Allen snapped his head to the right when he saw a light appear. A wave of relief passed over him. "I think I just found the light switch."

"Don't touch anything!" Hollman yelled. "You don't know what kind of traps they have in there."

"Understood." Lifting himself up, Allen dusted himself off. Leaning over, he felt along the floor for his missing flashlight. His hand flitted over the loose dirt on the floor. He came upon a small round object. Running his hand over it, he felt a lump well up in his throat. Grabbing the object, he lifted it up and held it in front of his face. "Dr. Hollman?"

"Go ahead, Private."

"I don't want to be down here anymore."

"Why?"

"Because I found a human skull in here." Allen stared into the empty eyes sockets of the partial skull. It looked to have been down here a long time. Most of the upper teeth were still intact, but the lower jaw was missing. Allen ran his hand over the brow, then back toward the skullcap. He found a gaping hole smashed into the top. Allen quickly dropped the skull and turned away. He hoped that whatever killed that man wasn't still down here.

Allen began to work his way toward the light source. He was running his hand against the wall as a guide. There was a bend in the tunnel just ahead of him, and beyond that, the source of the light. Passing around the corner, the landscape dramatically changed. The black stone was replaced with polished silver surfaces. The cave slowly melded into that of a corridor. Along its roof, there were oddly shaped lights embedded in the ceiling. They were triangular, but with a rounded bottom. They looked like arrows pointing down the corridor. Allen lifted the radio to his mouth. "Dr. Hollman?" Static. "Dr. Hollman, do you copy?" The static hissed at him through the tinny speaker. "Damn," Allen said as he placed the radio back on his belt. "Must be some kind of interference down here."

The corridor seemed to dip down again ahead of him. It looked like it extended several hundred more feet. Allen stood impatiently weighing his options. *I've lost radio contact,* he thought, *so I better head back. On the other hand, I could be very near the end.*

171

Curiosity won over reason as Allen turned and began to follow the corridor down. As he walked, he stared at his reflection in the walls. He had seen no seams, except where the lights on the roof were. This looked like one big piece of metal that had been hollowed out, rather than built here. Every floor and wall was perfectly polished. Not a single scratch or scuffmark was anywhere to be found. It looked as if no one had ever walked here before.

Finally, the corridor began to level off again. Up ahead, Allen could see the end of the tunnel. Two massive silver doors stood at the end of the hallway. They were closed tightly, leaving only the slightest seam between them. There were no windows in the doors, just a lone keypad and monitor located on the wall to the left of the doors. Allen cautiously approached the keypad and glanced over it. It had no numbers or letters, at least none that Allen recognized. Several black symbols were inscribed on each white key of the eighteen digit pad.

He ran his fingers lightly over the pad making sure not to depress any of the keys. The monitor above the pad jumped to life. A chain of symbols appeared on the small black screen. Allen quickly pulled his hand away from the pad. He watched the monitor repeat the string again, but this time, in red. Allen started to panic. Taking a few steps away from the panel, he started to turn to run, when he heard a loud siren begin to blare in the corridor. The echo was deafening. The blare of the horn was amplified tenfold by the smooth walls of the hallway.

Pressing his hands to his ears, Allen's

equilibrium began to be affected by the piercing sound. Stumbling around as if intoxicated, Allen tried to make his way back down the corridor. Ahead of him, four small panels slid open on the wall. Four long metallic tentacles began to snake out of their tubes inside the panels. As soon as Allen moved into striking distance, the tentacles shot out and wrapped themselves around Allen's limbs. They quickly began to retract into the wall while still gripping Allen.

Allen screamed in pain as the tentacles dislocated his shoulders. Then all at once, the tentacles retracted into the wall, ripping Allen apart. Pieces of Allen's body lay scattered about the corridor, his blood pooling on the polished silver floor.

Outside, everyone had moved away from the mouth of the cave as the alarms blared. The cave was acting like a speaker for the siren. It was amplifying the sound and pushing it forward. Men began to stumble down the slope of the volcano as they tried to retreat from the blaring sound. Anne and Hollman had turned and begun to do the same. Moving quickly down the slope, Anne caught her foot on an outcropping of volcanic rock and stumbled to the ground. Her momentum carried her forward, tossing her down the slope like a rag doll. After almost sixty seconds, the siren finally stopped. The camp began to breathe a sigh of relief and their balance and hearing began to return.

Hollman looked over at Anne, who was lying flat on the ground. "Are you all right, General?" He reached over and offered her a hand.

Anne rolled onto her back and grabbed

Hollman's hand. Pulling hard, she lifted herself off the ground. "What the hell was that?" she asked angrily.

"Probably one of those traps I was telling you about," Hollman answered in an "I told you so" voice.

Anne didn't appreciate the attitude. "See if you can reach Private Allen." Hollman nodded. Lifting the radio off his belt, he tapped and held the 'talk' button. "Private Allen, do you read?" Hollman listened for a moment. Nothing. "Private Allen, do you copy?" Still nothing. "I can't get him, General."

"Damn," Anne said under her breath. "I need to know what's in that cave." Anne made a split decision. "We're going down there tonight."

"I beg your pardon, General?" Hollman asked. "After what we just witnessed, *you* want us to go down there?"

Anne nodded. "We need to find out what's down there, Greg. If it's what I think it is, it can bring Area 51 back into power."

"Well," Hollman said, playing devil's advocate, "what if it's not?"

"Then I nuke this fucking little island off the map." Anne turned and began to walk away. "I want you and Dr. Cisan ready to go into the cave in one hour. Colonel Jannis and I will meet you there."

Chapter Twenty

The four men in black slipped easily into Jake's room. They had begun to pick the lock on his door, but found the door was flimsy enough that they could just push it open. Each man was dressed similarly. They all wore a pair of black slacks, a black shirt and a long billowing black trench coat. Each man had a bulletproof vest strapped around his chest and a holster attached to his hip. They were all wearing black masks, with the hood of their trench coats draped over them. Each had a pair of smoke colored goggles covering the eyeholes of their masks, giving them all an ominous appearance.

The four men stood quietly around Jake's bed. Jake had wrapped himself in the two blankets on this cool, winter night. He was sleeping peacefully while a small pool of drool was collecting on the pillow. The four men snickered while Jake unconsciously tried to wipe the drool from his face. The man standing the closest to the head of the bed leaned over and tapped Jake on the shoulder. "Mr. Silver?" he asked in his normal voice.

Groggily, Jake looked up at the man swathed in black standing before him. His eyes suddenly widened and he shot up out of bed. "Stay away from me!" he growled.

"Mr. Silver?" the man asked.

Jake was standing up on his bed and slowly pushing his way along the wall. "Don't come any closer."

The man grabbed his hood and slowly pushed it back. After carefully removing his goggles, he pulled off his mask. A familiar face stared up at

Jake.

"One?" Jake asked angrily.

One nodded. "I didn't mean to frighten you, Mr. Silver."

"What the hell are you doing?" Jake asked angrily. He carefully stepped off the bed and sat down on its edge. "You don't just come into a man's room and stand there staring at him!"

"I'm sorry," One reiterated, "but it's time."

Jake had lifted a pair of jeans off the floor and was beginning to pull them on. "Time for what?"

"Time to free your daughter," One replied.

Jake snapped his head around and looked at the alarm clock sitting on his nightstand. "It's three thirty in the morning, One. The exchange isn't until nine."

"We realize that, Mr. Silver."

"Then what the hell are you talking about?" Jake asked while buttoning up his pants.

"You remember when I told you about the Brotherhood?" One asked. Jake nodded.

"Then you know it is our job to protect the Divine Sanctuary." Something clicked inside Jake's head. He instantly realized what they were going to do. "You can't do it!"

"We must," One replied unemotionally. "It is our destiny," he smiled, "as well as yours."

"You're insane if you think you can take on a whole platoon of highly trained soldiers!" Jake yelled. "They'll slaughter you!"

"Perhaps," One conceded, "but we will die for our cause, and then we will truly be accepted into God's embrace."

"This is going too far!" Jake walked around to

face One. "My daughter is in there. If you go in there, guns blazing, they might decide to just kill her!"

"That's a risk we're—"

Jake grabbed One by the throat and began to squeeze. "If you say 'it's a risk you're willing to take', then I will personally kill you where you stand. My daughter's life is not trivial, nor is it part of your damned holy crusade!"

One pulled at Jake's hands, trying to break free. "Stop!" he gasped. The man standing behind Jake pulled his pistol out of its holster and pressed it into the back of Jake's head. "Let him go," the man said in broken English.

Jake stopped. In his anger, he had forgotten there were three other armed men standing in the room. Slowly, he removed his hand from One's throat and stepped away. He lifted his hands above his head. "My daughter's all I have anymore," Jake admitted.

"I know, Mr. Silver," One said while rubbing his throat. "I would not put her in harm's way. I promise." He stepped closer to Jake. "What I was going to say is that it *wasn't* a risk we were willing to take."

Jake slowly lowered his hands. A sullen look crossed his unshaven face. "I'm sorry."

"I completely understand." One looked over at his associates and snapped his fingers. The man lifted a black bag off the floor and tossed it to One. "I want you on this strike team," he said to Jake. "I've taken the liberty of preparing your gear." He handed Jake the bag.

Jake quickly unzipped it and peered inside. A

set of black clothes much like One was wearing was inside. A black pistol sat on top of the clothing. Jake looked up at One. "You are insane."

One remained motionless, his gaze unwavering.

Jake glanced at the other three men in the room. "Please tell me that you have more than the five of us going in there."

One shook his head. "Five is all that we will need."

Jake looked at the bag of clothes, then back up at One. A worried look crossed Jake's face, but was quickly replaced by one of confidence. "When do we leave?"

***

"Are you all right?" Faith asked while looking at Tulley's head. Tulley nodded. "I think I'll live."

Faith walked to her hall closet and opened the door. She rummaged around for a moment before returning with a washcloth. "Here," she said, handing the cloth to Tulley. "Don't bleed on my furniture."

Faith returned to her seat on the couch. Durard was sitting across from her with Tyler, while Tulley was seated next to her. "What happened?" here."

Durard sat forward on the couch and looked at Faith. "They know I'm

"Who knows?" Tyler asked.

"The government," Durard blurted out. He was still visibly shaking from the ordeal. His rush of adrenaline had worn off, leaving only the fear. "They found me here."

Faith quickly stood up and walked into the

178

kitchen without saying a word. Tyler watched his wife go, but paid no attention to it. "What happened?"

Tulley looked at the white cloth in his hand. It was beginning to turn a deep red from his blood. "We're sitting in a little coffee shop downtown, then suddenly, all hell broke loose and people were shooting at us."

"Christ," Tyler muttered. "How did you get away?"

"Some fancy driving on Durard's part," Tulley said with a smile. "What happened to the men pursuing you?"

"Wrecked," Durard blurted. "Hopefully dead."

Tyler stood up and began to pace the living room. "What are we going to do?"

"What do you mean 'we'?" Faith asked angrily from the kitchen. Stepping into the living room, she glared at Tyler. "We," she reiterated, "don't have to do anything."

"What are you saying?" Tyler asked.

Faith was tired of stepping around the issue. She was going to meet it head-on. "Jim needs to go."

"I thought we discussed this," Tyler said sternly.

"We didn't talk about anything!" Faith yelled. "I mentioned it, but you blew me off."

Durard stood up and looked at Faith. "I don't want to cause any inconvenience."

"It's too late for that, Jim," Faith shot back. "You've already brought the government back to our front door!"

"I had no intention of—"

179

"I don't care what you wanted," Faith said as she walked into the living room. "My husband and I have managed to live a completely normal life up to this point. I am not, under any circumstances, going to throw that away for you!"

Tulley saw the shells flying overhead and began to sink down into the couch. He hoped no one would notice him.

Durard turned away from Faith. "I just needed a place to stay for a while," he admitted. "The first people I thought of were you and Tyler."

"I'm sorry, Jim," Faith said with true apathy in her voice. "I just can't have you here anymore."

"Now just a damn minute, Faith," Tyler spat angrily. "This is my life, too. You can't just go around making all the decisions all the time!" Tyler pushed Durard out of the way and stepped in front of Faith. "Jim is our Goddamned friend. He helped save both our lives. If it weren't for him, we wouldn't even be here right now. You would've been fucking blown up on that radio tower in Las Vegas, and I would've still probably been wandering around North Carolina!" He looked away from Faith. "We owe him a little more than this."

Faith stumbled away from Tyler as if she had been slapped across the face. "I just don't want to lose you," she said while trying to hold back the tears.

Tyler gently placed his hands on her face, and drew her close to him. He stared into her soft brown eyes. Tears had begun to well up, but had not yet spilled out onto her cheeks. "I love you, Faith, but there's something more going on here."

Faith looked confused. "What?"

"I can't quite explain," Tyler admitted, "but I just have the feeling that you, Jim and I are all a part of some bigger picture."

Durard looked at Tyler. "How do you know?"

"I don't," Tyler said with a smile. "I think it has something to do with my alien abduction four years ago."

Tulley perked up. He rummaged around his person looking for his notebook. *Damn,* he thought. *I left it at the restaurant.*

"I just have this nagging feeling." Tyler looked at Faith. "You believe me, don't you?"

Faith thought for a moment. She thought about her training at Area 51 and the things she had seen while on duty there. It was hard for her to truly rule out anything within the scope of possibility. "I'm not sure," she admitted, "but I have no reason to doubt you."

"Good," Tyler said with a smile. "Everyone sit down, we need to talk."

Chapter Twenty-One

General Summers had a large yellow manila envelope tucked under his arm as he made his way through the hallways of NORAD. The halls were huge. They were designed to accommodate anything from several men walking side by side, to a jeep driving through. This base had been designed with a purpose in mind. They designers wanted the base to be able to handle anything thrown at it. The architects had even built the entire base on giant shock absorbers. The shocks consisted of huge iron springs that helped soak up and dissipate earthquakes, or the impact shock from a direct nuclear assault.

Walking briskly, he glanced down at his blue Air Force uniform. Using his free hand, he brushed a small bit of lint off of his collar. He passed several officers that saluted as they walked by, but Summers didn't return the gesture. Instead, he kept his mind focused on the impending meeting. This meeting was going to be imperative to the success of his plan.

For the past ten hours, he had taken no visitors or calls. Summers had sat alone in his large office working on a plan. He had tried to take into account every single detail he had available to him. He rubbed his hand over his face and tried to wipe off some of the grogginess. He couldn't remember the last time he slept. He had tried to catch a nap, but had been unable to sleep. This event was too big to just sit back and watch. He knew they had to take an active role in it, or the consequences would be dire.

Summers rounded a corner and stopped. He

stood facing a thick, silver door that had two armed guards standing on either side of it. It had six huge steel barrels built into it that locked it securely when the door was closed. The two guards saluted and moved to open the door. They easily pulled it open after sliding the barrels out. Summers marveled at the technology that went into its construction. It was at least a foot thick, but perfectly balanced so that one man could open and close it alone.

Stepping inside, Summers looked around the small, dark room. It consisted of a long oval shaped conference table surrounded on three sides by massive banks of monitors. A dark blue neon stripe circled the room about six inches from the ceiling. The monitors were quiet in this darkened room; only the light from the blue bar illuminated the room.

Sitting down at the head of the table, Summers laid the yellow envelope on the glossy black surface of the table. Leaning back in the high-backed padded leather chair, Summers checked his watch. The time had almost arrived. Reaching under the table, he grabbed the edge of a small keyboard drawer and pulled it out. He ran his fingers lightly over the low profile keys toward the upper right-hand corner. He felt a small round rubber button and pressed it. He listened as the room began to hum to life.

One by one, the monitors blinked on. Each one showed a headshot of different people around the country. None of them were paying attention to the camera, rather arranging their notes on their desks in front of them. On the large center screen in front of Summers, he could see the familiar trappings of the Oval Office, but no President. Summers checked his watch again. There were still a few minutes before the conference began.

He tapped in several commands on the keyboard and cleared his throat. "Good afternoon, gentlemen."

Each man on the monitor looked directly into the camera and nodded to Summers. On one of the monitors, a man in his sixties with light blonde hair and wearing a brown suit smiled when he saw Summers. "How the hell are you, you old hound dog?" he said with a southern accent.

"Well I'll be damned," Summers said with a smile. "What the hell are you doing at the Pentagon, Ricky?"

Rick Delane laughed. "Haven't you heard? I work here now."

"Doing what?" Summers asked.

Delane grabbed his jacket lapels and held them proudly. "I've been appointed to the President's cabinet. You're looking at the new Secretary of Defense."

Summers smiled. "You're harder to get rid of than a damn blood tick on a dog. How did you get this job?"

"After all my years of service in the Air Force, being an advisor to two previous presidents, and after figuring out that whole damned ballistic missile thing in back in '91, President Williams felt I would be perfect for the job." Delane said in his particular southern drawl. "I just happen to agree with the President on this one."

"At least someone does," Summers laughed.
"How long until we start?" Delane asked.

Summers checked his watch, "Looks like we've still got around three minutes."

"Kill the feed to the other offices for a minute," Delane instructed him. Summers quickly complied. Entering a code on his small keyboard, the sound from the other monitors went dead. "Done," Summers assured him. "Can you tell me a little about what we're facing here?" Delane asked seriously.

"Didn't you see the paper we sent over?"

"I did, but it left a lot to be desired. Who the hell taught you how to write a report?"

Summers smiled. "You did."

"Damn," Delane replied with a chuckle. "So what is the intent of the armada?"

"Frankly, we don't know, Ricky. All we do know is that there are close to fifty football field-sized ships heading in our direction."

"Is it possible they will pass right by us?" Delane asked.

"We don't think so." Summers sighed. "We've plotted their trajectory a hundred damn times now, and they always end up at the same place." Summers saw the Commander in Chief enter the Oval Office and sit down in front of the camera. "President's here," he advised Delane. Reaching over, he tapped his keyboard and turned the sound back on. Instantly, the glowing blue bar that ringed the room switched to a deep vibrant red.

"Good afternoon, gentlemen," the President said as he cleared his throat. President Dan Williams was a young and very charismatic man. He was wearing a black suit with a white shirt and dark blue tie. His brown hair was combed neatly

185

across his head, and his beard gave him an air of authority. His blue eyes softened his appearance and drew one in, while his stern face kept a person at a distance. He reached into his jacket pocket and removed a small pair of gold rimmed reading glasses. Sliding them onto his face, he flipped open a folder he had brought with him. "I've got a press conference in an hour," he announced in a deep voice, "so let's get going, shall we?" He looked up at the bank of monitors in front of him. "General Summers?"

Summer straightened up. "Yes, Mr. President?"

"Why don't you run down your plan for all of us?"

"It's very simple, gentlemen," Summers said, addressing the camera. "Once the armada enters our orbit, we target a couple of ICBMs and blow them out of the sky."

A man on a screen to his left laughed out loud. "That's your plan, General Summers?"

The President removed his glasses. "You would like to add something here, John?"

John Kendall was the Vice President. He appeared to be slightly older than Williams; his hair was beginning to gray at the temples, and his face was a road map of wrinkles from his life. "How can you even consider this idea, Dan? It's childish at best, and extremely dangerous."

Summers turned to face Kendall's monitor. "How so, Mr. Vice President?"

"Do we even know the intent of this armada yet?" Kendall asked. "They could be here on a mission of peace. I mean, how would we like it if we sent our ambassadors to Paraguay and they shoot at us before they even know why we're there."

Williams nodded. "I can see your point, John, but what if they are here to wipe us out and we hesitate? It could cost the lives of millions."

"Sir," Delane chimed in, "the Department of Defense happens to agree with General Summers. If this armada is hostile, we must strike first."

Kendall was getting visibly upset. "This armada could be a welcoming envoy! They could be coming to ask us to join an interstellar alliance or something. Think of the benefits to our civilization their technology could provide."

Delane laughed. "I think someone's been watching a little too much sci-fi lately."

"This could be our chance to advance our technology hundreds, if not thousands, of years!" Kendall argued.

Williams shook his head. "John, our boys down in Dreamland have had alien technology for over fifty years, and all we've gotten so far is a few stealth airplanes. Could their tech really be that great?"

"Why don't we ask General Caroll?" Summers asked.

Williams nodded. "General Caroll?" He scanned his set of monitors for her face. "Is she not part of this briefing?"

Delane checked his notes. "She was supposed to be, Mr. President." Williams looked away from the camera for a moment. A non-descript man standing behind him leaned over and whispered something in his ear. The man was presumably Secret Service. After a moment, Williams again

187

turned to the camera. "Gentlemen, we're going to have to cut this short. There's apparently been some trouble in the Middle East that requires my attention."

"What about the plan, Mr. President?" Delane jumped in.

Williams thought for a moment. "Let's go with Summers' plan for right now."

"We're risking turning these aliens violent, or at the very least, turning their armada into dangerous falling debris," Kendall argued.

"The issue is no longer open for debate, John," Williams shot back. "What's the armada's ETA?"

Summers checked his watch. "According to our latest data, less than two days away."

Williams rubbed his beard thoughtfully. "I want this panel to reconvene tomorrow at zero eight hundred hours, understood?"

"Mr. President?" Delane asked again.

"Yes, Mr. Delane?" Williams was annoyed. He had other matters he had to attend to.

"What do you want me to do about General Carroll's absence?"

Williams waved his hand. "Just get her to the next one. If she misses that one, then she's in trouble, and I'm going to hold you responsible, Mr. Delane."

Delane nodded. "Yes, Mr. President."

One by one, the various faces began to disappear from the monitors until only Delane and Summers were left. Summers looked at Delane for a moment before he began to speak. "What do really you think of the plan, Ricky?"

Delane shook his head. "Honestly," he bit his

lip, "I think it's dangerous. For as much as I don't like the Vice President, he may be right."

Summers leaned back in his chair and crossed his arms. "What if he's not?"

Delane leaned close to the camera. "Then God help us all." He clicked it off.

Summers was left sitting in a dark room. Tapping a key on his console, the red ring changed back to a cool blue color. It was deafeningly silent in this soundproof room. Summers sat with his arms crossed for a long time. Kendall had presented the group with an option he hadn't thought of and that bothered him. His plan had gone over well, but doubt had been placed in the minds of the President and his Cabinet. Summers lifted his envelope from the table and stood up. Turning around, he slowly walked out of the room.

Chapter Twenty-Two

Storms had entered into the area again early that morning. The small island of Rapa Nui had a tropical climate, making it not only wet, but also humid. Luckily for Jake though, they had come here during the winter. The usual humidity was gone, replaced with biting trade winds and cold rain.

Jake had changed into the outfit One had brought him. He now looked exactly like one of the members of the Brotherhood of the Divine Sanctuary. He was wearing a black t-shirt, a pair of black slacks and a long flowing black trench coat. There had also been a bulletproof vest and mask in the bag, but Jake had opted not to wear them. He had a black leather holster strapped around his chest, and a sleek black pistol in it. He was wearing a pair of black standard issue combat boots. *The Brotherhood must shop at 'Military Surplus 'R Us'*, Jake joked.

Turning around, he looked at the other five members of the group preparing on a small flat area of grass. They had hiked the entire distance from the hotel to an area just north of Rano Raraku. One had been informed the military had a base on the southern side of the ancient volcano.

Wind whipped at Jake's long black coat as he stood in the elements. The rain was beginning to freeze him to the core. He felt soggy and not ready for the battle he knew was at hand. Glancing down at his wristwatch, he checked the time. There were still hours before the prearranged meeting. The sun had just barely begun to peek above the horizon. It was casting a thick haze of orange against the dark storm clouds that filled the sky.

Jake lifted his head up. One told him that storms frequently blow in and out of Rapa Nui. The trade winds carried storm fronts quickly across the island, but this one appeared to be staying for a while. Jake let the rain hit his face and run down his cheeks. Cupping his hands over his face, he wiped the water out of his eyes.

Glancing south, he could see the mighty volcano looming ahead of them. It was a giant mass of blackness barely being backlit by the shimmering, reflective surface of the Pacific Ocean. Jake looked at it for a long time. He actually found it quite beautiful. The very force that had created this island in a storm of lava and molten rock was now dormant, standing as an ancient symbol of birth and destruction.

Turning away, Jake brought his attention back to his small band of rebels. They had gone from checking their equipment to standing in a circle and saying a prayer. Jake wondered if he should join the prayer. He didn't want to insult these men, but this wasn't his war. He wasn't here to do God's bidding. He was here to get his daughter back. That was all.

As soon as she was out of Anne's grasp, they were leaving this godforsaken island and heading back to Lake Tahoe. *As soon as I get back, I need to call Lindsay and tell her that Sam is staying with me.* Jake shook his head. He knew that wouldn't be fair to Samantha. She was an adult now. She needed to make her own choices, and as far as Jake knew, her life was in New York. He didn't want to drag her away from all she knew, but he didn't want to risk losing her again. He was torn inside. Jake decided not to dwell on the future before he knew what it held for him. She would have to make her own decision if—when she came home.

Jake looked down the slope at the men. They had pulled their masks and hoods over their heads and were walking toward him. He couldn't tell which of them was One. They all moved very similar, very languid and carefully. They looked as if their feet weren't even touching the ground, rather floating toward him with their coats billowing behind them.

The man stopped in front of Jake and placed his hand on his shoulder. "Are you ready, Mr. Silver?"

Jake recognized One's voice. "About as ready as I'm going to get," Jake assured him.

"Then it's time."

***

Anne stood impatiently at the mouth of the cave. She turned to look off at the ocean. Dawn had broken. It was casting a beautiful yellowish orange light across the camp. From up here, the tents of the base looked like a small city. There was a calm over everything at the moment. The men had started a shift change about half an hour ago, and it looked like each man had just gone and crashed. A few sentries moved back and forth through the maze of tents and technology as they kept watch over the camp.

Anne turned to look at the cave. Its gaping mouth was still dark, even with the enormous spotlights directed at it. This was a very ominous place. The rock was entirely black, making it

192

difficult to see where the cave's opening started and stopped. Something caught her attention. It was a quick flash of light in the cave. It lasted less than a second. Anne questioned herself. Did she really see that, or was she so tired, her eyes had begun to play tricks on her?

Curiosity overwhelmed her. Reaching down on her belt, she removed a small metal flashlight and clicked it on. A narrow and focused beam of light burst from it. Taking a few steps forward, Anne spotted the fleeting light again. A chill ran down her spine as a sudden gust of wind howled across the mouth of the cave in front of her. Stopping dead in her tracks, she found herself unable to move. Fear had locked up her entire body. She was unable to turn away from the cave. She couldn't even blink. The flashlight began to shake in her hand. The light began to grow in intensity as if it was approaching her. Another gust of wind whipped across the cave. She heard something…something very faint at first. She strained to hear what it was. To her horror, it was a voice.

"Help me...." it moaned as if carried on the very wind itself. "Help me," it said again.

Anne felt her heart begin to thump wildly in her chest. It was coming nearer. She wanted to step back, to look away, but couldn't. She was transfixed on the light.

"General?"

Anne jumped as she felt a hand touch her shoulder. Spinning around, she saw Jannis standing behind her. She quickly tried to calm her nerves. "Don't ever do that again!" she yelled.

"I'm sorry, General," Jannis apologized. "I saw

you just standing here and wondered what was the matter."

Anne spun back around to look at the cave. "I saw a light...." she let her words trail off. The light was gone, as was the wind.

Jannis peered into the inky blackness of the cave. "I don't see anything." Anne ran her free hand over her face. "I could've swore I just saw a light and...."

"And what, General?"

Anne looked back at the cave. "I thought I heard Allen's voice."

Jannis pulled his small black radio off his belt and checked it. Turning it on, he keyed the talk button. "Private Allen, do you copy?" He waited for a moment. "Allen, respond." He pressed the button again, "Private Allen, this is Colonel Jannis, do you—"

Anne grabbed the radio from Jannis' hand. "It wasn't on the radio," Anne scolded. "My radio is completely off."

Jannis studied Anne for a moment. "Maybe you need to get some rest, General."

Anne glared at Jannis. "I'm fine, Colonel," she spat. Anne looked into the cave one more time, then back at Jannis. "Where are Drs. Hollman and Cisan?"

"They should be along in a moment," Jannis responded. "I've put together a four man team to accompany us into the cave."

"Very good," Anne replied. "I want to be in that cave in five minutes." She glared at Jannis, "Make it happen."

"Yes, General," Jannis spun on his heel and

began to walk back down the slope toward the camp.

Anne turned back to the cave. She felt a general uneasiness fall over her. Goosebumps began to rise on her skin. There was something horrible waiting for them down there. She knew that for sure.

***

Alex lifted her head. She had tried to get some sleep strapped to the chair, but had been unsuccessful. She looked over at the wall of the tent. The blackness she had been seeing all night had slowly begun to lighten. The sun was beginning to rise. She tried to clear her mind. She needed to focus and find a way out of here. Her life, and Griggs', depended on it.

Glancing around the tent, she noticed the bottle of wine Hollman had left sitting on the green footlocker in front of her. Using all her strength, she jumped up and down with the chair and tried to turn around. After three quick bounces, her back was facing the footlocker. Her hands were strapped behind the chair, but she had a little bit of give. Looking over her shoulder, she pulled hard and tried to reach the bottle. She was still too far away. Bouncing again, she jumped the chair back toward the locker. Jumping too far, the leg of her chair hit the bottom of the locker. Whipping her head around, she watched the bottle teeter on its edge. She held her breath as the bottle wobbled back and forth. If it fell, she would be done. It rocked onto its edge and looked as if it were going to tumble.

She sighed in relief as the bottle came to a stop

and didn't fall. Carefully, she reached out. Her fingers ran over the curves of the bottle, but couldn't quite get a grasp on it. Using her feet, she leaned the chair back toward the footlocker. She closed her eyes and strained as hard as she could against the ropes. Her fingers again grazed the neck of the bottle, but this time, she snapped her hand closed. She smiled. Now came the hard part.

Using her other hand, she positioned the bottle between her hands. Titling it down, she let the alcohol pour out and onto the floor. Jostling the bottle again, she held it tightly by the neck. Swinging hard, she slammed it against the back of the chair. She heard the dull thud as it hit against the metal. Swinging it again, she hit the metal harder this time. Still nothing. Focusing all her energy, she swung one final time. She was greeted by the sound of glass shattering against the back of the chair. Running her hand down the neck, she felt the jagged edges of the broken bottle. *Perfect,* she thought. Flipping the neck upside down, she began to saw against the ropes. She only hoped she would finish before someone found her.

***

Samantha was lying quietly on the floor of her tent. Her body was exhausted. Her eyes were bleary and her body abused. She thought for a moment about her life back in New York. She would've had her third performance last night, and she would've been good. Out of exhaustion, she began to run her lines in her head. It was the only thing keeping her going.

"How could you do this to me?" she asked her imaginary co-star. "I have a husband and a family, and I threw it all away for you," she emoted angrily.

Sitting up, she looked at the boards on the floor. She desperately wanted to get out of here. She wanted to go home to her small studio apartment and watch the people on the street as she often did. She was a people watcher. Being an actor, she wondered what made people do the things they did. She would watch the pedestrians through her window and try to get into their heads. Her drama teacher in high school had taught her that. "You not only have to know the words," she always used to say, "but understand why this character is saying them. Find out why they are the way they are." A tear rolled down her cheek. She didn't want to be the character that died in this story.

Samantha stopped for a moment and listened. The camp was quiet and utterly still. This could be her chance. Summoning all her strength, she dug her fingers between two floor panels and lifted them up, exposing the dirt below. Clawing with her nails, she began to dig into the floor. She knew she only needed to dig a rut big enough for her to scoot under the tent flap. The muscles in her hands strained as she tore against the hard ground. Slowly, she began to move the dirt out of the way.

***

Griggs' eyes snapped open as his body began to convulse again. He sat straight up on his cot and tried to regain control. His hands were shaking as he pressed them to the sides of his head. He felt his heart beating irregularly in his chest, and the left side of his face becoming numb. Fear washed over him. He didn't want to die like this. He didn't even know where he was.

The muscles in his back started to spasm, knocking him over. He lay helplessly on his back as the seizure gripped his body. He tried to roll over onto his side to avoid swallowing his tongue, but it was useless. His body wasn't responding to his brain's instructions.

Then, as suddenly as it began, it stopped. Griggs' body lay motionless on the cot. He slowly tested his reflexes. One by one, he moved his fingers and toes. He relaxed. He still had full control of his faculties.

Griggs slowly leaned his head to the right and looked around. He was lying on a cot in a huge tent. He had an IV needle inserted into his left hand and sensor pads attached to his head and chest. There were several other cots, but none of them were occupied. Sitting up, he swung his legs over the edge of the cot and stood. He quickly began to pull the sensor pads off his body and toss them carelessly behind him. Looking over at his left hand, he began to undo the clear tape that was holding the needle in place. Slowly, he removed the final piece of tape. He could feel the needle jostling in his vein, scraping the walls. Grabbing the cord, he yanked hard and pulled the needle free. The wound immediately began to bleed. Snatching one of the discarded pieces of tape, he pressed it firmly over the bloody area. *That will stop it for now,* he told himself, n*ow to get the hell out of here and find Alex.*

Chapter Twenty-Three

The six man team stood in front of a row of Moai situated in front of the volcano. The statues were placed so they looked into the island and at the massive mountain in front of them. Jake and One were standing behind one of the statues. One passed a pair of binoculars over to Jake and pointed toward the base of the mighty volcano. "See there?"

Jake peered through the binoculars at the mountain. He saw a city of tents arranged at the base. "I see them. How do we sneak in?"

One thought for a moment. "The island's topography prevents that. It's pretty much flat around here with the exception of Rano Raraku."

Jake looked through again. "We just have to walk up there? Out in the open?" he asked in disbelief.

One nodded. "It's our only choice unless we want to go all the way around to the other side of the volcano and work our way back to the camp."

"Then we would have the element of surprise," Jake conjectured.

"But we will lose our timing," One argued. "If we walk all the way around, it'll be well into the morning before we arrive. The time to strike is now. We need to move so we are covered by the sunrise."

Jake looked over at the sun. It was beginning to peak over the horizon. He knew they only had about ten minutes before it was fully daylight. "All right," he sighed. "Let's do it your way."

One by one, the men set off across the plain toward the camp. They rapidly spread out in an effort not to be seen.

***

Anne, Jannis, Hollman and Cisan stood facing the mouth of the cave. A row of five soldiers stood behind them with their rifles cradled in their hands. Each person had a flashlight with them, and a wireless radio slipped over their head. Each was dressed in the traditional black fatigues of Area 51.

Anne turned around to address the soldiers. "I want radio and equipment checks right now." The men busily went to work at their task. Anne could hear them speaking into the radios on her headset. She looked over at Hollman. "Are you ready?"

Hollman nodded.

Anne smiled. "Then let's go. Jannis, you take point."

The nine members of the team led by Jannis walked slowly into the cave and out of the rain. Each member switched on the flashlights and began to search the cave. Goosebumps ran up Anne's body. She kept hearing Allen's voice in her head. The team followed the cave as it descended down into the depths of the volcano. They were all silent, not knowing what to expect when they reached their destination.

Anne heard the thump behind her and spun around. She ran her flashlight around the cave while doing a quick head count. One of her men was missing. "Private?" she called into the darkness. "Private?" She moved her light around the cave, but saw nothing except black rock. "Where the hell is he?"

Cisan stopped and looked behind her. "I don't

see him either. Private?" she called. Cisan took a few steps forward, then stopped suddenly. She let out a small gasp. "I found him."

Anne rushed to her side. "What the hell?" Anne gazed into a pit on the floor. "Where the hell did this come from?"

Cisan shrugged. "I don't know. It wasn't here when the rest of the team crossed."

Anne shone her light down into the pit. She saw the broken and lifeless body of one of the soldiers lying there. The pit was at least fifteen feet deep and six feet across. It stretched across the entire length of the floor. "Jesus."

Hollman limped toward the hole and stood next to Cisan. "It's a booby trap," he said.

"Someone must've triggered it," Anne thought. "That's the only possibility."

"Yeah," Cisan agreed, "but what triggered it?"

Anne turned around and shone her light on the floor. "I don't see anything," she confessed. She stopped to look at her team. "From this point on, I want everyone watching their step *very* carefully."

"General?" Jannis yelled anxiously.

"What is it, Colonel?" Anne said. Her skin was beginning to crawl. "I think you better come and take a look at this."

Anne turned to see Jannis standing a few feet in front of the group. His flashlight was trained on the ground. She quickly made her way over to his position. "What is it?"

"Look," he said while pointing down at the ground.

Anne brought her light to bear where Jannis was pointing. She was startled to see the skeletal remains of a person lying on the floor. The skull was smiling up at her with its lifeless eye sockets, as if it knew from beyond the grave what her ultimate fate was. "It's just a skeleton," she said half to herself, half to Jannis.

"Not that, General." Jannis reached over and pulled Anne's flashlight to the right. "This."

Anne uncontrollably gasped. She took two uneasy steps away. "What the hell is going on here?" Anne stared at Private Allen's head lying on the floor. It had been severed just below the base of the skull and its face was still twisted into a contorted grimace of horror.

Jannis knelt down beside Allen's head. Using the butt of his flashlight, he rolled it over to get a better look at the neck wound. "It looks like his head was ripped off by the look of the wound," Jannis speculated.

"Help me...."

Anne spun around. "Did you hear that?" she asked in terror. Her eyes were bulging, she was so scared. "Did you just hear that voice?"

"No," Jannis admitted calmly. Standing, he walked over to Anne. "Are you okay, General?"

"Please, help me...."

"There it was again," Anne said frantically.

Jannis grabbed a hold of her by the shoulders. "What the hell is going on, General?"

Anne didn't respond. Jannis could see that she was listening intently. "It's gone," she said.

"What was the voice saying?" Jannis asked.

"It said 'help me'." Anne took a deep breath to try and calm her nerves. "It was Allen's voice."

Jannis took a step back. "I don't think so,

General." He shone his light back onto Allen's decapitated head. "As you can see, he's in no condition to talk."

Anne knew Jannis didn't believe her. She took another deep breath and looked down into the darkness of the cave. "Let's keep moving."

"That's it?" Jannis asked confused. "You just have some kind of," he struggled to find the word, "experience, and you just want to keep going?"

Anne looked over at Jannis. Her face was calm and collected. "That's an order, *Colonel,*" she said, stressing his lower rank.

Jannis saluted. "Yes, General."

***

Jake glanced over at the sun as they approached the camp. It was about half exposed over the horizon. Its golden light was starting to filter down over the small triangular island. He looked back over toward the other men. From the way they moved, they looked like wraiths haunting the plain. They were all hunkered low to the ground, but moving as quickly as possible. Each man was holding an assault rifle in his hands as he moved. Jake returned his attention to the camp. They were less than twenty-five meters away now.

He stopped and sank down the ground. Reaching into his black trench coat, he pulled out his pistol. Hitting the release lever, the clip fell into his hands. It was fully loaded, and he had several more strapped to his belt. Slamming the clip back into the weapon, he pulled back on the slide and loaded it. The pistol made a resounding snap as it cocked into place. Holding it firmly in his hand, Jake took off toward the others. They were all gathering behind a small hill just in front of the camp. Each man gracefully spun around and lay with their back against the hill.

Jake looked over at the men. "This is it," he whispered. "What's our plan of attack?"

One of the men rolled over on his side to face Jake. He slowly opened his trench coat revealing several grenades attached to his belt. "We're going to blow up everything we see."

"You can't do that!" Jake argued. "My daughter's in there!"

"Keep your voice down," One instructed.

"You can't just go in there and start destroying everything!" Jake said with conviction. "You might accidentally hit Samantha!"

One pulled off his mask and looked at Jake. "We are here to protect the—"

"Protect the sanctity of the Divine Sanctuary, yeah, I've heard it all before," Jake said angrily. "Give me a chance to look for my daughter and get her to safety before you start blowing things up."

One's expression didn't change. It was a hardened look.

"I need a chance," Jake pleaded. "I have to get my daughter out safely." One rolled on to his back. "Fine," he said sternly. "We're wasting our cover. Let's move." Lifting up to his knees, he pulled his mask back on and raised his hood.

The six members of the team slowly lifted from their positions and began to stealthily approach the camp.

***

Griggs moved quickly out of the tent. He slowly craned his head around to see if anyone had spotted him. It was still early morning; the yellow rays of the sun were just beginning to filter over the camp. Crouching low to the ground, Griggs moved carefully through the maze of tents. He needed to find Alex, but he had no idea where she was. His only option was to go tent to tent.

Stopping in front of one of the tents, he ran his hand carefully down the flap, curled his fingers around it and began to lift it up. He poked his head inside. There was nothing there except several bunks arranged along the walls. Stepping inside, Griggs had an idea. He trotted to the nearest footlocker and cracked it open. Inside were several of the soldier's personal effects, and exactly what Griggs was looking for: one pair of black fatigues. Removing the clothing, Griggs began to peel his shirt off. Glancing down into the trunk, he noticed a silver .45 lying quietly in the bottom. Griggs reached inside and removed the weapon. "That's not standard issue," he said with a grin as he laid the weapon on the bunk. Pulling on the black shirt, he began to unbutton his jeans.

"What the in the hell are you doing, Private?" a voice boomed from the front of the tent.

Griggs looked up to see a burly man with the rank of major standing in front of him. Griggs instantly snapped to attention and saluted. "I was just preparing for duty, sir!"

The man studied Griggs for a moment, then

approached. "I don't remember your face, Private." The man balled up his fists and walked slowly around Griggs. "Name and rank!" the man yelled in Griggs' ear.

Griggs didn't even flinch. "Private Jason Griggs, sir!"

"Are you some kind of retard, Private?"

"Sir, no sir!"

The major moved back in front of Griggs. He leaned in close to Griggs' face. "Then why are you standing here with your pants around your ankles, Private?" The major smiled. "I get it," he said merrily, "you're a homo, aren't you?"

"Sir?" Griggs asked confused.

"You were just in here fucking your boyfriend, weren't you, you little faggot," the major said in a low and gravelly voice.

"Sir, no, sir!"

"Then what in the fuck are you doing, soldier?" the major screamed.

Griggs was tiring of this man. He was wasting time here. Slowly, Griggs balled up his fists, but kept at strict attention. "I was late for duty, sir. I needed to change quickly in order to make my post on time, sir!"

The major sneered. "I ought to kick your little faggoty ass, Private."

Griggs leaned closer to the man and smiled. "I don't think that would be in your best interest."

"What?" the major blared.

Griggs swung his fist hard and connected with the major's ribs. The older man stumbled away from Griggs, but quickly regained his balance. He threw himself into an attack. The major ducked under a wild punch thrown by Griggs and delivered a sharp uppercut into his jaw. Griggs shook off the blow. Swinging again, Griggs missed with his fist but connected with his elbow.

The major grabbed his chin. A trickle of blood was running down from his split lip. "You're gonna pay for that, you son of a bitch." The major launched another assault. Swinging his left hand, the major missed, but he quickly followed the miss with a kidney blast and two quick jabs to Griggs' ribs.

Griggs reflexes proved much faster than the major's. Thrusting his hand down, he grabbed the major's arm and twisted it painfully around. He heard the man's shoulder pop out of the socket. The major grunted, but refused to cry out. Griggs flipped the major around and pinned the man's arm behind his back.

"I don't have time for this," Griggs growled through his gritted teeth. "Let's make time then," the major smiled. Lifting his leg, he kicked backwards into Griggs' kneecap.

Griggs lost his grip and tumbled to the floor. The major spun around and delivered a sharp kick into Griggs' midsection. Dropping down, the major jabbed his knee into Griggs' chest and threw three quick punches across his chin. Countering, Griggs jerked his body up and tossed the major off. The older man hit the floor hard. Reaching up onto the bed, Griggs snatched the pistol. As the two men jumped to their feet, Griggs drew a hasty bead on the major.

"You don't have the balls, Private," The major announced confidently. Griggs smiled. "Please, call me Major." The man looked confused, but only for a moment. Griggs pulled the trigger. The major fell to the ground in a bloody heap.

Dropping the gun on the bed, Griggs pulled off his jeans and slipped on the pair of black pants. Hastily arranging the uniform, he tucked the gun into the holster on his belt and exited the tent. He knew his cover was blown, but he still needed to find Alex.

***

The group had just entered the outskirts of the camp when they heard the gunshot. They all quickly scattered. One and Jake moved toward a tent and crouched down behind it.

"What the hell was that?" Jake asked.

"Gunshot from inside the camp," One confirmed. "It looks like our plan has just been thrown out the window, Mr. Silver."

"Damn," Jake complained.

One stood up and signaled to the men. "Attack!" He turned his attention back to Jake. "Go find your daughter, Mr. Silver."

Jake nodded. Standing up, he made his way around the tent and into the camp. He could hear the other members of the Brotherhood discharging their weapons. "Shit," he muttered. "Have to find Samantha now."

***

"General Caroll?" a male voice crackled over the radio.

208

Anne reached up and pressed her hand against the earpiece on the headset. "Go ahead."

"We've got a situation at base camp," the man said frantically. "What's the problem?" Anne asked.

"We're under attack!"

Anne turned to Jannis and the group. They had all heard the message on their headsets. "Back to base camp on the double!"

Chapter Twenty-Four

Alex stood up. The chair was still lying on the floor with a mess of ropes tangled around it. Looking at the broken bottleneck in her bloody hands, she tossed it to the floor. She quickly wiped her hands on her pants. She had cut her hands several times while trying to hack through the rope and they were bleeding profusely now. Moving toward the front flap of the tent, she carefully peeked outside. She heard the crack of weapons fire echoing throughout the base.

Pulling her head back inside, she took a deep breath. *What the hell is going on out there?*

Stepping through the flap, she stood outside for a moment. Her eyes caught sight of a group of men dressed in black trench coats moving quickly toward her position through the maze of the camp. She didn't recognize their uniforms. Ducking around the side of the tent, she unconsciously began to hold her breath. She could hear the footfalls of the men as they moved past, as well as the thump of her own heart in her chest. The sound of machine gun fire erupted again. She heard the screams of men as they were gunned down in their bunks. Finally exhaling, Alex broke into a dead sprint down the long corridor in the camp. Flames had begun to lick the orange morning sky from several of the tents, and a thick smoke was beginning to settle over the camp. Her only relief was the light rain that was falling. It was helping to cool her overheated body.

"Stop there!" a man shouted.

Alex skidded to a stop and raised her hands.

Her chest was heaving as she tried to catch her breath. She was too out of breath to speak.

"What the hell is going on out here?" the man yelled from behind Alex. He had just emerged from his tent to see the destruction at hand.

"I don't know," Alex gasped. "Turn around."

Alex complied. The man she found standing before her was young, probably a private or a lieutenant, with dark hair and fearful brown eyes. He had probably not talked with his CO this morning, and the attack had taken him by surprise. He looked as if he were only eighteen or nineteen years old. He had the look of a man that knew he was about to die. "Let's get out of here," she said calmly to the man. She knew if she could play on his fears, she would have a better chance of surviving.

"Shut up!" the man yelled. His weapon was trembling in his hands. "Just shut up!"

Alex slowly took a step away from the man. She knew he had become irrational with fear. There was no use in even trying to convince him of anything. His mind was securely locked in self-preservation mode. The man glanced to his right just as an explosion rocked the camp. Several of the nearby tents were torn apart by the impact of the blast. Flames began to cross the grassy plain toward where Alex was standing. *Jesus,* Alex thought fearfully. *I hope Jason is all right.*

***

Griggs had no idea he had inadvertently started an all-out war. He pulled on the black hat he found with the uniform and briskly made his way out of the tent. He needed to know where Alex was, but he had no idea where to start looking. He quickly surveyed the camp. It was a disaster. Entire tents had been leveled and were now engulfed in flames. Dead bodies lay partially charred near the tents, while others were scattered randomly about the base. Griggs stopped and looked at the bodies. They were all Air Force personnel. "What the hell?" Griggs muttered.

Griggs heard the crack of gunshots to his right. Snapping his head around, he caught sight of a man in the distance in a long black trench coat emerging from a nearby tent. The man stopped and looked back. He began to move to the next tent, when he stopped. Griggs couldn't see the man's face, but he knew he had turned to look right at him. "Shit," he said. Jumping behind a tent, he swiftly moved around to the back of it. From his new vantage point, Griggs could see the man in the black trench coat more clearly. He watched as the man turned and started to jog toward a second tent. Slowly at first, Griggs moved out and began to follow the man.

***

Anne stood in horror looking down on her camp. She was standing with Jannis near the mouth of the cave listening to her headset. The radio chatter was filled with nothing but cries for help and static. Messages kept overlapping as her men frantically keyed their radios during an engagement. Anne watched the tan tents fall one by one in a burst of flames. She spun around to face her men standing behind her. "Get down there now!" she ordered them.

Jannis looked across the camp. He could see several dark forms moving through the corridors between the tents. "Who the hell are they?" he asked, unsheathing his weapon.

"I have no idea," Hollman responded from behind him.

"I don't give a flying fuck who these people are," Anne said in a deadly tone, "I want them all dead." Anne began to charge down the mountain with her men.

***

One had grabbed another member of the Brotherhood and was approaching the medical tent. He signaled for the man to check inside. Lifting the flap with the barrel of his rifle, the man peered inside. He turned back to One and shook his head.

"Burn it," One commanded him coolly.

The man pulled an incendiary grenade off his belt and pulled the pin. Tossing it inside the medical facilities, the two men quickly made their way away from it. Ducking down behind another adjoining tent, One felt a tremor ripple across the ground as the grenade exploded into a ball of fire. He peeked around the edge of their cover to see several men running and screaming. One of their comrades was on fire. They tossed him to the ground and began to pat him out.

One jumped up from his hiding place and began to fire his rifle at the men. He easily picked them off.

Letting the weapon fall limp to his side, he walked slowly toward the corpses. Guilt welled up inside him as he looked at their faces. *Damn,* he moaned. *They're all just kids.*

A gunshot startled him. Spinning, he saw his friend stumble out from behind the tent and fall to the ground. Moving closer, he saw the man had been shot in the head. Blood was beginning to pool on the ground around his wound. One quickly said a prayer for the deceased and made the sign of the cross on his chest.

Standing up, he walked around the edge of the tent to see two soldiers crouched down in the grass. They were trying to repair a jammed weapon. Lifting his weapon, One looked at the two men. "May God help us all," he said as he pulled the trigger.

***

Jake was running out of options. The Brotherhood was systematically destroying every single tent they came across. Fire's horrible tendrils were licking the sky as it spread across the camp. The sound of weapon fire echoed all over the base. The Brotherhood was almost unstoppable. A group of six men was destroying an entire base filled with highly trained military personnel. *I'm glad they're on my side,* Jake thought.

Stopping in front of a tent, Jake quickly lifted the flap and looked inside. There was nothing. Jake was starting to worry. He feared one of the enclosures the Brotherhood had destroyed had

Samantha inside. He had a sudden flash of finding her charred body in the aftermath. Jake took a deep breath and tried to push the thought from his mind. Walking around, he saw something out of the corner of his eye. Stopping, he looked over at the next tent. There was nothing. No sign of movement. Jake shook his head and began to continue on. He caught it again. It looked like someone's hands reaching out from beneath the ground, but it was gone too fast to be sure. He knew he needed to investigate.

Moving to the front of the tent, he listened inside for a moment. Nothing. Lifting the flap, Jake saw a dark form hunkered down in the far corner. The person had removed several of the floor panels and was trying to dig their way out. Lifting a flashlight off of his belt, Jake clicked the power button. "Oh, my God," tears began to well up in his eyes. "Samantha!"

The woman looked up from her kneeling position to see her father standing before her. Relief washed over her body. She felt a release as she began to stand up. Her emotions over the past few days came to a head and she began to sob uncontrollably. She took a few unsteady steps toward her father, then collapsed to the floor.

Jake moved in and fell to the floor next to her. He wrapped his arms tightly around his daughter. "I thought I would never see you again," he confessed.

"They told me you were coming," Samantha said between sobs, "and that they were going to kill you."

Jake ran his hand over her dirty hair. He pressed his cheek to her forehead. "It's all going to be over soon, Sam," he said in a comforting voice.

"We need to get you out of here."

Samantha tilted her head back and looked up at Jake. Her face was battered and bruised. Small lacerations crossed her cheeks and her usually joyful green eyes were now tired and bloodshot. "I knew you would come for me," she said as tears ran down her dirty cheeks.

Standing up, Jake helped his daughter to her feet. She was exhausted. Her body wanted to give up, but her spirit hadn't let it. She stood on rubbery legs next to her father, but found the strength to continue.

"Let's go," Jake said as he began to walk toward the front of the tent. He held her hand and kept one of his arms around her shoulders for support. He didn't want to rush her, but he knew they needed to hurry. Opening the flap, Jake helped Samantha outside.

Samantha cocked her head to the side and fear showed in her eyes.

"Dad, behind you!"

Jake swung around to see a soldier dressed in black coming around the side of the tent. Scrambling for his gun, he pushed Samantha down to the ground. Finally finding control of his weapon, he drew a bead on the soldier. "Stop," Jake commanded him. The soldier stepped out from behind the tent and reveled himself. Jake's eyes went wide in amazement. "What the hell are you doing here?"

Griggs smiled. This was the first stroke of luck he'd had all day. He reached out and shook Jake's outstretched hand. "Damn good to see you, Jake."

Jake reached down and lifted his daughter off

216

the ground and tried to dust her off. "Sorry about that, Sam."

Samantha nodded. "I know you were just trying to protect me," she said with a smile, "just next time, try not to protect me so hard." She rubbed her elbow.

Griggs looked at Samantha. "Who are you?"

Jake smiled. "We don't really have a lot of time to talk now, but this is my daughter, Samantha." Jake looked over at Samantha. "Samantha, this is Jason Griggs, an old friend of mine."

Samantha tried to muster a smile. "Nice to meet you."

Jake had an epiphany. "If you're here, does that mean Alex is too?" Griggs nodded. "She's here somewhere. I just haven't found her yet." Jake's mind whirred. "We need to find Alex, but I don't want my daughter down here in this mess." He looked up at Rano Raraku and spotted the giant gaping mouth of a cave. "There," Jake said, pointing to the cave. "Find Alex and meet us there."

Griggs nodded and patted Jake on the shoulder. "Good to see you again."

Jake smiled. "Same here." Jake turned and began to walk away from Griggs.

"Oh, hey, Jake?" Griggs yelled.

"Yeah?" Jake asked, turning his head back.

"Nice outfit," Griggs said with a laugh. "You've got that whole Keanu Reeves 'Matrix' thing going on there." Jake laughed. "Whoa."

Turning away from Jake, Griggs ran off back into the camp without another word. Looking down at his daughter, Jake smiled. Taking her by the hand, Jake began to move away from the tents toward the volcano.

Chapter Twenty-Five

Anne crept around the corner of two tents and stood with her pistol cradled in her hands. Flames from a nearby fire were throwing a lot of heat in her direction. Beads of sweat were beginning to roll down her forehead, but she was unable to give up her position. She looked across the corridor toward the next set of tents. Jannis and two of the soldiers had taken up position there. The three men stood with their weapons ready.

Anne had spotted two men in black trench coats moving toward them as they came off the slope of the volcano. Anne wanted to lay an ambush to capture the two hooded men. Snapping her fingers to get Jannis' attention, Anne twirled her hand in the air quickly, then tapped her nose. Jannis nodded understandingly at the gesture. Anne held up her hand with her palm facing Jannis. She flashed five twice. Jannis nodded again.

Counting down from ten in his head, Jannis readied himself. Tapping his two men on the shoulder, Jannis let them scoot in front of him. Reaching one, Jannis slapped the nearest soldier on the back. The two soldiers leapt from their hiding position into the open of the corridor. Immediately, the two men opened fire on the men in black trench coats.

The first man in black tried to dodge out of the way, but felt a bullet rip through his hip. He crumpled to the ground. Ignoring the pain, the man sat up and started to return fire. His companion had successfully moved out of the line of attack, but was now pinned down behind one of the tents. He realized it offered no protection, but it was all he had. He looked over at his friend sitting helplessly on the ground. He had to do something.

Ripping a grenade off his belt, he pulled the pin. Diving into the open, he lobbed the grenade toward the assailants. Firing wildly, he slipped his arm around his companion and lifted him off the ground. Behind him, the grenade exploded. The blast tore through the tents and started them on fire. Jannis and his two men scattered out of the way, but it was too late. The flames reached out and licked at Jannis' legs. Orange flames ran up his legs as his uniform caught fire.

The man in black helped his friend hobble out of harm's way. Setting him down behind a tent, the man ran back out into the flames. Covering his eyes, he charged through the wall of fire toward his attackers. Stopping on the other side, he fired flat-footed toward the two soldiers. The bullets slammed into their chests knocking them to the ground. Jannis had dropped and was trying to smother the flames by rolling. He didn't even look up as the man approached with his weapon aimed at Jannis' head.

"You have disrupted the sanctity of the Divine Sanctuary," the member of the Brotherhood said gravely. "For this, you will die." The man in black lifted his weapon to bear. He slowly slid his finger around the trigger and began to pull when he heard a familiar click behind him.

"I don't think so," Anne replied smugly. She pulled the trigger and felt the gun recoil in her hand. The member of the Brotherhood fell lifelessly to the ground in a bloody heap. Stepping over his body,

Anne slid her weapon into the waistband of her uniform. She extended her hand down to the burnt Jannis.

Reaching up, Jannis grabbed her hand. "Thank you, General." With Anne's help, Jannis got to his feet and dusted himself off.

Leaning over, Anne reached down and pulled the mask off the man she had just shot. A gaping exit wound in the middle of the man's forehead was letting blood drain through to the back of the man's head. Anne stared at the man's face. She didn't recognize him. She stood back up and looked at Jannis. "I want the rest of these fuckers dead," she commanded him.

Jannis nodded. "I'm on it."

***

"Move," the soldier instructed her as he pressed the gun hard into Alex's back.

Alex took an uncomfortable step forward when she felt the cold steel behind her. "Where are you taking me?" Alex asked the man. "Shouldn't you be more worried about this group that's attacking the base?"

"Maybe you're a member of that group," the man suggested. "Maybe I've just captured my first prisoner of war."

"And maybe you're an idiot," Alex shot back.

"Shut up," the man said, jabbing his gun into Alex's ribs. "Keep moving." The man was leading Alex away from the flames slowly engulfing the entire camp. Alex listened as she walked with her hands up. The sound of gunfire and explosions had been silenced. She wondered what had happened. Had the attacking group been defeated, or had they just been on a search and destroy mission?

Alex felt a hand slip on her shoulder. "Don't fucking touch me," she warned without turning around.

"You always let me before," a familiar voice replied.

Alex dropped her hands and spun around. "Jason!" she exclaimed. Griggs stood before her with a wide grin on his face. He pointed his thumb behind him. "You're friend got tired and had to rest."

Alex looked over his shoulder to see the man lying on the ground with a broken neck. She quickly wrapped her arms around Griggs' neck. "Why did you sneak up on me?"

"I didn't," Griggs smiled. "I snuck up on that guy."

"How are you feeling?"

"Better," Griggs said with a nod. He looked down into Alex's eyes. "Interesting news," he said with a bounce in his voice.

"What?" Alex asked.

"Jake is here on the island, too."

Alex pulled away from Griggs. "Why is he here?"

"He's here to rescue his daughter."

"What happened to his daughter?"

Griggs shook his head. "I don't know the whole story," he admitted. "You can ask him when we meet up with him."

"We're going to see him?" Alex asked with mixed feelings. Her mind quickly wandered back to the phone call she made from Egypt just days earlier. She didn't know how to feel about that.

***

One had crouched down behind one of the few tents still standing. Holding his weapon tightly in his hands, he leaned his head forward and rested it against the top of the weapon. He whispered a quick prayer, then looked up at the cloudy sky. A few scattered raindrops had begun to fall again, but it wasn't enough to slow the raging fires. One knew the Brotherhood had done its job.

They had destroyed most of the tents and taken no prisoners. The cost had been high, though. Out of the five members of the Brotherhood that had entered the camp, only two remained standing. One wondered how Jake was doing. Had he found his daughter?

He shook his head. He couldn't afford to let his mind wander. If he lost his focus for even a second, it could mean disaster. *One more tent,* he told himself. Standing up, he began to walk toward the front of the tent. A voice startled him. Stopping, he pulled back and listened. It sounded like a female's voice and she was talking to someone, but One wasn't sure to whom. Crouching down, One moved slowly toward the end of the tent. He carefully craned his neck around the corner. He saw a tall brunette woman speaking into her headset. She was wearing a black uniform, but she was wearing no rank insignia. One swallowed his guilt and slowly stood up. Lifting his assault rifle, he took a few steps toward the woman. One shot to the back of her head and it would all be over.

"I wouldn't do that," the woman warned him without even turning around. Hearing her voice unnerved One. He tried to think quickly. "Down on your knees and put your hands behind your back!"

Anne spun around and slapped the weapon out of One's hands. "I don't think so." She lifted her pistol and fired into One's midsection.

One stumbled back while trying to regain his composure. Steeling himself, he quickly recalled his hand-to-hand combat. Ignoring the pain, One leapt off his feet toward the Anne. Throwing a high punch, One caught Anne across the face. Anne's face snapped to the side, but she easily recovered. Whipping her pistol around, she smacked it against One's head. Grabbing One by the throat, Anne lifted him effortlessly off the ground. One latched his hands around Anne's arm and struggled to break free. Her grip around his throat was like iron. Kicking hard, he hit Anne directly in the chest.

Anne scoffed. "Is that all you have, little man?"

One's eyes widened. He knew that kick would've broken a normal person's rib cage. Kicking again, he felt his boot hit her jaw.

Anne smiled again, her teeth covered with blood. Turning her head, she spit out a mouthful of blood. Lifting her weapon, she pressed it to One's chest. "Why are you here?" she asked angrily.

"I know nothing," One gasped. He could feel the vertebrae in his neck starting to separate.

"You have one more chance, and then I'm going to kill you," Anne warned him. "Who are you and why are you here?"

"My soul is prepared to die," One announced

seriously.

Anne smiled. "Good." Rearing back, she tossed One away from her. One hit the ground hard. He summoned the strength to sit up and look Anne in the eyes. He wrapped his hand around his bruised throat. "Who are you?" he groaned in terror.

Anne smiled. "Your ticket to the afterlife." She targeted her weapon at One's head and pulled the trigger.

Chapter Twenty-Six

Jake stood facing the mouth of the giant cave. Samantha was next to him, trying to catch her breath after the long trek up the side of the volcano. Jake glanced around at the huge spotlights facing into the cave. Darkness permeated the mouth. Not even the light from the sun could penetrate it. Jake took an uneasy step back. "Maybe this wasn't such a good idea," he wondered.

"I don't know, Dad," Samantha said, "It doesn't look like we have a lot of options here." She turned around and glanced over the camp and the island. "By the way," she said, turning back to Jake. "Where is 'here'?"

Jake checked his watch. Griggs should've been there by now. He looked up at his daughter. "I'm sorry, what?"

"Where are we?" Samantha asked again.

"About two thousand miles from anywhere," Jake laughed. "Welcome to Easter Island. We're stuck in the middle of the South Pacific between Chile and Tahiti."

Samantha nodded. "We have less options than I thought."

Jake checked his watch again. "Two minutes and we go, with or without Griggs."

***

Jannis walked around the edge of a tent and stopped. He spotted a man in a long black trench coat trying to lift a wounded companion off the ground. He watched the man set down his weapon

226

and slide his hands under the wounded man's arms. The second man looked like the one Jannis' men had injured just moments earlier.

Jannis had slowly circled around the flaming tents in search of the remaining attackers. He stood now with his M-16 ready. Running his hand over his baldhead, he took two steps toward the men and raised his weapon. Clicking off the safety, he pulled the butt of the gun into his shoulder and steadied himself.

Jannis stared down the sights at the two men. Holding his breath, he pulled the trigger.

The men cried out for a moment as the hail of bullets rained down on them, but stopped as quickly as they began. Jannis slowly lowered his weapon and stared at the two men in black lying silently on the ground, their bodies now glistening with their own dark, red blood.

Two soldiers charged around a second tent toward Jannis. The first man stopped. "Sir, we heard gunfire."

Jannis nodded, "I found two of the attackers."

The men looked over at the two bodies. "Good hunting, sir."

"Mobilize every man you can find," Jannis instructed. "I want this mess cleaned up before midday."

The two men snapped to attention and saluted. "Yes, sir."

Jannis lifted the strap on his M-16 and slung it over his shoulder. Looking up at the cloudy sky, he searched for a glimpse of the sun, but found only more darkness. Letting his eyes slowly fall back down to the ground, he stopped on the slope of

Rano Raraku. From here, he could only make out shapes, but he could tell that two figures were standing near the mouth of the cave. Jannis cursed under his breath. He tapped a button situated on the earpiece of the headset. "General Caroll?"

The radio hissed for a moment before crackling to life. "Yes, Colonel?" Anne's voice replied coldly over the speaker.

He paused for a moment, "We have a problem."

***

Griggs and Alex were running hand in hand up the slope of the volcano. Alex looked up to see Jake and his daughter motioning for them to hurry. A barrage off bullets tore into the ground directly behind them. Alex stumbled to the ground as her foot caught on a hole in the lava rock. Griggs skidded to a stop and reached down and grabbed Alex. Another salvo of bullets tore into the rock around them, narrowly missing Alex and Griggs.

Lifting Alex off the ground, the two sprinted off toward the cave. Holding their arms over their faces to shield themselves from flying debris, they zigzagged across the face of the volcano. The sound of machine gun fire echoed behind them again. A piece of debris shot up, hitting Griggs in the chin. His hands instantly wrapped around the bleeding wound. They were almost at the top.

Jake reached down and scooped up a discarded flashlight. Grabbing Samantha by the hand, he led her quickly toward the mouth of the cave. Alex and Griggs were close behind after they reached the

228

plateau. The four fled into the darkness of the cave.

**

"Damn," Anne cursed. She turned around to face Jannis. "You missed." Jannis slowly lowered his weapon to his side. "Sorry, General." He looked up at the slope again. "They were just too far away."

"I don't want to hear excuses!" Anne lashed out and slapped Jannis angrily across the face. "I've had to deal with this kind of failure for six years now!" she yelled. "I will not deal with this anymore!"

Jannis wanted to cradle his face, but kept at attention. "Sorry, General." Anne began to pace back and forth in front of Jannis. She clasped her hands behind her back. "At least we have them cornered," she sneered. Stopping, she looked back at Jannis. "I want Doctors Hollman and Cisan here ASAP."

Jannis started to turn, but then hesitated. "May I ask why, General?" he asked cautiously.

Anne licked her lips. "We're going in after them." She turned and looked up at the volcano. "There'll be no escape for them this time."

Chapter Twenty-Seven

Tyler was awake. He glanced out his window. The sky was beginning to brighten as morning broke. He had been lying there all night, only closing his eyes to blink. The idea of sleep hadn't even crossed his mind. The house was quiet. Durard and Tulley had finally gone to bed about an hour ago. They had been up talking all night long recounting Durard's previous adventures with Jake and Alex. Tyler knew Durard fascinated Tulley. Never had he met a man who had experienced so much and not been able to tell his story. Tyler wondered what Tulley was going to do with all this information once he had it all collected. He smiled for a moment. Maybe Tulley would write a book, then a major Hollywood studio would pick up the movie rights. He wondered who would play him in the movie version...Brad Pitt? Matt Damon? That kid who played Urkel? Tyler shuddered and allowed himself a brief laugh.

Rolling over, he looked over the body of his sleeping wife. Her face was peaceful, and her body completely relaxed. He loved to watch her sleep. He tried to imagine what she was dreaming about. Running his hand over the curve of her hips, he watched a smile cross her face. *Hopefully, she's dreaming about me....*

Tyler rolled onto his back and stared at the ceiling. His mind returned to the subject it had been thinking about all night, a more morbid subject. He wondered what Faith would do with herself after he was dead.

He knew a normal person of his age sometimes

thought about death, but most of them didn't know when it would happen. Late last evening, Tyler was blessed, or cursed, with that information. He truly understood now what the aliens that abducted him meant by calling him the "savior". He would indeed save all of mankind, but die in the process. He thought about the vision he had of his death. It wasn't pleasant. He shook the thought. He had been dwelling on this long enough. It was time to enjoy what little time he had left with his wife.

Rolling onto his side, he slid his hand over her stomach and pulled her close to him. He gently began to kiss the back of her neck.

Faith slowly opened her eyes and rolled into his arms. She smiled ever so softly, her green eyes glistening in the early morning light. "Well, good morning," she said softly as she draped her arm around his neck. "To what do I owe the honor of this wake-up call?"

Tyler stared into her eyes. "I just wanted you to know that I love you, and I always will."

***

A few meters into the cave, Jake stopped. He handed the flashlight to Samantha and took a few steps toward Alex and Griggs. Alex held her position, but felt uneasy. She had no idea what to expect. Jake stopped and just looked at Alex for a moment with a serious face. Jake's stern glance suddenly gave way to a smile. He opened his arms wide and hugged Alex. "So good to see you!"

Alex was relieved. She returned the embrace. "It's good to see you too, Jake."

Letting go, Jake stepped back. He placed his hands on her shoulders.

"I'm sorry we don't have more time to catch up." Alex nodded. "Me, too."

Griggs placed his hand on Jake's shoulder. "Aren't you going to introduce your daughter to Alex?"

"Oh," Jake said with a smile. "I'm sorry." He reached back and pulled Samantha closer. "This is my daughter, Samantha Silver. We all call her Sam." Alex reached out and shook Samantha's hand. "Very nice to meet you." Samantha smiled. "Same here."

Jake turned and looked into the darkness of the cave. "We better get going."

"Where are we going?" Alex asked. "Into the cave," Jake assured her.

"But what if the cave leads nowhere?" Alex asked.

Jake smiled. "I've been assured by a reliable source that this cave leads somewhere very important."

"Where?" Samantha asked.

"Apparently, to the 'Divine Sanctuary'," Jake replied.

"What the hell is the 'Divine Sanctuary'?" Griggs wondered. Jake shrugged. "I don't really know."

"Well," Alex said with a smile, "let's find out then." Jake laughed. "Ever the explorer."

Turning around, Samantha returned the flashlight to Jake. He quickly flashed the light around the cave and looked over the black igneous rock. It was laden with holes that used to be ancient air bubbles. None of the holes were larger than a few inches, but they knew that they could still be potentially dangerous if they stepped wrong.

Jake began to walk further into the cave. "Everyone stay behind me. Samantha?"

"Yes?" Samantha chimed. "Stay right behind me, okay?"

Samantha looked around the darkness with a touch of fear in her heart. Ever since she was a child, she had had an irrational fear of dark, enclosed spaces. "You don't have to worry about me."

Jake stopped suddenly. "Whoa," he said to the group. "Take a look at this," he said, moving the flashlight down to the floor.

Griggs moved closer to Jake. "Wow," he exclaimed as he stared into the massive hole in the middle of the floor.

Jake took a step closer and shone the light down into the hole. "Jesus, look at that."

Griggs peered inside. "He doesn't look like he died a happy death," Griggs said, looking at the broken man lying in the pit dressed in black fatigues. "Looks like one of Anne's men."

Jake nodded. "They must've already been in here."

"What were they looking for?" Alex asked. "Probably the Divine Sanctuary," Jake guessed.

"It would help if we knew a little more about what this sanctuary is," Alex said.

Jake shone his light to the far side of the pit. There was a bridge over it that was no more than a foot wide. Jake moved toward the bridge. "From what I know," he started, "the Divine Sanctuary was a place that God himself touched."

"Really?" Samantha asked curiously. "Who told you that?"

"I met a man from 'The Brotherhood of the Divine Sanctuary'. He informed me that a Spanish priest found this place around the eighth century A.D. while he was here as a missionary. That's really all I know. One could tell you more." Jake suddenly realized he had forgotten about One. He wondered if he survived the battle. Jake hoped so; he hadn't had a chance to say thanks.

"Who's One?" Alex asked.

"He's part of the Brotherhood. He doesn't have a name, so I just called him 'One'."

"Where is he?" Griggs asked.

"I don't know." Jake wanted to change the subject. He looked down at the bridge. He took a step on it, then stopped. "I think this thing will be able to hold our weight if we go over it one at a time."

"Good," Samantha said nervously. "Let's get going."

***

Stewart checked his readings again. He hoped to God the new calculations weren't correct. Tapping the numbers into his database, he waited a few moments for the monitor to display the answer. The screen flickered briefly as the answer appeared. Stewart cursed under his breath and stood up. Looking around the small office he was in, he tried to make sense of these new figures. *They don't match up,* he argued with himself. *There has to be an error in my...wait....*

Moving toward the glass door, he pushed it open and walked into the hallway. He was a level above the command center of NORAD, but he knew it would only take a minute to reach it. Running his hand through his red hair, he threw open the door to the stairwell and started down the metal stairs. Emerging, he looked out over the darkened command room. The three huge monitors at the front of the room were constantly displaying tactical information on the intruder. Command had grown quiet over the past few hours. Deadly quiet. Each was dealing with the situation in his/her own way, while still trying to perform their duties. A single cough echoed from the left side of the room. Stewart watched a sea of heads turn almost in synch toward the sound. It was too quiet.

Stewart checked his watch. It was still two full hours before he was scheduled to start his shift at six in the morning. Pressing into the command center, he briskly made his way toward his station. Slumping down in his plush black chair, he quickly keyed in his security password. His fingers flew over the keys with purpose. He had to check this new information against the satellite data. He had to be absolutely sure before he took this to Summers.

With one last keystroke, his station whirred to life. Lights on the console began to flash a bright white as various readouts were accessed. Tapping in the numbers from memory, he waited for the computer to compile the data. A message appeared on the screen: "WORKING." Stewart shook his head. He didn't have time for this. He needed these figures now.

Leaning uneasily back in his chair, he stared intently at the monitor as if an act of sheer willpower would somehow speed up the computer. He ran his hand nervously through his hair again. Stewart reached up and wiped a bit of sleep out of the corner of his eye. In his haste this morning, he hadn't taken a shower. He had been awakened an hour earlier by the night watch when a set of numbers weren't corresponding with the data on hand. He had gotten out of his bunk, pulled on his pants and hastily tied his shoes. He hadn't even fully buttoned his white shirt yet, nor had he made any attempts to tuck it in.

This was too important to waste time on such trivial things, he assured himself. If the General saw him, he would surely understand the circumstances. Stewart glanced down at the screen again. It hadn't moved. Leaning forward onto his console, he hit the screen with the back of his hand. "Damned computers," he said.

Stewart looked up to see a member of the night shift approaching his station. The man was younger than Stewart, but not by much. He had his dark hair closely cropped to his head, and his uniform was neatly pressed. Stewart glanced at the man's rank on his collar. "What can I do for you, Private?"

The man stopped in front of Stewart's console and placed his hands on top of it. The tap of his gold wedding band made a light clinking sound as it hit the console. "Is there anything I can do to help, sir?"

Stewart shook his head. "No, just keep at your post. That's all any of us can do."

"Sir," the young man said slowly, "what's

236

going to happen?"

"I don't know," Stewart replied honestly. "I—" Steward stopped; he was glaring at his monitor. The screen was flashing the answer he didn't want to see.

The young man stood straight up. "What?"

Stewart jumped up. "Assemble the command staff," he commanded the private. He quickly began to run toward the command station at the front of the room. Grabbing a phone from the station, he dialed a four digit number from memory. He listened intently as the phone rang on the other end. "Pick up, pick up," he muttered.

"What?" a gruff voice finally responded.

"General Summers, I'm sorry to wake you," Stewart said nervously. "This is Lieutenant Stewart in Command, sir."

"What is it, Lieutenant?"

"Sir, I've rechecked the data on the intruders."

"And?" Summers responded angrily.

Stewart hated giving bad news in the middle of the night. "Sir, they've sped up."

"What?" Summers asked, surprised.

"I've ran the numbers five times now, sir, and there's no denying it," Stewart admitted, "they will now reach Earth in twenty-three hours." There was silence on the line. "Sir?"

"I'm on my way."

***

Cisan and Hollman had almost reached the plateau when she stopped. They could both see Anne and Jannis standing near the top. Cisan

237

brushed a strand of blonde hair and grabbed Hollman's shoulder. Hollman looked over at his colleague angrily. "General Caroll is waiting for us," he said.

"I don't care," Cisan replied in a soft tone. "I need to tell you something." Hollman used his cane and turned toward Cisan. "What is it?"

"Please," Cisan started, "listen to me very carefully." She glanced up at Anne, but quickly returned her attention to Hollman. "I have a bad feeling about this."

Hollman rolled his eyes. "I don't have time for this." He started to walk away from Cisan.

She grabbed his arm forcefully. "Listen to me." Hollman turned to look at her. "What?"

"Turn around right now and walk away."

"What?" Hollman asked in shock. "What are you talking about?"

Cisan bit her lip. "If you go into that cave, you're going to die." She placed her slender hands on his shoulders, "And I will, too."

"How do you know that?" Hollman asked seriously. Cisan shook her head. "I just have this gut feeling."

"A gut feeling?" Hollman echoed. "You're a scientist. You shouldn't believe in that kind of garbage."

"I know," Cisan said as she lowered her gaze, "but the sensation is so strong. I can't get it out of my head."

Hollman laughed. "Everything is going to be fine," he assured her. "We're going to go inside that cave and we're all going to be fine."

Cisan smiled. "Maybe you're right," she

conceded.

"I know I'm right," Hollman announced. He patted Cisan on the back. "Let's go."

Cisan nodded. Hollman had gone a little way to ease her fears, but he hadn't erased them. They had settled in her belly and begun to eat at her.

***

Anne looked at the cave. She hated that place now. She didn't want to go back inside, not after hearing the voices again. A light breeze was kicking up a patch of dirt in front of her. She squinted her eyes to try and keep the flying debris out. She was standing completely still cradling her flashlight in her arms. She stared unblinkingly at the giant mouth. She kept expecting to see the flash of light again. She wanted to see the light again. She needed to prove to herself that she wasn't going insane. There was nothing but darkness. Chills ran up her spine. She didn't like it here.

"General...."

Anne slowly turned around to see the rotting corpse that used to be Private Allen standing behind her. His face was a twisted mess of scars and gashes. One of his eyes had been removed from the socket leaving only a gaping black hole. His uniform was tattered and torn and stained with his blood.

Anne froze in terror. Allen began to lift his arms toward her. Several of his fingers looked to have been bitten or torn off. His mouth was agape and a dark fluid was oozing out of it. Anne began to stumble away from Allen's bloody hands. She watched as his face turned angry, his eye hardened. "No," she screamed as he drew nearer. An angry moan welled up from the chest cavity of Allen. Anne turned to run just as Allen reached out and grabbed a handful of her hair. She screamed again as he began to pull fistfuls of hair out by the roots. Sliding his hand around her throat, Allen pulled her close to his chest. Leaning close, he flicked out his tongue and licked her cheek. Anne shuddered and screamed again. Closing her eyes, she felt Allen pushing her to the ground....

"General Caroll!"

Anne refused to open her eyes. She screamed at the top of her lungs as she felt hands against her back.

"General Caroll? Are you all right?"

Anne slowly opened her eyes to see Jannis kneeling down next to her with Hollman and Cisan standing around her. Jannis had his hands on her shoulders. "What happened?"

"You just started screaming and fell down," Jannis replied. "You don't remember?"

"No, I saw...." she let her words trail off when she realized how insane she would sound.

"What did you see?" Hollman asked. Anne didn't want to reply. "Nothing."

"Nothing?" Hollman repeated. "How could you see nothing? You were lying on the ground screaming!"

Anne lifted herself off the ground and proceeded to dust her black uniform off. "I don't want to discuss it."

"But, General," Hollman prodded.

"That's the end of it, Doctor!" Anne shouted

angrily. Hollman quickly buttoned his lip.

Anne cocked her head to the side and popped her neck. "Are we ready?" Jannis nodded. "As close as we're going to get."

"Let's go then," Anne said as she marched toward the awaiting mouth of the cave. Jannis turned and followed her into the darkness. Hollman and Cisan were close behind. One by one, each member of the team was engulfed by the darkness of the cave. The worried feeling in the pit of Cisan's stomach was getting worse.

Chapter Twenty-Eight

The group was moving close together through the cave. Jake was leading, while Samantha, Alex and Griggs walked slowly behind. Each person had their hand firmly on the back of the person in front of them. The darkness was so dense, they were afraid to lose each other in it. It enveloped them. It swallowed them whole in one mighty gulp.

"Do you see that?" Jake asked, pausing for a moment. Samantha looked around her father. "What is that?"

Alex couldn't resist. "It looks like the light at the end of the tunnel."

"Very funny," Jake said with a dry laugh. "Seriously, what do you think it is?"

"Maybe it's the exit," Griggs guessed. Samantha felt herself smile. "God, I hope so." Jake nodded. "Let's find out."

The team moved slowly through the cave toward the ever growing light.

Rounding the final corner, they stopped dead in their tracks and stared at the sight before them. The black lava rock gave way to smooth polished walls and floors that were shimmering silver. Large triangular lights were embedded into the ceiling in a regular pattern. Stepping onto the polished floors, Jake clicked off the flashlight and looked down. He could see his reflection in the floors. The group slowly spread out in the hallway.

Griggs ran his hand over the walls. "There are no seams."

"How can that be?" Alex asked.

"I don't know," Griggs replied, "but it looks

like this whole hallway is one continuous piece of metal."

Jake had an uneasy feeling. "Let's keep moving."

With Jake in the lead, the group made their way down the long corridor. Alex turned and glanced behind her. She could see no trace of the cave they had been in, only the reflective surface of this hallway. Their footfalls echoed throughout the hall and made it sound like there was an entire army marching through, not just four people. Rounding a final corner, the group came to a stop. They stared at the two huge silver metal doors closed in front of them.

Samantha gasped and took an uncomfortable step back. "Oh, my God." Jake turned around to look at his daughter. "Wha...." before he could finish the question, he spotted it. Three fingers and a portion of a right hand were hanging out of a small slot in the wall. "Probably one of Anne's men."

Griggs turned and looked at the hand. "Not anymore."

Alex caught sight of the entry pad next to the door. "We need to get in there."

Jake's unease was quickly growing. "I don't think this is such a good idea, Alex. Maybe we should turn back."

Alex turned to look at Jake. "We've come this far, might as well finish the journey."

Jake took a deep breath. "All right, you're in charge here. Let's go." The four moved cautiously toward the panel located next to the doors.

Alex gave the keypad the once over. She smiled when she recognized the symbols on the twenty keys. "It's Egyptian," she said triumphantly.

"We have no idea what the code is though," Griggs shot back. "I can decipher it," Alex said assuredly.

"Are you sure?" Jake asked. "Pretty sure."

Jake looked over at his daughter. She looked way out of her depth here. He glanced back at Alex, "Okay, let's do it."

Without another word, Alex turned back to the keypad. She held her hands just above it for a moment in anticipation. She wasn't sure where to begin. The keys were all colored a light cream except for one blue button in the upper right-hand corner. Making up her mind, she pressed the blue key. The monitor above the keypad flickered to life. A line of hieroglyphs ran across the screen. Alex began to quickly decipher. "I think it's a riddle," she said as she ran her eyes over the text.

"What does it say?" Jake asked.

"It's just four letters: E - G - B - D. There's a blank space behind the fourth letter. I think it wants us to finish the string."

"What the hell does that mean?" Griggs asked. Alex shrugged. "I don't know."

"I know," Samantha said quietly.

"Wait," Jake said. "I'm good at these word puzzles. Give me a second."

"I know what it is," Samantha said again, but her words fell on deaf ears. "Take a guess," Griggs said.

"Take a guess?" Alex shot back.

"Yeah," Griggs replied. "You know you've got a one in twenty chance of getting it right."

"Are you joking?" She turned and pointed at

the hand in the wall. "There's what's left of the last guy who took a guess."

Griggs kept his vision on Alex as she turned back to the pad. "Well, whatever you're going to do here, you better make it fast."

Alex's eyes widened as the white text shifted to red. "I think we're running out of time here!" A siren began to blare loudly in the hallway. The smooth walls of the corridor acted like an amplifier, raising the siren's wail to dangerous decibels.

"I know what the answer is!" Samantha shouted. Everyone turned to look at Samantha standing at the rear of the group. "It's Music Theory."

Unbeknownst to the group, four slots in the walls slowly slid open. Silvery tentacles still stained with Private Allen's blood began to creep out of the wall.

"Tell us!" Griggs snapped.

"Didn't you ever learn music in school?" Samantha asked.

Jake caught sight of one of the tentacles creeping along the wall toward Samantha. "Look out!" He tried to push her out of the way, but he was too late. The tentacle whipped out with speed and accuracy and wrapped tightly around Samantha's throat. It yanked her to the ground, just as three more tentacles wrapped around her head and shoulders. Jake dropped to the ground and began trying to pull them off, but they were like steel coils in his hands. He couldn't get his fingers around them. Samantha was choking.

"The answer!" Jake shouted. "Tell us the answer, Samantha!"

Samantha was gasping for air. The tentacles had begun to constrict. She tried to push the word out of her mouth but failed. Griggs dropped down next to her and started to help Jake pull off the tentacles.

"We need the answer, Sam!" Jake shouted frantically. "F," Samantha gasped.

Jake turned his head toward Alex, who was still standing near the keypad. "Hit the "F" key!" he yelled.

Alex turned around and ran her hands over the keys searching for the F. Pressing the key hard, the red lettering changed back to white, then a new message appeared. Alex turned around to look at Samantha. The tentacles were slowly unwrapping themselves and retracting back into the wall. The siren had stopped. Samantha sat up on the floor. Tears were streaming from her eyes as she tried to catch her breath.

Jake looked up at Griggs. "Why is it always tentacles?" Griggs shrugged.

Jake turned his attention to his daughter. He patted her on the back. "Are you okay?"

Samantha nodded. "I'll live," she said in a gruff voice. The tentacles had bruised her larynx.

"How did you know what the answer was?" Griggs asked.

"I'm an actress," she said quietly. "We had to study Music Theory in our classes just in case we wanted to be in a musical. E G B D and F are the notes on a treble staff."

Jake smiled. "Thank God you're smarter than your old man." Samantha started to laugh, but stopped. It hurt her throat too much.

"Thanks, Dad."

"I think you better come look at this," Alex said.

Jake and Griggs stood up and helped Samantha off the floor. The three turned around and fell silent. The double doors had silently slid open revealing the secret they had been constructed to keep. A bright white light spilled into the sliver corridor. The silver surface was reflecting the light, bouncing it around. Each member of the team held their hands over their eyes to try and see through the doors. Slowly, their eyes began to adjust to the light and the vague silhouettes of shapes began to come into view. Jake looked on in awe. "The Divine Sanctuary," he gasped.

***

"I've just advised the President of our current situation," Summers said gravely as he placed the red phone back into its cradle. "Needless to say, he wasn't overly happy to hear that."

"Sir," Stewart said tentatively, "what are we going to do?"

Summers lowered his head and began to rub the bridge of his nose. He was exhausted. Tonight, he had actually intended on trying to get some rest. He had gone almost seventy-two hours without sleep during this crisis. Looking up, he tapped a command onto his console. A brief claxon sounded, then stopped. Two brightly lit signs on either side of the two main monitors shifted from green to yellow. "We've officially been upgraded to DEFCON two."

Stewart's eyes widened. During his lifetime,

they had never been above DEFCON three. DEFCON one meant they were at full-on war. He hoped it wouldn't have to go that far. "Sir?"

"The President has agreed with me," Summers took a deep breath, "that we need to launch a full scale nuclear assault against the intruders."

"Sir," Stewart said again, "how can we do that? We'll irradiate the entire planet. We'll not only destroy them, but most of the life on this planet."

"I've gone over this with the President, Lieutenant." Summers clasped his hands behind his back and began to walk down the steps toward the main monitors. "We feel that if we launch the warheads early enough, we can avoid the risk of nuclear fallout."

"You can't be serious!" Stewart said angrily.

Summers spun around and glared at his junior officer. "You're damned right I am. Whatever the intruder's motives are, I don't want to find out. I don't give a fuck if they're here to apply for a green card! It is my job to protect this country from hostile invaders and I fully intend to do that!"

Stewart was undaunted by the General's words. "This can't be allowed to happen!" He slammed his fist against a nearby console. "I won't allow this to happen!" He took a step closer to Summers and lowered his voice. "For God's sake, General, think of our kids, and the generations after that. What legacy are we leaving them, a burned out planet that can barely support life? I implore you, General, please rethink this plan. There have to be alternatives."

Summers shook his head. "I'm sorry," he said quietly. "The decision has already been made."

With that, he turned and began to walk away.

Stewart's first reaction was to go after him; to further argue his case, but he knew it was useless. With the intruders less than twenty-four hours from Earth, rash decisions had been made. He knew they were trying to act in the best interests of the planet, but how could the Earth's best interest be total annihilation?

Chapter Twenty-Nine

Awe wouldn't even come close to describing the feeling Jake was having as he walked into the Divine Sanctuary. The click of his boot heels echoed through the cavernous room. The floors, walls and ceiling were constructed of the same seamless material as the corridor. There wasn't a scratch or a scuff anywhere to be seen. It looked as if no one had ever walked in here, and the more he looked around, he wasn't sure "walked" was the correct term to use. The beings that created this room were obviously light years beyond just walking.

He cocked his head back and gazed up. The ceiling was barely visible, it was so high. Only a faint glimmer of silver assured Jake it was there. A faint buzzing sound permeated the room; Jake assumed it was coming from the machinery. About a hundred feet up, there was a maze of silver pipes and wires. They looked like a giant spider web ready to catch its prey.

He looked over at Alex and Griggs. They were both wandering around like children in a toy store. Every sight was brand new and full of surprises. Jake turned and looked back at his daughter. Samantha was walking uneasily behind them. She was biting her nails, probably unconsciously. He reached back and pulled her close to him as wrapped his arm around her shoulders.

The double doors had led them into the huge room on the far side. They all stood in front of a massive video screen that was displaying a constantly changing thermal map of the Earth. The bright yellows and reds stood out against the polished silver of the room. The group watched the screen for a moment, and then turned to face each other.

Alex was the first to speak. "This is incredible." Jake nodded. He was at a total lack for words.

Alex pointed toward the opposite end of the room. "Let's see what's down there."

With Alex in the lead, the group slowly walked through the cavernous room, their eyes dancing from one marvelous sight to the next. Alex glimpsed a computer monitor to her right that appeared to be studying human DNA. Just to its left, there was a six foot tall screen that had the entire human nervous system mapped on it. "Incredible," she muttered again. Turning her attention forward, she screeched to a sudden halt. "Oh, my God." The rest of the group hadn't seen it yet.

Griggs glanced over at Alex's unblinking stare. "What is it?" Alex slowly raised her hand and pointed in front of her. "Look."

"Holy shit," Griggs gasped.

Their eyes slowly moved from the bottom to the top of the structure trying to process the information. It was much too big to see all at once. The silver floor slowly melded into the biggest structure any of them had ever seen. Each curve, each corner, had been meticulously crafted to be perfectly symmetrical with its counterpart on the opposite side. Its skin was as smooth and reflective as the rest of the surfaces in this place, but curiously, they had no reflection. Two rectangular eyes glowed an intense yellow near the top, but the mouth was nothing more than a slit. At the top, the spider web of tubes and wires connected into the structure. This seemed to be the central core of the Divine Sanctuary.

"It looks like one of those statues," Jake said, "but on a much grander scale."

"The Moai," Alex corrected. "It's exactly like the Moai here on Easter Island. This must be where they got the idea to carve all those statues."

"Why is this here, though?" Samantha asked.

Alex laughed. "We have no idea."

Griggs walked closer to the giant Moai. "This thing has to be at least nine or ten stories tall." He let the tips of his finger glide over the Moai's skin. "Why don't we have a reflection?" He stared at the silver finish. "Everything else does."

Alex took a step closer. "I don't know." She pressed the palm of her hand against the Moai's skin. It was cold, but she could feel a warmth radiating from inside. She had the sudden flash of a great intelligence.

"I don't think we should be that close to this thing until we know a little more about it," Jake warned.

"Relax," Alex said with a smile. "If we were in any danger—" A loud hiss cut her off.

Jake looked over to see a large door had opened to the left of the Moai. The shimmering silver floor ended at the door and was replaced with a dark gray metal floor. "What's going on here?" Jake asked nervously.

Alex took a step toward the door. "I don't know, but I think it wants us to go in there."

"It?" Jake asked.

"Don't ask me why," Alex said, "but I think the

Moai is alive in some way. It wants to show us something."

"Or it wants to kill us," Griggs theorized.

Alex glared at Griggs for a moment. "Aren't you all curious about what's behind that door? We will probably be experiencing something no human being has ever seen before."

"I can live without seeing it," Samantha quipped.

Jake nodded. "I'm with Sam. I don't think it's a good idea that we just go where this thing wants. I think we should get the hell out of here and off this island."

"Jake is right," Griggs said. "We don't have time for this. Anne's forces could be right behind us."

"Closer than you think, Major Griggs."

Griggs spun around to see Anne, Jannis, Hollman and Cisan standing behind them. They each had their weapon drawn and trained on the group. "Like I said...."

Jake looked at Anne with disdain. "I thought you were dead."

"I get that a lot," Anne said with a smile. She turned to Jannis. "Colonel, would you please relieve them of their weapons?"

Jannis nodded. He quickly walked toward Jake. "Hands up."

Jake lifted his hands into the air. "You know, we don't have to do this little dance again. You could just turn around and let us walk away."

Jannis pulled open Jake's black trench coat. He pulled his pistol from its holster and tucked it into his belt. Moving to Griggs, Jannis repeated the process.

"It doesn't work that way," Anne said cynically. "I want you dead, so if you leave, I won't achieve that goal."

"Why are you doing this to us?" Samantha cried. She had hoped never to see Anne again.

Anne took a step closer to Samantha. Jake jumped between them and assumed a defensive posture. "If you so much as touch a hair on my daughter's head, I'll kill you."

Anne pressed the barrel of her gun against Jake's chin. "If you don't move, I'll kill you right now." Jake didn't budge. Anne looked around at Samantha. "Your father is either ultra-brave," she looked back at Jake, "or ultra-stupid. I haven't decided which yet." Anne took a step back from Jake. "You know, I went through a whole lot of trouble to set up your death, Jake, and you ruined it."

Jake shot Anne an unconcerned look. "Sorry."

"Don't be," Anne said. "This will be much better. I get to kill all of you at once now, but first, we're going to find out what's behind door number one." Anne walked seductively toward Alex. "You were so intent on going through the door, Dr. Robinson, I'm going to give you your chance."

Alex turned away from Anne. "Fuck off. I'm not doing anything for you."

"Colonel?"

Jannis stepped forward. "Yes, General?"

Anne sneered at Alex. "Why don't you give the good doctor some motivation?"

Jannis walked briskly toward Griggs and pressed the barrel of his pistol to Griggs' head. "Do

254

what the General asks, or I kill the clone."

Terror welled up inside Alex. She stared at Griggs. His deep blue eyes were pleading for her not to do it, but she couldn't let him die. "I'll go."

"See? You are capable of good decisions when correctly motivated." Anne pushed Alex toward the door. "You have twenty minutes. If you're not back in that time, I start killing your friends. Inside. Now."

Alex turned to take on more glance at the group. Griggs was standing silently next to the immense silver Moai, while Samantha had her arms wrapped around Jake's waist. She looked especially frightened, but Alex couldn't blame her. She turned her attention back to Griggs and nodded once. Griggs silently returned the gesture. She had just told him that she loved him, and he understood.

Anne jabbed her pistol into Alex's back. "What in the fuck are you waiting for?"

Alex ignored her. Taking an uneasy step toward the doorway, she stopped and peered inside. It was nothing like the exterior. The dark gray metal was riddled with electrical panels and cables hanging from the ceiling. The dank hallway inside was barely six feet high, and only about four feet wide. Taking a step into the hallway, Alex waited for her eyes to adjust to the dimness. The hall was bathed in an unnatural red light, giving everything an ominous appearance. An open panel to her right crackled, sending a shower of red-hot sparks raining down into the hallway. Alex accelerated past the shower, succeeding in not getting burned.

She ran her hand against the wall. The hair on her arms stood up due to the static electric charge.

Pulling her hand away, she walked carefully through the corridor. There were no connecting passages, just one long hallway. Ducking down, she moved beneath an exposed section of wiring. Inch thick cables were dangling from the ceiling.

Alex stopped. There was a bend in the hallway just ahead. She checked her watch. Three minutes had already gone by. Letting her arms fall to her side, she considered whether to proceed or not. She wasn't sure how far this passage went.

Glancing to her right, she noticed a line of text on the wall. She slowly turned and looked closely at it. It was also written in Egyptian Hieroglyphs. She ran her fingers over the recessed symbols carved into the metal. She read them out loud as she translated, "It reads like some kind of design schematic," she theorized. Three words of the text immediately jumped out at her. She ran her hand over the symbols again. "The Keeper," she translated. "What the hell is 'The Keeper'?" She quickly ran her fingers down the text. "Oh, wow," she said like a child who had just unwrapped her favorite Christmas present. "Atlantis," she said, allowing the words to just roll off her tongue. She read the entire line: "'The Keeper's main subsystem was constructed on the continent of Atlantis in the early days of man'. This is incredible."

Her curiosity had now been piqued. She had to know where this passage went. She checked her watch again. An additional three minutes were gone. She didn't have a lot of time left. She had to hurry. She moved into a brisk jog as she moved through the passage.

Coming around the corner in the hallway, Alex

came upon a small room littered with small dark monitors and wires. The room was at least ten feet wide and eight feet tall. The same horrid red light permeated the area. Alex cautiously stepped inside and stood in the middle of the room. She heard the door to the room hiss shut. Running toward it, she pounded on it with her fists. Pressing her hands against it, she tried to force the door open, but couldn't budge it.

"Damn," she said under her breath. Walking back into the center of the room, she glanced around. This place differed from the rest of the structure. The floor and ceiling was made of a metal grating, while the walls were nothing but monitors. She peered down through the metal grating. There was no floor in sight, just darkness below. Returning her attention to the monitors, she waited for something to happen. There were no control panels or keypads in here. There was nothing she could do but wait. "I'm here," she said to no one. "Now what?"

***

Anne tapped her fingers angrily against the silvery skin of the Moai. She rubbed the barrel of her gun against the back of her head to scratch an itch. She looked into the Moai at her missing reflection. She wondered if this was how Dracula felt when he looked into a mirror. Flipping her hand over, she checked the time on her bulky digital watch.

"Where the hell is she? Her twenty minutes are almost up." Anne moved away from the Moai

257

toward Jannis and Hollman. They were both standing and staring up at the megalith in front of them. Anne tapped Jannis on the shoulder to get his attention. "Get one of the prisoners ready for execution."

Jannis looked at the group standing in the corner guarded by Cisan. "Which one?"

"I don't care," Anne replied, "but leave Jake for me."

"Understood." Jannis moved toward the group. Jake and Griggs were standing with their backs to the Moai with Samantha in between. Jannis glanced over at Cisan. He wondered if she had ever held a gun before. She looked very nervous with her hands wrapped tightly around it. "Doctor," Jannis said addressing Cisan, "why don't you take a break?"

Cisan nodded. "Thanks."

Jannis stepped in front of the prisoners. "Take one step away from the wall." He waited for them to comply. Moving around behind them, he cocked his weapon. "Down on your knees with your hands behind your back."

Jake looked over at Griggs, and then at Samantha. "Come on, you don't have to do this," he said to Jannis.

"I'm afraid I do," Jannis replied. "Now get down on your knees."

The three slowly complied. Jake sank to his knees with Samantha next to him. He looked over at his daughter. She was quietly crying. He marveled for a moment at her soft features. She looked so much like her mother. He slowly reached around and rubbed his hand against her back. "Everything's going to be okay, Sam. I promise."

"Face forward," Jannis instructed the trio. Pacing back and forth behind the three, he finally decided. Stopping, he pulled the hammer on his pistol back with his thumb startling the three prisoners. Looking up at Anne for approval, she slowly nodded once. Jannis slowly lifted his weapon to the back of the prisoner's head and slipped his finger around the trigger.

***

Alex had pressed into the corner of the small room. She looked down at her watch. She cursed under her breath when she saw that her twenty minutes were up. She ran frantically toward the door and tried to lift it open again. "I have to get out of here!" She slammed her fists against the door until they began to bruise. "Let me out of here!"

She was startled to hear a lone electronic beep behind her. She turned around to see one of the center monitors had lit up. Walking slowly toward it, she was amazed to see a line of hieroglyphics appear on it. The message was instantly translated to English. "Hold for transmission," she read. "What the hell does that mean?"

Several more monitors flickered to life. Alex took a step back from them. She watched as they began to cycle through five thousand years of human history. The main monitor's message changed. It now read: "Transmission commencing."

She gazed in astonishment as the screens began to replay key moments from human history. One of the monitors showed the atomic bombs being dropped on Hiroshima and Nagasaki, another showed Hitler giving a speech to his assembled armies, and yet another was relaying the text of the United States Constitution. She took a step closer and stared at the screens. She watched Columbus' boats arriving at Plymouth Rock, the first Moon landing, the bombing of Pearl Harbor, the Nazi concentration camps and the Aztecs worshiping at one of their many temples in Mexico. Many of the screens were sequencing through the data much too fast for Alex to catch more than a glimpse. She wondered where all this footage came from. "You've been here watching since the beginning, haven't you?" she asked the room.

Several other screens flickered to life on the walls, until the entire room was awash with human history unfolding in front of her. A lone screen in front of her faded to black. A simple word in English appeared on the screen. "Yes."

Alex was startled. She hadn't expected a reply. "Why?" The computer responded again. "It is our task."

"Who's?" Alex asked.

"Ours."

"Where are you sending this information?"

The computer processed the information for a moment, then replied. "To the Keeper."

"What's the Keeper?" Alex wondered.

"It is the one that catalogues the evolution of this planet's civilization."

"Where is the Keeper?" The screen displayed two sets of two digit numbers. Alex quickly recognized them as latitude and longitude coordinates. She memorized the numbers. "Why are you sending this information to the Keeper?"

"Transmission is imminent," the monitor replied.

Alex studied the reply for a moment. "Transmission to who?"

"Our makers." The screen flickered for a moment, then showed a picture of the approaching armada.

Alex stumbled back. "Aliens?" she asked. "They're coming here?"

"They are returning on schedule."

Alex shook her head. "I need to get back to my friends. Can you open this door?" The door slid open behind her. Alex walked slowly away from the screens toward the door. Once outside, she hit a dead sprint back down the passage.

***

"Time's up." Anne looked over to Jannis and nodded. "Pull the trigger." Jannis felt the cold metal trigger below his finger for a moment.

Squeezing the weapon in his hand, he settled his nerves. "Stop!" Alex shouted from the doorway.

Anne turned to look at Alex, who was standing there panting, completely out of breath. Anne casually looked down at her watch, "You're late." She turned back to Jannis. "Kill the prisoner anyway."

"No!" Alex screamed as Jannis lifted his weapon to the back of Griggs' head. "I did what you asked!"

Anne smiled casually and waved her hand at Jannis. Jannis slowly lowered his pistol, but kept it at the ready. "You did," Anne agreed, "but you

261

were late. Tardiness is something I do not tolerate. I should, by all rights, kill one of the prisoners. Give me one reason why I shouldn't."

Alex was thinking on the fly. "I found what you wanted."

"Oh?" Anne said in amusement, "and what is it you think I want?"

"Technology, and lots of it," Alex replied.

"Very good," Anne purred. She turned to look at Hollman and Cisan. "You two, come with me. Colonel Jannis?"

"Yes, General?" Jannis replied.

"You stay here and guard the prisoners," Anne instructed. "The doctors and I are going to take a look."

"Yes, General."

Anne motioned for Hollman and Cisan to follow her into the passage. Jannis turned toward Alex. "Over here, Dr. Robinson." He pointed to a spot next to Griggs. "Get down on your knees and put your hands behind your back."

Alex quietly followed Jannis' instructions. She hadn't come this far just to die. Stopping next to Griggs, she knelt down and clasped her hands behind her back. She carefully leaned over to Griggs. "I have a plan," she whispered.

Griggs turned his mouth toward her ear. "Now would be a good time to tell us about it."

"Shut up!" Jannis yelled from behind them. He ran his hand over his shaven head as he paced back and forth. "I don't want to have to kill you."

Samantha turned her head back to look at Jannis. She recognized him as the man that brought her water. "Andrew?" she asked cautiously.

262

Jannis stopped and looked down at Samantha. He wasn't sure if she had remembered him or not. "What is it?" he asked.

Jake, Alex and Griggs were amazed when Jannis answered. Jake leaned over and placed his hand over her mouth in fear for her life. "Nothing," he said to Jannis. "She must be delirious."

Samantha pulled her father's hand away from her mouth. "I am not delirious," she assured. "Andrew brought me water while I was being held captive."

Jake let his hand slip away. "This man?"

"I said shut up, Silver!" Jannis yelled. He pressed his weapon to the back of Jake's head. "I don't want to hear another word out of any of you!"

"Why are you doing this, Andrew?" Samantha asked. "Shut the fuck up!" Jannis yelled.

Samantha shook her head. Standing up, she turned to face Jannis. "I know this isn't you. You don't want to kill any of us," she explained.

Jannis took a step closer and held his pistol to her temple. "Are you willing to bet your life on that theory?"

Samantha was frightened, but stood her ground. "Yes."

Jannis hadn't expected that. Pulling the gun away, he took a step back and looked at the woman standing before him. "Why are you doing this to me?"

Samantha didn't know how to reply. "Why don't you just put the gun down and let us go?"

"You don't understand," Jannis pleaded. "General Caroll will have my ass if I do that."

Jake was in awe of the situation unfolding

263

around him. He knew Jannis to be a cold-blooded killer capable of serious destruction. Now here he was, a fragile human being pleading with a young woman. Jake looked over at his daughter. He suddenly realized how brave she was. She was signaling to Jake with her hands behind her back. Jake didn't fully understand the sign, but he had a pretty good idea of what she had in mind. He slowly lifted off his knees onto the balls of his feet.

"Why are you taking orders from that witch in the first place?" Samantha asked. "You're obviously the brains of this operation. You should be leading." She hoped he found her convincing.

"I should," Jannis agreed. "General Caroll doesn't know her ass from a hole in the ground. I have to do everything for her." He turned and began to lean on the Moai. He let his weapon fall limp to his side.

"You don't have to take that," Samantha reassured him. She opened her fingers wide behind her back and began to count down from five.

"You're right," Jannis said with a smile.

Jake snapped his fingers to get Griggs' attention. Jake pointed at Samantha. Griggs looked over and understood the signal. He cautiously nodded back to Jake. Just as Samantha was about to reach one, Jake and Griggs jumped up and rushed Jannis.

Jannis tried to lift his weapon to defend himself, but it was too late. Jake hit him squarely in the side, while Griggs wrapped his meaty arms around Jannis' arms. All three men toppled to the ground. Griggs pinned Jannis to the ground and delivered a vicious head butt. Jannis' head snapped back, bloody and limp. Scrambling for the gun, Jake scooped it up. Jumping back toward Jannis, he pressed it hard against Jannis' chin and prepared to pull the trigger. He held up his opposite hand as a shield from the blood that was sure to splatter backward.

"No!" Samantha yelled. "Don't shoot!"

Jake looked up to see his daughter standing over them. He suddenly felt very guilty under her gaze. "This man is a killer," he rationalized.

"I don't care," Samantha shot back. "He really did bring me water when I was being held captive. He doesn't deserve to die."

Jake looked down at Jannis. Griggs had broken his nose, and two black bags were beginning to form under his eyes. He slowly pulled the gun away from Jannis' head and sat up. "She's right," he admitted to Griggs. "I can't kill him."

Griggs tried to snatch the gun from Jake's hand. "I can."

"Stop it," Jake said angrily. "We need to get out of here while we can. Jannis isn't going anywhere."

Griggs conceded the fact. "All right," he said forcefully. "Let's go." The two men stood up off Jannis. Jake slipped the pistol into his belt. The four quickly began to move toward the exit.

Chapter Thirty

Anne, Hollman and Cisan followed the passage around to the transmission room. One by one, they slowly stepped inside. Hollman began to excitedly look around the room at the many monitors displaying human history, and then he caught sight of a center screen still showing a picture of the approaching armada.

"What the hell is that?" Hollman asked, pointing to the picture.

Anne took a step closer and looked over it. "That's what we've been looking for, Dr. Hollman, alien technology." She studied the picture carefully. "This must be a photo of their ships in space," she concluded.

Cisan was watching a screen that was showing scenes from the Revolutionary War. "How did they get these?" she asked. "All our photos from that time were in black and white and done on metal plates."

Anne found herself staring at a screen with two sets of numbers on it. She quickly understood they were longitude and latitude coordinates. Pulling a small pen from her pocket, she jotted the numbers neatly on her hand. These numbers would be useful, she just didn't know how yet.

Hollman moved over to look at the screen Cisan was watching. "They must've been here watching this whole time, somehow cataloguing our history."

"Why?" Cisan asked.

"We must be a very interesting species," Hollman said with pride. He looked over at Anne.

She was studying one of the screens. She pulled a small silver tool out of a belt pouch, flipped out a knife blade, and began to pry out the screen. "What the are you doing?" he asked while hobbling toward her.

"What we're here for, Dr. Hollman," Anne said without looking at him, "trying to salvage this alien technology."

"I don't think you should be doing that," Hollman warned her.

"Why not?" Anne asked as she dug her knife blade deeper into the frame of the screen. Pressing hard with the knife, she heard a snap. A smile crossed her face as the screen fell out of its slot. "See?" she asked sarcastically. "Nothing bad happened."

"General!" Cisan screamed.

Anne turned to see the door they had entered was rapidly sliding shut. Dropping her knife and the screen, she snatched Hollman's cane and jumped toward it. She succeeded in wedging the metal cane in between the closing hatch and the jam. The motor whined as it tried to close. The hollow cane bent in half, but still held, with the opening just big enough for Anne to crawl under. Sliding on her belly, Anne just barely made it under. She looked back to see Cisan and Hollman crawling toward the opening. She knew they weren't going to make it. The motor was whining louder now, and a thick white smoke was falling from the top of the mechanism. Cisan slid her hand through the opening for Anne to grab. The metal cane began to buckle under the pressure. She heard the metal creak as it began to give way. "Get back," Anne shouted. Cisan yanked her hand back under just as the hatch slammed shut, crushing the cane. Anne tapped on it. "Stay put, I'll try and find the release lever." She was lying. This place had no value to her. In her opinion, the technology wasn't salvageable. This was nothing more than a waste of her time. Moving briskly through the passage, she stopped when she went by an open electrical panel. Pulling four small silver grenades off her belt, she pulled the pins and tossed them into the panel. Taking off in a dead sprint, she emerged from the passage to see Jannis lying unconscious on the floor. *The idiot,* she thought. *He let the prisoners escape!*

Her first instinct was to let him die here, but she thought better of it. She would enjoy killing him much more herself. Running to him, she lifted him off the floor and slapped him hard across the face. His eyes slowly opened to look at her. "Come on," she said angrily. "We need to get out of here." She felt the first of four grenades explode. An impact tremor ran through the passage and into the silver room. The next set of grenades exploded, shredding the passage and all the hardware around them.

The massive Moai shook as the tremors went through it. It felt its circuits being destroyed by the ensuing explosions. It knew a vital system had been hit.

There was no time to repair it. It only hoped the Keeper had received its transmission.

Anne was moving Jannis quickly across the floor as the first of the explosions knocked her off her feet. Standing back up, she turned to see the giant face of the Moai behind her. Its yellow eyes had changed to red as pieces of wire and tubing

268

began to fall from the ceiling. Her grenades had done more damage than she'd thought they would. Looking back at Jannis, she lifted him off the floor and began to move toward the exit.

Another explosion rocked the Divine Sanctuary. The blast had destroyed the systems that held the flow of lava in the mountain in check. Plumes of the mighty red liquid began to burst through the silver floor and coalesce everywhere. Anne looked behind her to see the mighty Moai being engulfed by the molten lava. It was slowly sinking into the flow, as was this whole structure.

The scraping sound of bending metal filled the room as the support beams in the ceiling began to give way under the pressure. Mighty columns of metal fell from their perch and into the steaming red river.

The flow was moving quickly across the floor toward Anne. With Jannis in tow, she ran out of the Sanctuary and into the silver corridor. Reaching over, she smashed the keypad with her fist. The double doors slid shut behind her containing the flow, but she knew that was only temporary. The lava would eat through those doors like they were tin foil.

Moving quickly, the two began to race toward the darkness of the cave. Anne reached down onto her belt to grab her flashlight, but it wasn't there. *Damn,* she thought, *I must've dropped it somewhere.* There was no choice; they had to run the cave blind.

***

Jake was almost pulling Samantha behind him, he was running so fast. Griggs and Alex were having a hard time keeping up as they made their way through the darkness of the cave. Jake's small flashlight was illuminating the way, but dimly. He guessed the batteries were about to die. A tremor from an explosion rumbled through the cave. Jake stumbled and almost lost his balance. Recovering quickly, he glanced back at Griggs and Alex. They were still running hard to get out of the cave.

Pieces of debris had started to rain down from the ceiling onto the group. A jagged rock sliced across Alex's forehead as she ran. Not even slowing, she pressed her hand to her head to try and stop the bleeding. She wondered where they were. It felt like they should have been out by now.

Lifting their arms over their heads to curtail the falling rock, Jake spotted a welcome sight ahead. A patch of daylight was filtering into the cave. "We're almost there!" he yelled.

A second explosion rocked the Sanctuary. The tremors slithered their way up through the cave like a snake. Glancing behind him, he could see an immense dust cloud approaching them. He knew they wouldn't make it; the cloud would certainly engulf them. Stopping, he pulled Samantha in front of him and scooped her up into his arms. Pumping his legs hard, he tried to make headway against the porous rock. The entrance was just ahead.

Running as fast as he could, he dove into the air just as he reached the entrance. Using all his strength, he tossed Samantha out of his arms. She landed hard on the ground, but she was out of harm's way. Jake hit the ground just as Alex and

Griggs did. Burying their faces, they felt the dust cloud move by like sandpaper over their skin. Bits of rocks and debris were moving at almost bullet speeds as they whizzed by. Holding his breath, Griggs felt a rock careen off the tip of his ear. Pain shot up through the side of his head. After a few moments, the dust cloud began to settle. The air around the mouth of the cave was a thick brown from the dust content. Taking a breath felt like inhaling a mouth full of sand. Lifting themselves off the ground, the group began to make their way down to the camp, and out of harm's way.

Once there, Jake skidded to a halt. "Shit," he said out loud.

Griggs stopped just behind him. "What is it?" he asked nervously. Jake slowly knelt down to the ground. "It's One." He looked over the lifeless corpse in front of him. His black clothing was stained with his own deep, red blood. Jake reached down and grabbed One's hand and looked into his still open eyes. "Thank you," he said softly. Laying One's hand over his chest, Jake reached up and carefully shut his eyelids.

Standing back up, he looked across the camp. Soldiers were working their extinguishers, frantic to put out the fires still blazing in many parts. No one even stopped to look at the group. Cautiously, they began to walk away from the city of tents. A third explosion rumbled from deep inside the volcano, shaking the ground. Alex looked back at the volcano. "Look!"

Jake, Samantha and Griggs spun around to see plumes of smoke rising up from the peak of the mountain and rivers of molten lava beginning to

271

erupt from all sides. "What the hell happened in there?" Griggs wondered.

***

Moving along the wall, Anne kept her hand against it to guide her. They had slowed to an almost trot in the darkness. She didn't want to lose her bearings. She was running blind and she feared that if she let go of the wall, she would get turned around. Jannis stumbled over a rock and toppled to the ground.

Anne stopped and reached down to pick him up. "I should've left you back there," she said angrily. Returning her hand to its former position, the two continued to make the treacherous trek to the surface.

Anne turned to look behind her. The molten lava had eaten through the door and was bubbling toward the surface. She could see its ominous red glow behind them. Turning her attention forward, she saw the welcome glow of the exit. Pumping her legs hard, she ran the last few meters through the entrance and out into the daylight. Moving swiftly down the slope toward the base camp, she headed directly for the landing pad where her personal helicopter was still perched. Tossing Jannis into the passenger seat, she climbed in and started the rotors. The massive chopper whirred to life as the blades began to build speed. Glancing back at the volcano, she saw several lava flows had burst from the mountain and were heading down the slope. Most of them would burn harmlessly into the ocean, but a few of them were headed for Mataveri Airport, and one was moving toward the base camp. She watched men scrambling in every direction trying to evade the flow, but it was hopeless. Looking down at her instruments, she flipped a set of silver toggle switches and pulled back on her yoke. The helicopter lifted vertically into the air and away from Rapa Nui. She knew if she made it, then so did Jake. She would find him. She opened her hand and looked down at the numbers inscribed on it. She knew where they were going.

***

Hollman and Cisan were huddled in the corner of the small transmission room. The explosions had knocked out all most all the screens in here, leaving only the dull red light filtering in from the ceiling grates. They weren't sure why, but the temperature in the room had jumped dramatically in the past five minutes. They were both fairly certain, though, that Anne wasn't coming back.

Hollman glanced over at the door. The bottom was beginning to turn a bright red. He turned to look at Cisan. "Something wicked this way comes."

Cisan tried to laugh, but couldn't. She was scared to death. She watched as the door turned from a red to a super-heated white. It wouldn't be long now. She looked over at Hollman. "It's been nice working with you, Dr. Hollman."

Hollman smiled. "Same here, Dr. Cisan."

The two turned to see the door give way. A flow of lava slowly moved into the room and began to eat away at the grating on the floor. Reaching over, Hollman grabbed Cisan's hand and held it

273

tightly as the lava moved toward them. Without warning, the lava ate away the support structure of the grating and the floor broke open. The two doctors toppled silently into the abyss.

*****

The sun was fully in the sky now. The shades of red and orange had been replaced by the more tranquil blue and white. It had turned out to be a fairly calm day on Rapa Nui. The dark storm clouds of the morning had parted, leaving only the dark smoke billowing out of Rano Raraku. Jake, Samantha, Alex and Griggs had slowly made their way back to the small cottage they had rented. All four were standing on the cobblestones that comprised the porch.

"It's actually quite beautiful," Samantha commented as she looked at the active volcano.

Jake was standing with his arm around her shoulders. "Yes it is." Griggs looked over at Alex. "You're thinking about her, aren't you?"

Alex was standing quietly with her back against the wooden doorframe of the cottage. Her face was twisted into a grimace of deep thought. "I am. I wonder if she made it out alive."

Jake looked over at Alex. "Personally, I couldn't care less. I hope Anne is finally dead."

Griggs scooped Alex into his arms and hugged her tightly. "Let's not think about her anymore, okay?"

Alex nodded. "Okay." She leaned her head forward and kissed Griggs on the lips.

Samantha was still staring at the volcano.

"What now?"

Jake patted his daughter on the back. "We get to go home."

"We can't!" Alex interrupted. "Not yet."

Jake turned to face Alex. "Why not?"

"We have to finish the journey," she exclaimed.

"I thought we *were* done," Griggs said with a smile.

Alex shook her head. "When I was inside the transmission room, it showed me something. Something very important."

"What?" Griggs asked. "A set of coordinates."

Jake ran his hand over his face. "To where?" Alex smiled. "I have no idea."

"Great." Jake turned around and took a few steps away from Alex.

"Another crusade."

Alex's mood turned dark. "How can you say that?" she asked angrily.

"The Moai showed me there was an alien armada approaching. This is important, Jake!"

Jake disagreed. "My job here is done. I came to get my daughter, and I did that. Now we're going home. End of story."

Alex was awestruck. She couldn't believe she was hearing this from the same man that helped destroy Area 51 and S-4. "You're incredible, Jake Silver, do you know that?"

Jake reached over and grabbed Samantha by the hand. "We're leaving on the next flight off this damned island." He began to walk away.

Alex started to chase him, but stopped. She turned back to Griggs with tears in her eyes. "How can he not want to be a part of this? How can he not want to be with me?"

Griggs pulled Alex into his arms. He pressed her head against his chest. "I'm sorry, but you've just got to let him go his own way."

Alex wiped the tears from her eyes and looked up at Griggs. "We're going to find out where these coordinates are," she assured. A plan began to form in her mind. "Do you still have Faith and Tyler's phone number?"

Chapter Thirty-One

The flight off Rapa Nui was tedious. Jake and Samantha had been lucky enough to be able to board a commercial jetliner bound for Chile, but they had been unlucky in the fact they were sitting across the aisle from Alex and Griggs. The four hadn't even tried to make small talk, instead kept glancing over at each other uneasily. Samantha had tried to keep herself occupied by reading some of the in-flight material, but found it extremely boring. Griggs had his seat leaned back and was trying to take a nap, but Alex kept waking him up. She didn't want to be alone right now. Jake, meanwhile, had chosen to drown his sorrows in several tiny bottles of airline alcohol.

Eight hours later, the plane touched down in Chile. Jake and Samantha stood up immediately and exited the plane, while Alex and Griggs were the last two off. None of them knew why they were acting this way. They had been through life and death situations together. There was no need for the uncomfortable silence, or the off glances. They were friends above all else.

Making his way to the ticket counter, Jake weaved in and out of the tourists in the busy terminal. After his last encounter in the Chilean Airport, he didn't want to be here that long. Pulling off his black trench coat, he hung it over his arm and leaned on the edge of the counter. A pretty young brunette was standing behind her terminal busily typing on her keyboard. Jake cleared his throat to get her attention.

The flight attendant looked up with soft brown

eyes. "Can I help you?" she asked sweetly.

Jake smiled. "In more ways than you can imagine."

Samantha kicked Jake in the shins. "Knock it off. You're old enough to be her father."

Jake shot a dirty glance at his daughter before returning his attention to the young woman behind the ticket counter. "We need to book a flight."

The woman poised her fingers above her keyboard. "Destination?"

"San Francisco," Jake replied.

"Return trip, or one way?" the woman asked as she tapped her long fingernails against the keyboard as she typed.

Jake smiled. "I have no burning desire to ever see your country again, so one way will be fine."

"Very good, let me check out available flights." Her fingers flew over the keyboard as she tapped in the information. Moving her hand over to a small tan mouse, she guided it rapidly over its small blue pad. After double-clicking several times, the computer returned the information she was looking for. "You're in luck, we have a flight leaving for San Francisco in a few hours."

Jake reached for his wallet in his back pocket. "Great, two tickets please." After a few minutes, Jake left the counter with the tickets in hand. He had laughed when the flight attendant was worried about either of them having any luggage. *If she only knew what we had just been through,* he told himself, *she wouldn't be half as worried about our luggage.* Samantha was walking about two steps behind him and staring at the floor. She was still dirty, battered and bruised, but the rest, not to mention the food,

278

she had on the plane had helped her tremendously. Jake stopped and looked back at his daughter. "What's wrong, Sam?"

Samantha shook her head. "It's nothing."

Jake glanced around the terminal. There were an empty section of seats just across from them. Wrapping his arm around Samantha's shoulder, he led her toward them. "Well, you heard the lady, we have a couple hours to waste here."

Samantha slipped slowly into the curved yellow plastic chair as Jake sat down next to her. "I don't think it's any of my business."

Jake smiled. "Everything that has to do with me is your business. You're my daughter, after all."

Samantha wished the circumstances were different, but she was enjoying seeing her dad. He had always been her favorite because she considered herself daddy's little girl. She knew she was always free to say what she wanted, and be herself around Jake. "Why aren't you going to help Jason and Alex?"

Jake's smile faded. "I don't really want to talk about that."

"You said we could," Samantha protested. "I want to know."

Jake looked at his daughter. He wasn't sure he wanted to be talking to her about this, but he realized she was an adult now. He shook his head. "It's petty."

Samantha held up two fingers. "I'll still respect you, scout's honor."

"You were never a scout." Jake turned away from his daughter and swallowed his pride. He might never get the chance to come clean again, so

279

he might as well take the opportunity while he had it. "I love Alex."

A warm smile crossed Samantha's face. "I already knew that." Jake was surprised. "How?"

"As an actress, I've learned how to study people. I can tell when they're hiding something." Samantha placed her hand on her father's knee. "You were pretty easy to read."

"I'm that transparent, huh?" Jake blushed. "You are definitely smarter than your old man."

"Why don't you just tell her how you feel?"

"I can't do that," Jake said sitting back. "She's with Griggs. It wouldn't be right."

"You're going to run out of chances sooner or later, Dad. Even if she doesn't return the sentiment, at least she'll know."

Jake shook his head. "Her and I just weren't meant to be. It's better if I just keep quiet. She's happier with Griggs than she could ever be with me."

"I still think she deserves to know," Samantha countered.

Jake ran his hand over Samantha's hair. "I can't. I think it's just better if she never knows how I feel."

Samantha stood up in front of Jake. Leaning over, she kissed her father on the forehead. "Whoever said chivalry was dead never knew you."

Jake reached up and held Samantha's hand. "I love you, too, you know."

"I know."

Standing up, Jake wrapped his arms around his daughter and hugged her tightly. "I'm just glad you're okay."

"Thanks."

Pulling away, Jake looked into his daughter's green eyes. "Well," he said glancing around the terminal, "what do you want to do for a few hours?"

"How about you buy me lunch?" Samantha said with a smirk.

"I think I can handle that," Jake admitted. Turning, the two walked hand in hand through the busy terminal. All of their problems seemed to suddenly fade away as they felt the warmth of each other's hands. Looking down into his daughter's eyes, Jake found a peace he hadn't known in years. All he had become lately melted away and he was once again a father leading his child through life. This was possibly the best moment of Jake's life.

***

Close to four hours later, Jake heard the boarding call for their flight over the public address system. Reaching over, he pressed his hand against Samantha's arm and gently shook her. She had fallen asleep on his shoulder almost an hour ago. He had draped his long black trench coat over her as a blanket. He didn't have the heart to wake her; he knew she needed the sleep.

"Samantha?" he said softly.

Taking a deep breath, Samantha opened her eyes and looked up. "Yeah?" she asked with a yawn.

"Our flight is boarding."

Samantha slowly sat up and stretched her arms. Yawning again, she looked over at Jake. "Good, I need some more sleep."

Jake patted her on the back. "I second that."

Standing up, the two slowly made their way toward the announced gate. They weren't in any rush. Night had fallen in Santiago, Chile. The huge windows on either side of the terminal allowed the stars to shine brilliantly inside. The once busy area had now cleared, and only a few passengers could be found loitering around waiting for their flights. Moving past several gates, Jake spotted theirs.

There was no one waiting to board, and only one male flight attendant stood behind the ticket counter in an ugly red vest.

"Tickets?" he asked casually in a monotone. Jake could see the Hispanic descent in his face, even though his skin was a creamy white and his hair was blonde.

Pulling the rectangular stubs out of his back pocket, Jake laid them on the counter. Behind the ticket counter and through the windows, Jake could see the front fuselage of the 747 they were about to board. The plane was white with a blue stripe that appeared to run tip to aft. Technicians in orange vests were making their pre-flight inspections of the craft.

The attendant handed the tickets back to Jake. "You two are in business class, you can begin boarding as soon as the first class passengers are seated."

Jake looked over the row of seats situated in the waiting area. "There's no one here but us," Jake said with amusement.

"I'm sorry, sir," the blonde attendant said unapologetically, "you'll have to wait your turn. We'll begin boarding business class in about five minutes."

"But—"

The attendant held his hand palm up toward Jake in a 'stop' gesture. "I'm sorry, sir."

With a sigh, Jake gave up. He turned and looked down at his daughter. "Let's go sit down for a minute."

"Jake, wait!"

Jake spun around to see Alex running toward him across the terminal. A lump instantly began to well up in his throat. He had hoped he wouldn't see her again. He placed his hand on Samantha's shoulder. "Go sit down, okay?"

Samantha smiled. "Tell her."

Jake's expression didn't change. "Go sit down."

Samantha nodded as she turned away. She walked around the first row of chairs and sank down into a plastic yellow chair in the third row facing Jake. "He won't do it," she muttered to herself.

"Jake," Alex said as she trotted to a stop. "I'm glad I caught you before you boarded."

"Why are you two still here?" Jake asked, getting right to the point. "We had to wait for a few friends to arrive," she admitted. "Friends?" Jake asked inquisitively.

Alex turned and pointed back down the terminal. "Those friends."

Jake spotted Griggs walking with four other people. As they neared, Jake instantly recognized most of them. Jake moved past Alex toward the group. He met Durard first. Jake smiled and shook his hand firmly. "Damn good to see you again, Jim."

Durard reached over and slapped Jake on the shoulder. "It's good to see you again too, you old dog."

Moving around Durard, Jake opened his arms wide to Faith. Faith stepped into Jake's embrace. "How's the newlyweds?"

Faith looked up and smiled. "We're wonderful."

Jake extended his hand to Tyler. "What've you been up to, Tyler?" Tyler reached out and shook Jake's hand. "Being married."

Jake laughed, "So not much of anything."

Faith took a step back and slapped Jake in the stomach. "Careful now," she said with a grin.

Jake looked over at the fourth member of the party. He stepped toward him and extended his hand. "Hi, my name is—"

"Jake Silver, yeah, I know." Tulley grabbed Jake's hand and shook it. "My name's Tulley, Jeff Tulley. I'm a reporter."

Jake took a step back. "Who brought a reporter?"

"He's tagging along with me," Durard admitted. Jake smiled. "What are you guys doing here?"

Faith pointed to Alex. "She invited us. She said she had a job for us."

"Oh, did she?" Jake asked uneasily. He didn't like where this was heading. Turning around, he motioned for Alex to join them. "What's this I hear about a 'job'?"

Alex looked over at Samantha sitting in the waiting area, then back at Jake. "I have a proposal for you, Jake."

Jake dropped his head and sighed. "I knew it had to be something."

"Will you listen to me before you dismiss my idea altogether?" Alex argued.

Faith, Tyler and Durard were shocked at Jake and Alex's behavior. The last time they had seen them together, over four years ago, they would've been happy to help each other. Now they seemed almost at odds. *It's strange how time affects people,* Durard commented to himself.

Jake glanced down at his watch, and then over to the flight attendant still standing behind the ticket counter. "Okay," he said, "you have until my flight starts boarding."

"That's not enough time," Alex argued.

Jake tapped the face of his watch. "Tick, tick, Alex."

Alex was visibly flustered now. They could tell she hadn't expected this reaction from Jake. "I need you on this mission with me, Jake."

"I don't have time for this," Jake said. "I'm going to get on my flight, and take my daughter home." He pointed his finger at Alex, "No more adventures!" Jake turned and began to walk away. "I'm sorry you all came out here for nothing," he said over his shoulder.

Alex charged after him. Grabbing him by the shoulder, she spun him around to face her. "Goddamn it, Jake, listen to me for a minute. Stop being so damned pig-headed!"

Jake couldn't look her in the eye. "Say what you've got to say, and let me go."

"Jim, Tyler and Faith are here to take Samantha home. They flew out here from San Francisco just

285

to do this for you. They're going to keep an eye on her until you get back. I've already chartered a plane, and it's waiting for us right now on the tarmac."

Jake's eyes widened. "How could you even suggest that?" He stepped up and got right in Alex's face and lowered his voice. "I just got my daughter back, and now you want me to send her away so I can go on your little treasure hunt?

Are you out of your fucking mind?" Jake asked angrily.

Alex was tired of this run-around from Jake. "No, Jake," she said, starting to raise her voice, "I think it's you who's out of your fucking mind. When I first met you, you went out of your way to save a young girl and me from one of the most highly guarded bases in the world, then you made me help you stop Anne when she let loose The Yellow Death in the southwest. You used to want to help and make a difference." Alex turned away from Jake. "You've changed, Jake. I don't know who you are anymore."

Her words cut deeply into Jake's heart. It was like she had just verbally slapped him across the face. "It's a little different when I have my daughter to worry about."

"I realize that, Jake." Alex turned around to face him again. "That's why I had Jim, Tyler and Faith come down here. I have everything covered." Jake shook his head.

"Do this for me," Alex pleaded. "Come on, one last adventure with me." She looked up into his rugged face, "It ends here."

Jake stared at her for a moment. He was

awestruck by what she had suggested. He mulled the idea over in his head for a moment, then turned to look at Samantha. She was sitting quietly in her seat watching events unfold. He turned back and looked at Alex's face. Tears had begun to well up in her eyes, but she was trying to remain strong. Jake reached out and pulled her close to him. The two wrapped their arms around each other for a long moment.

Alex felt the tears starting to run down her face. "Then you'll go with us?" she asked with a twinge of hope in her voice.

"No," Jake replied quietly. Pulling away from Alex, he began to walk toward Samantha.

"Don't do this to me, Jake!" Alex cried.

Samantha slowly stood up and wrapped her arm around her father's waist. The two walked toward the ticket counter, not looking back. The attendant nodded for them to pass. Jake and Samantha slowly disappeared into the skyway.

Alex turned to look at the group standing behind her. She hastily wiped the tears off her face with her fingers as she began to walk toward them. "I'm really sorry I hauled you guys all the way out here for nothing."

Tyler stepped forward and placed his hand on her shoulder. "It's okay," he comforted her. "Since we don't have to take Jake's daughter back to San Francisco, we were wondering if we could come with you."

Alex looked over at the rest of the group. "You guys want to tag along?" They all nodded in unison.

Alex laughed. She looked over at Griggs. "Okay with you?"

"Sure," Griggs said. "The more the merrier, I guess."

Alex looked over to see Jake's plane beginning to taxi away from the terminal. It would only be minutes before they were airborne. She started to search her feelings. She wasn't angry at Jake, just hurt that he didn't want to go with her. In a way, she understood. She knew his daughter was the most important thing to him, and her safety was his top priority.

She found herself walking toward the windows, watching the mighty plane. It had slowly turned and rolled onto the runway. There was no traffic ahead of it, so it was free to take off at any time. Alex felt a hand on her shoulder. She looked behind her to see Griggs standing there. She reached up and wrapped her fingers tightly around his hand. The rest of the group joined her at the window. They watched the massive craft begin to accelerate along the runway, then lift into the air. They watched it for a long time in silence, until all they could see was the plane's blinking anti-collision lights. Alex was about to turn away, when she saw a bright flash in the sky. In horror, she pressed her hands to the glass. All she could see was a bright ball of fire that seemed to be suspended in mid-air.

"Jake's plane just exploded!" she screamed. Tears rolled down from her eyes as she watched the fireball that used to be the plane scream toward Earth. Fragments had broken off and looked like shooting stars as they crossed the night-time sky. "Oh my God," she said softly. She slowly sank down to her knees. "He's dead," she muttered. She watched as the last of the fiery debris rained down beyond the horizon. A wave of nausea passed over her as her stomach began to turn.

Durard had run toward the flight attendant, who was still standing at the ticket counter. "What the hell just happened?"

The blonde attendant looked confused. "What?"

"That 747 that just took off," Durard pointed out at the tarmac, "it just exploded in mid-air!"

The attendant became ghostly pale instantly. "Dear lord," he muttered. Picking up the phone at the desk, he began to dial frantically. "Get me the tower immediately," he shouted.

Griggs dropped down next to Alex and wrapped his arms around her. "I'm so sorry," it was all he could think to say.

Faith and Tyler squatted down next to her and placed their hands on her back to try and comfort her. Tulley looked out the window to see several rescue vehicles tear away from the airport toward the crash site, their sirens blaring. He already knew there were no survivors. Tulley heard footsteps behind him and quickly turned to see who it was.

"Hands up," the man commanded.

Tulley dropped his notepad on the floor and raised his hands above his head. He stared at the man in front of him, his dark goggles and ski mask completely covering his face. He had an assault rifle pointed directly at Tulley's chest. Eight more soldiers charged into the terminal and quickly brought their weapons to bear on the group. One by one, they all stood and raised their hands above their heads.

Alex and Griggs were the last to stand. Griggs

looked at the soldiers. "Come on, guys, can't you give it a rest?"

Alex snapped. "You killed him!" she screamed. She charged the first soldier she saw and began to pound on him. The soldier fell to the ground as he tried to defend himself. A second soldier quickly moved to his aid. He delivered a vicious blow to Alex's head with the butt of his rifle. Alex fell to the floor limp.

Anger welled up inside Griggs. "You sons a bitches!" He charged the soldier and threw a right hook across the man's chin.

The soldier stumbled back, but quickly regained his composure. He drew a bead on Griggs. "Move, and you're dead," he warned Griggs.

Griggs stopped dead in his tracks. He knew, at this range, the soldier's rifle would tear a hole the size of a bowling ball in him. He slowly knelt down next to Alex and pressed his fingers to her throat. She was still breathing.

The soldier looked back at the rest of his squadron. "Round them up and take 'em down to the tarmac. The helicopter is waiting." The other soldiers nodded and quickly followed their instructions.

Griggs scooped Alex off the floor and into his arms. Lifting her up, they began to walk slowly through the terminal toward the exit. As they walked, he glanced out the window one last time toward where Jake's plane had gone down. A bright orange light was filtering over the horizon. It looked as if the plane started a fire when it impacted. *Goodbye old friend,* Griggs thought.

Chapter Thirty-Two

"Time?" Summers asked anxiously.

Stewart looked at his monitor. "The armada is nine hours and twenty- three minutes from Earth at present speed," he reported gravely.

Summers looked up at the two main monitors at the front of the control room. The first monitor was showing the inside of one of the many missile silos located throughout North America. A team of technicians and engineers were busily rearming the ballistic missile. A majority of the warheads had been removed during Reagan's administration after the peace accord with the then Soviet Union. Summers cursed under his breath. *Now, in our time of need, we don't have them ready.* The second screen was showing a tactical map of the world and surrounding space in green. Summers could clearly see the armada approaching Earth.

Summers shook his head. This wasn't right. His whole life he had been trained to detect, and stop, an Earth based attack. He had spent much of his younger years monitoring the former Soviet Union for missile launches. Thinking about the situation he was in now, he missed the cold war. Rubbing his hands together, he walked up the stairs away from the monitors. He was tired of looking at them. It was like watching the timer on a bomb slowly tick away in front of your face and there was nothing you could do about it. He had no idea what wire to cut.

Wrapping his plump fingers around the bottom of his blue uniform jacket, he gave it one quick tug to straighten it out. Even though he was scared to death, he had to keep a calm exterior for the men under his command. He knew if they caught even the slightest hint that he was at all worried, they would begin to fall apart. He was the rock these men and women depended on for their survival. He had to remain strong, even if he felt like everything he knew and loved had come crashing down around his ears.

Summers glanced over at the Defense control sign hanging in the corner. It was still firmly fixed on DEFCON two. The odd yellow light from the number two was illuminating the corner of the dark room. Summers found himself transfixed by it. He knew when they hit DEFCON one, they would have the President's clearance to launch their missiles. Summers had never seen DEFCON one in his lifetime. He unconsciously looked up at the screens again. "Time until we can launch?"

Stewart tapped in a series of commands on his console. "Estimated time until launch: seven hours." A small green graphic appeared in the corner of the tactical display showing the time until launch.

"Damn," Summers said. "We're cutting this awfully close."

"We don't have much of a choice, General," Stewart said.

"I know, Lieutenant," Summers answered unemotionally. "I just want to put Earth in as little danger as possible."

Stewart frowned. "I think it's a little late for that, sir." Stewart stood up and walked toward Summers. "Either we launch our missiles and destroy the advancing armada, or they arrive and wipe us out." Summers turned around and folded his hands behind his back. He shook his head when he found himself staring at the tactical map again.

***

It was a warm night in Southern Chile. A blanket of dark clouds had moved in and a light sprinkling of rain was falling on the tarmac. The runway was empty. All flights had been suspended until the cause of the crash could be explained. Most of the night crew and the emergency teams had made their way to the crash site, leaving the airport almost empty.

The group was standing silently out in the open surrounded by soldiers with the rain falling lightly on them. Griggs was still holding Alex in his arms, while Tyler and Faith were standing hand in hand awaiting their destiny. Tulley was pacing uneasily behind the four. He had lost his notebook back in the terminal.

He wasn't even thinking of the men pointing weapons at them, just the wealth of information he had dropped.

One of the soldiers lowered his weapon and walked toward the group just as a bolt of lightning tore through the sky. "Appropriate," he said, pointing to the sky, "don't you think?"

Faith glared at the man. "How's that?"

The soldier slipped his goggles off and pulled off his mask. Looking up into the dark sky, he let the raindrops roll off his face. "The Earth uses rain and lightning to cleanse itself. The lightning reaches down and destroys, then the rain washes the evidence away." The man stared at the group with his steely blue eyes. "That's what General Caroll wants me to do to you. I am the lightning, and the rain has arrived."

Griggs laughed out loud. "Fantastic, a killer with the soul of a poet." The man pulled his pistol off his belt and pointed toward Griggs and pulled the trigger. Griggs felt the bullet whiz past his ear. "Whoa," he yelled, taking a step back from the soldier, "whoa!"

"That was just a warning, Mr. Griggs," the soldier holstered his weapon. "The next time you smart off, you will be dead."

"Does it matter?" Tyler asked. "We're all going to be dead anyway."

The soldier smiled. "Yeah, you're right." Lifting his rifle from his side, he brought it to bear directly on Tyler. "Since you were so anxious to get things rolling, I'll kill you first. Get down on your knees and put your hands behind your back."

"Fuck you," Tyler spat.

The soldier moved angrily toward Tyler. Reaching out, he threw him hard to the ground. "I said, down on your knees!"

Faith swung around and knocked the weapon from the soldier's hands. Without a word, she threw herself on top of the man, sending them both crumbling to the ground. Using all her strength, Faith dug her nails into the soft flesh of his face and ripped, creating five angry, bleeding cuts.

The soldier yelled in pain. "You bitch!" Rearing back, he punched Faith in the mouth, knocking her off him.

"Don't you ever touch my wife again," Tyler warned him, now on his feet.

Reaching up, he wiped a trickle of blood off of his lip.

"What are you going to do, *boy*?" the soldier asked in amusement. Slowly standing up, he took a step closer to Tyler. He towered a full foot above the younger man. "Let's see what you've got, son."

Tyler balled up his fists. Tensing every muscle in his body, Tyler uncoiled like a compressed spring and flew headfirst at the larger man. Hitting him in the chest with his shoulder, Tyler sent the soldier reeling back. Leaping forward, Tyler delivered a heavy right left combo to the man's face.

Griggs slowly turned to look at the other eight soldiers standing around them. They had moved away from the group to watch the fight. Griggs slowly set Alex on the wet tarmac. Moving quickly, he made his way behind one of the soldiers. Lifting his hands, Griggs grabbed the man's head and quickly snapped his neck. As the man fell, Griggs lifted the man's weapon. Looking over at the amazed Tulley, Griggs winked and pulled the trigger. He easily mowed down the eight soldiers.

Tulley stared in awe at the carnage. "Oh, my."

Tyler and the soldier stopped and turned around. The soldier looked at his dead squad lying on the ground. "What the hell?"

Tyler took the opportunity and attacked again. Grabbing the man's shirt, he yanked him hard toward him and slammed his knee into the soldier's stomach. As he took a step back and doubled over, Tyler balled his fist again and swung up into his opponent's face. The force of the impact was so hard, it knocked the soldier off his feet. Dropping down onto his opponent, Tyler grabbed the sides of his head and looked him in the eyes. "I told you not to touch my wife." Tyler threw one final head butt that connected with the bridge of the soldier's nose. Tyler heard a crack as his nose broke. Letting go of his head, Tyler let the soldier fall limp to the ground. Standing up, Tyler stumbled back from the man on the ground. His knees were weak. Using the palms of his hands, Tyler wiped the blood off his face.

Faith grabbed Tyler by the shoulders and twisted him around. She wrapped her arms around his chest and hugged him tightly. "Thank you."

Tyler placed his hands on her shoulders and smiled. "Anything for my wife," he said softly.

"Time to go!" Griggs yelled. Lifting Alex off the ground, he tossed her over his shoulder. "We need to get to the plane."

The group set off across the tarmac toward their waiting plane. It was a small white twin propeller Cessna with a black stripe down its side. The pilot was sitting in the open hatch reading a magazine, his feet dangling near the ground. Looking up, he watched the four people running toward him. Standing, he moved out of the way so they could board. Faith and Tyler first in, followed by Tulley.

Griggs stopped to greet the pilot. "Are you Jack Sonera?"

The pilot, a scruffy man in his thirties with a partial beard, nodded. "Yeah."

"My name's Griggs, and this," he pointed to Alex on his shoulder, "is Dr. Robinson. We're your charter."

"Hell," he remarked with a slightly Texan accent, "get on board then. I'm ready to get the hell out of here."

Griggs nodded to the man and then climbed on board. The cabin of the Cessna was small and cramped, but designed to accommodate ten people, including the pilot. The small brown leather chairs were arranged along either side of the tan cabin. Sliding Alex into one of the front seats, Griggs quickly buckled her in before taking his seat up front next to the pilot. Looking back around the cabin, Griggs watched as everyone fastened their safety belts.

Jack climbed into the small plane and shut the door behind him. Twisting the lever, he locked it securely in place. "Everyone comfortable?" Jack took his seat and began to work through various switches on the control panel. He looked over at Griggs. "I managed to get all the equipment stuffed into my cargo hold just before you got here."

Griggs smiled. They'd had the foresight to bring all their gear to the plane before intercepting Jake. "Let's get the hell out of here then."

"We're off." Jack gripped the stick and sent the plane lurching forward. Once on the runway, the small plane accelerated and then finally, lifted into the air.

Chapter Thirty-Three

The silvery hull of the armada glistened against the light of this system's sun. Each ship was roughly shaped like a saucer, but slightly elongated. The nose of the ship tapered toward the front into a rounded point. There were no visible seams on the massive ships, just smooth curves of silver.

They had passed into the inner system of planets a few hours ago, and were now rapidly approaching the third planet from the sun. Scans of the fourth planet revealed nothing new or out of the ordinary. The once shimmering, green orb was now a completely dead world, devoid of any life. Only the frozen ice caps of the planet hinted at its former glory and splendor. The Keeper inside Mars had long since been deactivated and destroyed, negating the need for the armada to stop.

One of the massive ship's subsystems signaled its success. Contact had finally been established with their Keeper inside the Earth's moon. The Keeper had signaled its readiness to transmit its data. The ship slowed into a geo- synchronous orbit around the lifeless moon and transmitted its access codes. In its final step, the ship angled itself so its nose was pointing at the moon.

The great machine buried deep within the moon acknowledged and keyed the final transmission sequence. Pure energy, on which the data was to be carried, began to accumulate inside the transmission chamber. Checking the levels one last time, the Keeper released the beam. A bright blue pulse of energy shot out of the Keeper and into the rock of the moon. The moon began to shake violently as the beam worked its way to the surface. After a few brief moments, the beam erupted from the moon's crust and shot toward the awaiting ship above. It connected directly with the nose of the craft.

The ship began to relay the information directly toward its central computer. Five thousand years of information on the Earth's climate, orbit, and manned missions away from their planet was changed into digital form inside the ship's databanks. Once the last bit of data had been recorded, the transmission ceased. The bright blue beam vanished as quickly as it appeared, leaving only a few random sheets of blue electricity to dissipate into the galaxy.

The ship relayed a message down to the Keeper: BEGIN RECORDING AGAIN.

The Keeper acknowledged. It wiped its memory banks and performed a quick self-diagnostic to assure that all systems were still working properly. Once it was finished, it started the five thousand year process over again and began to record the data from the small, blue planet.

Breaking out of orbit, the ship re-joined the rest of the armada. As its systems continued to process and archive the data, the machine relayed its success to the rest of the ships. Once all were satisfied, they returned to their trek toward their final destination: Earth.

***

Alex slowly opened her eyes. Reaching up, she ran her fingers over the lump on her forehead. Straightening up in her seat, a rush of pain shot through her head. She pressed both hands to her temples to try and stifle it. Once it had gone, she looked around the cabin of the small plane. Sitting across the aisle from her was Tyler. Reaching over, she rested her hand on his leg.

Tyler looked over in surprise. "Welcome back to the land of the living," he smirked.

Alex rubbed her throbbing head again. "Where are we?"

Tyler smiled. "In a small airplane somewhere over Southern Chile."

"How long have I been out?"

Tyler checked his watch, "About three hours or so."

The haze on Alex's mind was suddenly lifted and she remembered everything. "Jake!" she said in horror.

Griggs spun around in his seat when he heard Alex's voice. He reached over and placed his hand on her shoulder. "Are you okay?" he asked caringly.

"Jake's dead!" Alex moaned. She allowed herself to slump back down into her seat as tears began to streak down her cheeks. "He's dead," she said again.

Griggs looked over at Tyler. "Trade seats with me for a minute."

Tyler nodded. Standing, he took a step back and let Griggs slide into the empty chair. Moving past them, he fell into the co-pilot's chair and began to scan the controls.

Griggs lifted Alex's hand and pressed it inside his own. "Everything's going to be all right, I promise."

Alex tried to wipe the tears from her face with

300

her free hand. "How do you know?"

Griggs smiled. "I just do."

Alex leaned forward and rested her arm and head on the back of the seat in front of her. She slowly pulled her brown hair out of her face so she could look at Griggs. "I never got a chance to tell him how I felt about him, Jason."

"I think he knew," Griggs comforted.

"I don't think he had any idea," Alex sobbed. "If it weren't for you and Jake, I'd probably still be stuck in cold storage at Area 51. You two risked your lives for me."

"Yes we did."

"After he and I escaped from S-4, he was all I had to depend on for a whole year. You were...."

Griggs smiled, "Dead?"

Alex nodded. "He saved me so many times during that year we were running from the government, and I never once said 'thank you'." Alex took a deep breath and tried to stop crying. "Then you came back into my life and I basically just tossed him aside like he was nothing more than garbage."

Faith reached over the back of Alex's seat and began to rub her back. "Jake was a good man, and he lived a good life. It's his daughter that I think we should be mourning. I mean, she was my age, just at the beginning of her life, and it was all taken away," Faith snapped her fingers, "just like that."

"I don't mean to interrupt, little lady," Jack said from the pilot's seat, "but if you keep both of them in your heart, they're never really dead."

Alex looked up at Jack with a bewildered look

on her face. "What the hell was that?" she asked. "Did you just remember that line from some cheesy '80's movie?"

"I'm just saying," Jack defended himself.

"When we get back home," Durard interjected, "we need to have a funeral service for the two of them. I think it will help with the grieving process."

Alex turned to look at Durard. "Thanks, Jim, that's a really good idea." Sitting up, she took another deep breath and wiped the tears off her face.

Griggs patted her on the leg. "No more sorrow right now, I think Jake and Samantha would've wanted it that way." Griggs tapped Jack on the shoulder. "Hey, Jack, how long until we reach Punta Arenas?"

Jack looked at the silver watch on his wrist, "Well, I'd say about an hour or so. Once we're there, give me about twenty minutes to refuel the plane, and we'll head out for McMurdo."

"Great," Griggs said with a smile, sitting back in his seat. "Where are we going?" Durard asked.

Griggs turned back to face the group. "Our next stop is in Punta Arenas, Chile. Once we're there, it's only a little hop over to McMurdo, Antarctica."

"Why are we going to Antarctica?" Faith asked with amusement. "We had a chance earlier this afternoon to do a little research," Alex admitted. "The numbers the alien computer on Easter Island gave me turned out to be coordinates. Jason and I checked them against a map, and they point to a mountain on the western side of Antarctica: Mount Vinson."

Tyler laughed uneasily. "I think we're all a little underdressed for the coldest place on Earth."

Griggs shook his head. "We took the liberty of rounding up gear for everyone this morning. We have enough cold weather gear to clothe an army."

"How did you know we would come?" Durard asked.

Alex shrugged. "We really didn't. We just wanted to have enough," she smiled, "just in case."

Durard mulled over the information for a moment. "What do you expect to find there?"

"Answers," Alex said seriously.

"Answers to what?" Tulley interrupted from his position in the rear. "We don't have any idea," Griggs said with a twinkle in his eye.

***

Claxons began to sound inside NORAD. Summers turned uneasily to look at the two monitors in front of the room. The timer on the second screen had less than ten minutes left on it. He took a deep breath and began to walk toward the Command Console. "Shut that damned alarm off," he instructed. The alarms fell silent. "I want an update now."

"Sir," Stewart started, "the armada is about to breach Earth's perimeter."

"Damn," Summers said under his breath. For the past hour, he had been hoping they would change direction and pass right by. It was now clear their target was Earth. Summer lifted the receiver of the red phone off its base and pressed it to his ear. Tapping the only button on the phone, he waited for an answer. He heard a click on the other end of the line. "Mr. President, we await your final confirmation of deployment." There was silence on the line. "Mr. President?" Summers asked.

"Deploy," the President said and hung up the phone.

304

Chapter Thirty-Four

The small white Cessna touched down gracefully on the runway in Punta Arenas. After taxiing toward the small, one level terminal, Jack brought the plane to a halt. Running through his postflight checklist, Jack began to flip off the switches on the control panel. The twin propellers sputtered once, then cut off. Jack unbuckled his seat belt and stood up. Walking to the rear of the plane, he twisted open the latch on the door and popped the hatch.

"Everyone out," he announced. He stepped out of the way as everyone onboard exited single file.

Griggs was the last one out. Turning, he looked back at Jack still standing inside the plane's cabin. "How long until we can get underway?"

"Give me about twenty minutes, and we'll be back in the air."

Griggs nodded. Spinning around, he broke into a light jog to catch up with the rest of the group.

***

General Summers watched ominously as the launch timer hit zero.

Taking a deep breath, he looked down at the gold wedding band on his left hand. He closed his eyes for a moment and thought of his wife and children. "May God have mercy on our souls," he prayed. Running his fingers over his keyboard, he tapped in the final launch command. "Launch on my mark," he said loudly. "Three...two...." He glanced around the room at the young officers manning their stations. He was signing all their death certificates with this one action. "One...launch."

Looking up at the left screen, he saw the booster rockets on the ballistic missile heat up, and then fire. The missile, slowly at first, lifted out of the tube and beyond the view of the camera. "Lieutenant Stewart, give me a full tactical view on both screens."

"Yes, sir." Stewart quickly complied. The two main screens began to move on small motors toward each other. Once next to each other, their views changed into a giant tactical map showing the Earth and the approaching armada. "Three missiles are away, General," Stewart confirmed.

Summers watched as the three solid white triangles representing the missiles roared up through the Earth's atmosphere toward the approaching armada. It would be less than a minute before they knew if they had a hit or not.

***

The ships in the armada slowly eased to a halt. They had all detected the launch. Communications were moving quickly between ships as they discussed the problem, then the chatter abruptly stopped. Two ships moved out of formation toward the approaching missiles.

***

"Sir, the armada's stopped," Stewart yelled across the control center, "and two ships have

306

broken off from the rest."

Summers rubbed his chin as he looked at the green and white display in front of him. "What the hell are they doing?"

***

A small slit opened at the front of each of the shimmering, silver crafts and a long slender tube emerged. Rerouting the energy from the rest of their systems, they focused it all on the shafts. The chrome cylinders began to glow a bright blue as each of them began to collect the energy.

***

"Time!" Summers yelled.

"Ten seconds until impact, General!"

Summer leaned forward and placed both of his hands on the command console. He watched intently as the missiles drew nearer to their targets.

"Five seconds, General," Stewart announced.

***

The ships released the energy. An intense white beam erupted from the end of each cylinder and crackled through the darkness like lightning. The beams instantly obliterated the approaching missiles. The blast wave from the three ballistic missiles tore through space like a blue wave, obliterating everything in its path, but the armada remained. The ships held their position as the wave ran its course through them. Advanced stabilizers on the crafts kept them from even moving an inch. The cylinders on each of the craft quickly retracted, and the slits closed seamlessly, showing no signs of ever being there.

***

"What the hell happened?" Summers demanded. "Did the missiles hit their targets, or were they destroyed?" He stood up and walked briskly toward Stewart's console.

"Checking," Stewart replied as his fingers flew over the keyboard. "I can't get a solid reading as yet, General, we lost two of our satellites in the blast, and the electro-magnetic pulse has knocked out several others."

"Is the second salvo ready to launch?" Summers asked as he moved back toward his console.

"Yes, sir," another lieutenant replied. "Prepare to launch."

***

The ship to ship communication resumed. This event was unexpected. They had never encountered this type of resistance before. Maybe this barbaric world wasn't worth studying after all. The armada came to an agreement. The data must be recovered, at any cost. It was much more valuable than even the civilization it was studying.

A round aperture on each ship's hull slid open. Out of each, a small silver ball, no larger than a basketball, emerged and hovered below the ships.

308

The balls' instructions were quickly relayed and each rocketed off toward its destination around Earth. The fifty balls took up strategic positions around the globe and stopped. They hovered in position, awaiting their final instructions.

***

"Sir," Stewart said in horror, "the armada has released something around Earth."

Summers' eyes widened. "What the hell is it?"

Stewart shook his head. "I don't know yet, but there are a lot of them."

***

The armada signaled their instructions to the balls. A moment went by before the balls reacted. Then, in an explosion of blinding white light, each ball was obliterated, sending a wave of electromagnetic energy raining down on Earth. The wave was designed to disrupt, and even destroy, technology, according to its proximity to the blast. The satellites were the first to go. The wave of energy covered the globe and began to ripple around it as if a rock had been dropped into a calm pond. The wave covered the Earth in a matter of seconds, and everything stopped. The Earth was enveloped in darkness as every light died. Everything from cars, to stoplights, to computers, to household appliances, and anything with technology in it ceased functioning

.

***

NORAD was completely dark. "What's going on?" Summers asked through the darkness.

"Everything's dead, General. All systems are off-line."

"Backup power?"

"Nothing, sir. Whatever they just did, it knocked out everything."

"Shit," Summers said to himself. "We're completely defenseless now."

*****

The lights inside the terminal flickered once, and then died. Alex, Griggs, Durard, Tulley, Tyler and Faith were all sitting in the waiting area. They waited for a moment for the backup emergency lights to come on. Nothing happened. The terminal remained dark.

"Power outage?" Alex asked.

"Probably," Tulley answered. "These small countries always have the worst power grids."

Griggs stood up and stretched his arms. "I'm going to run back out to the plane and check on Jack."

"Sounds like a good idea," Durard agreed.

Moving back out onto the tarmac, the group walked casually toward the small white Cessna. Jack had attached a large gray nozzle to the underbelly of the plane and was in the midst of refueling. He was currently hunched over a small opening in the concrete, looking at the pressure gauge on the fuel tank.

Alex stopped in front of him. "Problems?"

"Damned power failure." Jack said as he began unscrewing the nozzle. "Can't pump gas with no power."

"How much did you get before the power went out?" Griggs asked.

Jack jumped up and stepped into the cabin of the plane. Sliding down into the pilot's seat, he flicked on the power to the control panel. "Looks like I have a little over three quarters of a tank."

"Can we make it to McMurdo on that?" Alex asked as she stepped into the cabin.

Jack thought for a moment, "Yeah, I think so."

"You *think* so?" Alex asked warily. "Do you *think* so, or do you *know* so?" Jack smiled. "Stop worrying your pretty little head about this. I know we can make it to McMurdo. Hell, it's a little less than three hours from here."

"Let's get going then."

Jack half-heartedly saluted Alex while her back was turned. "Yes, ma'am."

Chapter Thirty-Five

The armada loomed above Earth for close to four hours after neutralizing it. They had never attempted this procedure on an entire planet before. Such drastic measures had never been needed. They felt this was a wonderful chance to observe what the species did after it was robbed of all its marvelous technology, and they did. For hours, they hung motionlessly in the sky while the humans scurried about trying to restore power to their precious technology. This was interesting to the machines. They had saved this culture because of its uniqueness. They had never encountered anything like them before. They used to build massive monuments and pray to their various gods, and now they seemed to do the same for their technology. They seemed lost without it, unable to complete simple tasks such as preparing food, or communicating with each other. Technology had truly become this culture's god. The machines quickly entered this fact into their database. No matter how this civilization evolved, at the core, they remained the same. Perhaps they were worth studying after all.

The lead ship left its position in the armada and loomed closer to Earth. It instructed its subsystems to contact the Keeper to begin transmitting the data it had accumulated. The subsystem beeped a warning back at the ship. Uplink with the Keeper could not be established. It tried again with the same end result. They were unable to contact the Keeper.

The lead ship sent a message back to the

armada on the Keeper's status. This was odd; they had never before had any kind of problem with a Keeper. The armada wondered if they had somehow damaged the Keeper when they released the EMP. They realized this could not be the case. Their systems ran on entirely different principals than the Earth systems did. Machine technology was impervious to the EMP blast.

A solution was achieved. The armada transmitted a message to the lead ship:

DATA MUST BE MANUALLY REMOVED. DESCEND, ANALYZE AND REPAIR THE KEEPER. USE WHATEVER MEANS DEEMED NECESSARY.

The lead ship acknowledged. Summoning three other vessels, they began to slowly sink into the Earth's atmosphere. They set their course for the southern polar region, specifically Antarctica.

***

The darkness of winter covered their arrival, but the white blanket of snow that covered the continent of Antarctica was visible as the small Cessna approached. It appeared out of the dark like a ghost ship in the fog. It was the coldest place on Earth, and at the same time, the driest. It was considered, for all purposes, a desert. There was little to no rainfall here, and yet eighty percent of the world's fresh water was locked up in the ice caps. The ice was so heavy, it actually dented the Earth, making it slightly pear-shaped at the bottom.

In most places, the ice was over a mile thick, and in others, over three miles thick. It was a desolate and unforgiving place; it was truly one of the last frontiers to be conquered on the planet.

The small Cessna banked down and headed toward the Eastern Sheet. There would be no sunlight for the next five months, only darkness. Coming in low, Jack guided the plane toward the runway built into the volcanic rock on its coast. Throttling back, he touched the plane down lightly and brought it to a complete stop near the terminal building. The building itself only consisted of a small one room structure with a tall tower constructed next to it. It wasn't much to look at, but it served their needs.

"This is it?" Faith asked as she looked out at McMurdo, Antarctica through her window. McMurdo was the most populated town on the entire continent, with an average of fifteen to thirty residents.

Jack stood up out of the pilot's seat and walked toward the rear of the cabin. "Welcome to Antarctica," he said as he popped open the hatch. The cabin of the plane was instantly flooded with cold air.

Everyone slowly stood up and exited the plane. They had broken out most of their cold weather gear before they left Punta Arenas earlier, and were glad they did. The cold wind bit at them, and their breath was visible before them. Moisture instantly began to freeze to their exposed skin.

"Nice place," Durard said smugly as he looked around. He looked down at his watch. "This is weird," he remarked. "My watch says it's close to seven in the morning, and it's dark here. I don't think I could ever get used to six months of darkness." Turning back to the plane, he began to help Jack unload their equipment from the cargo hold.

"Yeah," Griggs agreed, looking up into the clear sky, "it would be strange." Walking back toward the plane, Griggs lifted a few bags off the ground.

Tulley laughed. "I was on this fishing trip once in Northern Alaska during the summer. My buddy and I were sitting on the front porch of this small cottage we had rented, smoking some cigars and just talking. It was still light out, but I felt exhausted. I couldn't figure it out until I looked down at my watch. It was close to midnight! I had forgotten that the sun never sets there during the summer." Tulley smiled, "The body never truly adjusts to daylight or darkness all the time."

Griggs pulled one of the bags over his shoulder and held another in his hands. "I guess it wouldn't," he admitted, trying to keep his mind off of the cold. "Grab a few of those bags," he instructed Tulley, "make yourself useful."

Tulley nodded. Walking toward the plane, he stopped behind Durard. Durard turned around to see Tulley with his arms outstretched in front of him. Lifting two bags of equipment off the ground, he dropped them into Tulley's arms. Tulley's knees almost buckled under the weight. Smiling at Durard, he turned and began to quickly walk toward the terminal.

Stepping through the doors of the small building, Tulley instantly began to feel the warmth inside. Setting the bags down carefully next to the door, he unzipped the thick winter coat he had on and pulled it off. Dropping it next to the bags, he began to walk around the cozy room. The walls were painted an off- white, while the floors were covered with a yellowish tile. The walls were covered with black and white photos of previous explorers that had trekked into this barren wasteland. He spied Alex, Faith and Tyler standing near a small booth on one side of the terminal.

"What's the plan?" Tulley asked as he walked toward them.

Tyler spun around to greet him. "Alex is trying to rent us a few snow cats."

"Why?" Tulley wondered. "Can't we just use the plane and hop to where we're going?"

Tyler shook his head. "The nearest base, a U.S. research facility named Siple, doesn't have a runway. It's only accessible by snow cat."

"A person would think every base had a runway in case of emergencies."

"Most of their equipment and personnel are delivered by helicopter," Tyler explained, "so they are air accessible, just not by our little Cessna out there." Tulley thought for a moment. "Why don't we just use a helicopter then?" Alex turned around and walked by him, "Because the closest helicopter is parked on a tarmac in New Zealand, and they've lost all communication with the mainland for some reason." She had an angry look on her face.

"Communications are out?" Tyler asked from behind her.

Alex stopped. Slowly turning around, she tried to get control of her anger. She didn't want to take it out on them just because they were standing there. "There's nothing but complete radio silence."

"How can that be?" Tulley asked.

"We're not sure." Alex looked down at the two sets of keys in her hand. "There's just no one listening right now."

Griggs, Jack and Durard burst through the doors with their arms full of equipment. Setting it down, they all took a moment to catch their breath. Griggs looked up at Alex and smiled. "It's cold out there."

Alex tossed Griggs one of the sets of keys. "Pack up the equipment, we're leaving."

"What?" Durard asked with amusement. "We just got it all in here."

Alex walked over and lifted several bags. Zipping up her coat, she walked through the exit without saying another word.

Jack looked over at Griggs. "What's her problem?"

"Her best friend died," Griggs replied solemnly.

Jack nodded and slowly walked out into the cold. Griggs stopped for a moment and looked back. Turning back to the equipment, he felt a sharp pain in his chest and his breathing became shallow. He gritted his teeth hard. *Not now,* he pleaded. Dropping to his knees, he doubled over in pain. Wrapping his arms around his chest, he tried to take a deep breath, but found only more pain. Tossing his head back, he forced himself to breathe. Swallowing hard, Griggs lifted himself off the floor. Pressing one hand against the wall to steady himself, he held the other in front of his face. It was shaking violently, despite his best efforts to stop it. Clenching his fist, he forced another deep breath and stood up. *Just a little more....*

***

The four silvery ships slowly sank through the layers of atmosphere. Due to their sheer size, they created a lot of resistance as they went through the various layers. The bottom of the ships began to heat up. They glowed a bright red. The heat became so intense, it began to ignite the oxygen around them. They were enveloped in a ball of fire as they made their final approach.

Finally breaking through the upper atmosphere, the ships slowed their descent. Automatic repair systems began to activate all over the ships, making sure nothing was damaged in the entry. These vessels weren't designed for atmosphere entry, rather long, weightless voyages through space. Their smaller counterparts were usually the ones who did this, but this mission was far too important to give to a worker. It had to be handled by the upper echelon of the machine's society. That's why only the oldest of the race were allowed to participate in the data gathering missions.

The ship began to access its databanks. It was there when the decision was made to save this race from their inevitable fate on the dying world of Mars. It had ferried the first humans to this small planet within its great hull, and it had been here every five thousand years after that to collect the data from the Keeper. The machine found this race fascinating. They were unlike any other sentient

318

beings it had ever encountered during its long lifetime. They were capable of creating the most wondrous works of art and design, and at the same time, capable of mass destruction. After all this time watching this culture, the machine was still captivated by them. It knew now that saving them was the correct choice.

Its diagnostic systems signaled their completion. There was nothing wrong with the ship. Moving slowly over the glistening waters of the South Pacific, the ships neared their destination. It was only a matter of time now.

Chapter Thirty-Six

"This is incredible," Anne said as she looked around. "This makes that base we found on Rapa Nui look like it was built with an erector set." Anne was dressed in a heavy dark blue winter coat, and thick pants. The collar of her coat was made out of a synthetic fur, making it extremely warm.

Anne looked around the cavernous room. Unlike the base on Rapa Nui with its glistening silver floors and walls, this place had a more sinister and alien appearance. The walls were black with occasional patches of tan that appeared to be letting light filter into the room. The tan sections looked as if they were made of bee's honeycomb, as they were comprised of geometric patterns. The floor and walls looked like decomposing tissue from a corpse. They were unsymmetrical, and rough to the touch. She estimated the room was at least a mile tall, and probably double that in width. Massive, oddly shaped view screens on every wall were displaying information on Earth. Some were showing climate information, while others were displaying television broadcasts from all over the world.

She had entered through two massive doors in the middle of the room. It was so long, she couldn't see either side with her eyes. A network of tubes and wires ran in and out of the walls and floors, casting an eerie appearance over the room. Anne walked carefully around and through the tangled mess of wires as she moved further into the room. The walls and floor seemed to meld into each other, giving the space an almost oval shaped appearance.

She tried to move carefully over the rugged floor, bet kept stumbling because of her heavy rubber boots. Looking to her left, she noticed a small terminal jutting out of the wall.

Making her way toward it, she felt her coat get snagged on the jagged edge of a pipe running perpendicular to the floor. Pulling hard, she heard the fabric give way and rip. Looking at her shoulder, she could see the massive tear in her coat. The soft white lining had been exposed. "Christ," she muttered.

Stopping in front of the console, she smiled as she looked at it. This place was what she had been looking for. She knew the technology contained here would surely put Area 51 back on the map. The console stuck out about six inches from the wall. Its top arched gracefully back like a drafting table. Recessed into the top was a small, black screen with a dull green outline of a handprint on it. The handprint was obviously alien, as a second opposable thumb jutted out from the opposite side. Pulling the thick glove off her hand, she reached out toward the handprint. Stopping, her hand hovered just above the pad. *What am I doing?*

"General...." She heard a voice from out of the darkness. "General Caroll...." the voice said again.

"What?" She turned around and glanced uneasily into the darkness. "Who's there?" She stood utterly still as the silence of the room washed over her. Moments passed, and still nothing. Running her hand over her face, she closed her eyes for a moment. She realized she was hearing things. Her mind had begun to play tricks on her in this place. Shaking her head, she turned back around to the panel. Stretching out her bare hand, she laid it gently on the panel. A bright white line appeared at the top of the screen and slowly moved down. After a moment, a green light appeared in the upper right-hand corner of the screen. Lights in the walls began to flicker on.

Pulling her hand away, she turned to her left and gasped. The huge black face of a Moai was staring back at her from the far side of the room. It was monstrous in size, easily reaching the roof. Its rectangular eyes burned a harsh yellow as the mouth had been molded as an eternal frown. A wicked smile spread across her face. Lifting her small radio off her belt, she keyed the talk button. "Jannis, are you there?" Static hissed back at her. "Colonel Jannis, do you read?" There was still nothing but static. Hitting the radio with her hand, she pressed the button again. "Colonel Jannis, do you read? This is General Caroll, do you copy?" She waited for a response, but none came. "Fucking technology," she said as she placed the radio back on her belt. Turning around, she began to make her way back toward the door.

"Anne, why...?" the voice asked.

Snapping around, Anne searched the room. Her eyes quickly moved everywhere, but found nothing. Reaching her hand into her coat, she slowly pulled her pistol from her shoulder harness. Cradling it in both hands, she scanned the room again. Lowering her guard, she turned around. Her eyes widened and her mouth fell agape.

"Why did you kill me?" Allen asked as he looked at her through empty eye sockets. The skin was beginning to rot off his body. He lifted his hands toward her. "Why?"

Anne instinctively raised her weapon and fired. The bullets seemed to pass right through his body. Anne fired again with the same results. Dropping her gun, she turned and tried to escape, but Allen was upon her. He grabbed the back of her coat and whipped her around. Grabbing her by the throat, he pulled her close to his face and sneered. Anne could see that his teeth had fallen out and his tongue was missing.

"Are you ready to die?" Allen asked in a harsh voice.

"Please God!" Anne whimpered as she tried to break free. "Let me go!" Allen lifted his hand and slapped Anne hard across the face. "Since when do you believe in God?" Wrapping his other hand around her throat, he began to squeeze. Anne felt his fingers tighten, cutting off the oxygen to her brain. A gurgling noise welled up from her throat as her arms fell limp. She tried, but she couldn't fight it anymore. She felt her eyelids becoming heavy and begin to close, and then she lost consciousness.

***

Workers with flashlights moved quickly around the Command Room of NORAD. They were desperately trying to restore power. General Summers was standing with his hands on the command console. A tall lantern sat in front of him, its bluish light casting an eerie glow. Lifting a hand, he rubbed his fingers against the bridge of his nose. He needed to know what was happening out there.

"General!" Stewart yelled from across the

room. "I've got one console back up."

Summers turned around to see Stewart's face light up by the glow from the monitor in front of him. Summer walked quickly toward him. "Damned good job, son." Summers leaned over and looked at Stewart's console. It was a mess of wires and electrical tape. The entire face had been pulled off to gain access. Summers smiled. He didn't care how. He glanced down at the picture on the screen. "What am I looking at?"

"Not much, General," Stewart admitted as he tapped several keys on his console. "There's not much working out there." He tapped another command into the keyboard. "We have one satellite working. It seems to be the only one that wasn't knocked out by the armada."

Summers stared at the tactical map on the screen. "Is that what I think it is?"

"Appears to be, General." Stewart tried to adjust his readings. "Four ships seem to have entered the Earth's atmosphere."

"Heading?"

"From what little data I have here," Stewart paused for a moment, "it looks like they're heading for Antarctica."

Summers stood up. "Why?"

"Don't know, General."

Summers patted Stewart on the back. "Good job, Lieutenant. Keep trying to restore power."

Just as the words had left Summers mouth, Stewart's console exploded in a shower of sparks and his monitor went dead. "So much for that console," Stewart said.

"Damn!" Summers yelled. His words echoed

across the quiet room. "I need to know what's happening!"

***

Six hours driving across the barren landscape of Antarctica hadn't made anyone happy. The group had split up into two teams: Snow cat one contained Alex, Griggs and Tulley. Snow cat two was carrying Durard, Faith and Tyler, as well as most of the equipment. Both cats' headlights had frosted over about an hour ago, leaving them navigating with only GPS.

Each snow cat was a behemoth vehicle built on top of two tank treads. The front was built like the cab of a truck, while the back of each was just a flatbed that they could strap their equipment to. Mighty chrome smoke stacks, affixed to either side of the cabs, were billowing black smoke into the already dark skies. Each was painted a dull orange with the company's logo they had rented them from on each door.

They had gone through the small U.S. base known as Siple about forty minutes ago. They had only stopped long enough to fill up the fuel tanks on the cats, and make sure their bearings were correct. There were only three researchers at Siple. They explained that most of the crew left during the winter, and then returned during summer. The three researchers stayed and conducted astrological studies during the winter. They had explained that the sky wasn't tainted here. No light from a nearby city, no pollution, and it was night-time for six months straight—*perfect conditions for sky*

325

watching.

Griggs was leaning over the steering wheel of the cat as he drove. Ice and frost had begun to collect on the windshield, but the wipers were useless. They had frozen to the window shortly after they had left McMurdo. Wiping his gloved hand across the window, he tried to wipe off some of the condensation that had begun to form. Looking out the window, his eyes widened. Smashing the brake pedal to the floor, Griggs sat back in his seat. "Alex," he reached over to the passenger seat and shook her, "wake up."

Alex had fallen asleep with her head leaning on the passenger window. Slowly, her eyes opened and she sat up. Pulling off one of her gloves, she wiped the sleep out of her eyes. "What is it?"

Griggs pointed out the front window. "Do you see what I see?"

Alex leaned forward and glanced out the window. A look of awe crept over her face. "Oh, my God!"

Four sets of lights were slowly passing over them heading in the same direction. Alex couldn't make out much detail on the ships, only the bright pattern of lights on their underside. Opening the passenger door, she stepped out into the cold night and looked up. The ships were tremendous in size, each easily the length of a football field.

"What the fuck are you doing, Alex! Get back in the cat!" Griggs yelled. Tulley slowly lifted his head up to see what the commotion was about.

"Hey, close the door! You're letting all the heat out...." his words trailed off as he stared out the front window. Sitting straight up, he tapped Griggs

326

on the shoulder. "Is that...?"

"Yeah," Griggs replied, still looking over at Alex. "Alex! Get back in the cat!"

Alex felt like a child full of wonder as she stared up at the lights. They were a mixture of red and green, running in a triangular pattern across the front edge of the ship. Lifting her hand toward the sky, she felt as if she could reach up and feel the underbelly as it passed by.

The radio inside the cat crackled to life. "Snow cat one, this is two," it was Durard's voice. "What the hell is Alex doing?"

Griggs threw the cat into neutral. Sliding across the front seat, he jumped out of the cat and grabbed Alex around the waist. It was then that a bright light from the last ship enveloped them. Alex lifted her hand in front of her face as she looked up into the light. Pulling hard, Griggs sent the two of them flying back into the cab of the cat. Slamming the door, Griggs scooted back behind the wheel and kicked the cat into gear. Pressing the gas pedal to the floor, he sent the vehicle skittering across the ice and away from the light.

Alex and Tulley looked out the rear window of the vehicle. They watched as the light beam from the ship abruptly stopped and darkness again swallowed the landscape again. The ship began to hover in the direction of the other vessels.

"What the hell was that?" Tulley asked.

"A UFO," Alex responded, still awestruck from the experience.

"What the hell were you doing back there?" Griggs asked angrily. "I wanted to get a closer look."

"You almost had an extreme close-up!" Griggs shouted. "They were going to take you!"

Static erupted from the radio again. "Is everyone all right?" Durard asked. Griggs lifted the radio from its cradle on the dashboard. "We're fine. How's everyone in cat two?"

"Everyone accounted for," Durard replied.

Tulley leaned over the back of the seat and pointed at the lights still visible on the horizon. "Hey, isn't that where we're going?"

Alex lifted the small black GPS box off the seat and looked at it, then back up at the lights. "It appears that way."

"Did you hear that, Jim?" Griggs asked into the radio. "Every word," Durard replied.

Griggs looked over at Alex. "Well," he said with a sigh, "what's the plan, chief?"

Alex smiled. "I'm more curious now than ever."

"I knew it," Griggs said with a shake of his head. He keyed the talk button on the radio. "We're going ahead with the plan." Silence.

"Understood," Durard reluctantly responded.

Pressing the accelerator to the floor, Griggs sent the cat tearing across the snow toward Mount Vinson, and the awaiting ships. He didn't like this. He remembered the stories Tyler told him about his abduction experience. Griggs didn't want to be their guinea pig. Reaching into his coat pocket, he made sure his pistol was close at his side.

Chapter Thirty-Seven

"General?"

Slowly at first, Anne opened her eyes. Her mind suddenly began to remember what had happened. Her eyes shot open and she sat straight up. She flailed her arms wildly as she tried to lift herself off the cold, black floor.

Jannis grabbed her by the collar and held her tightly on the floor. "General Caroll!" he shouted.

Anne looked up at her first officer. "Jannis?" Slowly, she glanced around the alien chamber. "What the hell happened to me?"

Jannis shook his head. "I don't know, General. I was escorting the prisoners in here, just as you asked, when I found you lying on the floor." Jannis stood up. Lowering his hand, he slowly helped her up.

Anne tried to wipe off some of the sludge on her coat but stopped. She remembered. "Look at my neck," she ordered Jannis, "do I have bruises?"

Jannis gently placed his fingers on Anne's face and pushed it to the side. He looked over her neck. "I don't see any kind of bruising, or any kind of marks for that matter."

"That can't be," she argued. Anne pushed Jannis away from her. Pulling off her gloves, she ran her fingers over her neck. There were no sore spots. She knew Jannis was right. She suddenly became very worried. "What the hell is the matter with me?" she wondered.

"General?" Jannis asked.

Anne slowly looked up to see the confused look on Jannis' face. "Nothing. I just...."

"General?" Jannis asked, reaching for her.

Anne fell back to the ground, her back arching up in pain. She twisted sideways, then curled up in a ball. She began to gasp and cough. "Janni—" Her words were cut short as her body began to convulse.

Jannis dropped down to his knees beside her. "General? What can I do to help?"

She tried to reach her coat pocket, but couldn't. Her body didn't seem to be obeying her commands anymore. She shook violently again, all the while gasping for air. "Pocket...." she croaked.

Jannis dug his hands frantically into her coat pockets, searching for anything she might be talking about. Coming up empty, he zipped open her jacket and dug his hand into her inner pockets. His fingertips glanced over a gold surface and stopped. His eyes widened. Removing the bottle, he glanced at its red contents. He knew what this was. Reaching back into her coat pocket, he found the syringe he knew would be there.

"Hurry," Anne breathed.

There was a tone in her voice he had never heard before. It was fear. Pure fear. Pulling the plastic tip off the needle, he pressed it firmly into the top of the bottle and into the red liquid. Drawing in the exact amount of medication, he dropped the ampoule to the floor. Reaching over, he twisted Anne's head to the side and jabbed the needle into her neck. Pressing his thumb down on the plunger, he watched the fluid drain into her body. Jannis tossed the needle aside and sat quietly for a moment next to his superior officer. He had no doubt the medication would do its job, and quickly.

Anne convulsed again, then stopped. She took a

long, deep breath and slowly opened her eyes. Turning her head toward Jannis, she glared angrily at him. He knew now. That was unacceptable. "You should've let me die," she said slowly. Taking another deep breath, she began to pull her gloves back on and compose herself. "Where are the prisoners?" she asked, changing the subject.

Jannis pointed toward the far side of the room near the entrance. "I have both sedated and tied securely to a large pipe."

"Very good." Anne looked at Jannis' face. "How's the nose?"

Jannis carefully ran his fingers over the large butterfly bandage that covered his nose. Two large black bags had also formed under his eyes. "Broken," he replied with a half-smile.

"I want—" Anne was interrupted by a loud alarm that seemed to come from nowhere and everywhere simultaneously. Lifting her hands, she cupped them over her ears to try and dampen the noise. "What the fuck is that?"

Tremors began to filter through the alien base. Wires and pipes started to break free and fall dangerously to the ground. Anne and Jannis wisely moved out of the middle of the floor toward a wall. About twenty feet away from them, one of the massive monitors flickered once, and then died in a shower of sparks. The mighty screen began to tumble as it broke away from the wall. It impacted the floor and shattered into millions of tiny shards of glass. A large wire swung down from the roof toward Anne and Jannis. Diving out of the way, the wire slammed against the wall with a thud.

Anne looked over at Jannis after lifting herself

off the floor. "What the hell is going on?"

"Earthquake?" Jannis speculated. "Go find out!"

***

"You still want to go there?" Griggs asked as he brought the cat to a stop. The four vessels had taken up position around Mount Vinson. They had aligned themselves vertically above the mountain, with their noses pointing down at it. Bright blue beams of energy were being directed at the mountain. Steam was beginning to rise around them, form into snowflakes and fall back to the ground.

"They're melting the ice!" Alex said in horror.

"Why is that such a bad thing?" Tulley asked. "Maybe we'll finally get a good look at the land around here."

"No, you idiot," Alex snapped. "If they melt the ice, it could have catastrophic results."

Griggs looked over at Alex. "What do you mean, 'catastrophic'?"

"I mean that if they melt the Eastern Sheet, it would cause the planet's oceans to rise around two hundred feet."

"And?" Tulley asked.

"Reno, Nevada would become ocean front property," Alex said gravely. "The cities of New York, Los Angeles, Washington D.C., London, and many others would all be under water. You could pretty much kiss Hawaii, California, and Florida good-bye. Millions of people would die."

"Damn," Griggs said under his breath.

Alex nodded. "The key has to be in that mountain."

Griggs looked at the ships for a moment. Grabbing the stick shift, he pulled the cat back into gear and pressed the gas pedal to the floor. The wide treads of the cat began to kick off patches of snow as it tore off toward the mountain.

***

Anne stood at the ready near the center of the room as the base shook beneath her feet. Her eyes kept scanning back and forth for falling debris. Taking a few steps back, she remembered that Jannis had tied the prisoners to a pipe on the far side of the room. "Fuck," she muttered. She wanted them dead, but not this way.

Moving at a quick pace across the room, she weaved in and under the wires hanging from the ceiling. Massive pieces of debris had fallen to the floor, making it difficult to pass. One such piece, a large chunk of metal piping, had been buried beneath several layers of metal girders and portions of the roof. Grabbing the side of the pile, Anne gave it a quick shake to see if it was sturdy enough to support her weight if she climbed over it. The mountain of debris began to sway back and forth, threatening to fall. Anne looked in both directions. The pile looked to extend to both sides of the room. Looking for other options, she noticed a pipe that intersected it. Running toward it, she quickly sized it up. It was large enough for her to walk through. Stepping inside, the pipe pitched sideways into the debris, sending Anne shooting through it. Anne

333

emerged on the opposite side of the rubble.

Standing up, she broke back into a brisk jog as she crossed the room.

Out of the darkness, she could see her two prisoners sitting on the floor with their backs to a large pipe that ran vertically to the ceiling. Anne heard the angry sound of metal beginning to give way. Looking up, she saw a massive metal bar swinging toward her. With no time to dodge, she braced herself for the impact. The bar hit her hard in the midsection, knocking her off her feet. Anne landed hard on her back, getting the wind knocked out of her. Forcing herself to breathe, Anne rolled out of the way just as the bar made a return trip.

She let herself lay on the floor for a moment until she caught her breath. Lifting onto her hands and knees, she looked over at her two prisoners. They were completely drugged, unaware of the mayhem happening around them. Anne glanced over at the doors. They were thankfully still clear of debris. She had the sudden urge to cut her losses and leave. Restoring the glory of Area 51 wasn't worth her life.

***

Griggs and Alex piled out of the snow cat and looked up at Mount Vinson. The beams from the ships seemed to be cutting entire blocks of snow and ice off the mountain at once. Griggs looked over at Alex. "This is not a good idea."

Alex walked back to the rear of the cat and pulled one of the bags off. Unzipping it, she pulled out a pistol and tucked it into the pocket of her coat.

334

"Yeah, but it has to be done."

Durard, Faith and Tyler met them at the rear of the cat. "What's the battle plan?" Faith asked.

"Go in," Griggs started, "and whup some alien ass." Durard laughed. "I guess that's as good as any."

Lifting a bag off the back of the cat, he slipped it over his shoulder and began to walk toward the mountain. "Let's go."

The group walked cautiously toward the mountain. Durard tapped Griggs on the shoulder. "Look over there."

Griggs turned to see a lone helicopter parked just in front of the mountain.

"Shit." Pulling out his pistol, he began to run headlong for the mountain. Stopping in front of the helicopter, Griggs peered cautiously around the side. It was empty. No pilot or crew. He returned his weapon to his pocket. Spinning around, he looked at Alex. "How do we get into the mountain?"

Alex shrugged. "I don't know."

Tyler pushed past them. "Follow me."

Alex looked at him in confusion. "Do you know where you're going?"

"The voice will tell me," Tyler replied quietly.

"Okay," Alex said uneasily.

"It's all right," Faith assured Alex. "Tyler explained it to all of us."

"Explained what?" Griggs asked.

"When the aliens took him four years ago, they did something to his mind," Faith explained. "It allows him to communicate with alien technology."

"Incredible," Alex said.

Tyler stopped and pointed toward a large hole

in the mountain. "We can get in through there."

Griggs and Durard moved carefully toward the hole. It was as big, if not bigger, than the cave back on Rapa Nui. Stepping in front of the cave, Griggs saw something flash inside the cave. "That was strange," Griggs commented, "I think I just saw a flash of light."

Machine gun fire erupted from the cave, hitting the ground in front of them. Diving away from the mouth, Durard and Griggs pressed themselves against the ice outside. Reaching around the corner, Griggs fired blindly into the cave.

"We just can't get away from these guys, can we?" Durard said as a bullet ricocheted off the rock face next to him. Durard dove in front of the cave and fired inside. He jumped out of the way just as another volley of lead flew past him.

Dropping to his knees, Griggs pulled the small black gear bag off his shoulder and set it on the ground. "Cover me," he instructed them. Unzipping the bag, Griggs lifted two small grenades out of it.

Durard looked over at Griggs. "You can't use those."

"Why not?" Griggs asked as he pulled the pin on the first one. "You could collapse the cave," Durard warned him.

Smiling, Griggs stepping in front of the cave and lobbed the first grenade inside. He quickly stepped back. "Cover yourself."

Durard ducked down and buried his face in his body just as the grenade exploded. A cloud of smoke poured out of the hole in the side of the mountain. Standing up, Durard turned around and began to fire into the darkness. After emptying his entire clip, he stopped and waited. "I think you got them." Just then a lone shot rang out. It hit Durard in the stomach, dropping him to the ground.

"Nope," Griggs said. "Missed one." Pulling the pin on the second grenade, he tossed it into the cave. Running across the mouth, he lifted Durard and pulled him out of the way. A second explosion rocked the cave.

After helping Durard to his feet, Griggs signaled for the rest of the group to join them. He looked over at Durard. "Are you going to live?"

Durard moaned. "I think so."

"Good, we need to get going." Standing next to Durard, Griggs lifted Durard's arm and put it over his shoulder. Supporting his weight, Griggs helped him into the cave.

***

Lifting herself off the floor, Anne walked toward the prisoners and smiled. She had been waiting a long time for this, too bad she wouldn't be able to kill all of them at the same time. She would just have to settle for these two. Pulling her pistol out of her shoulder harness, she knelt down next to the prisoners and looked them over. Their eyes were still closed, while thick, white ropes bound their hands and feet.

Anne began to undo the ropes. "It's too bad I have to kill you, Jake." She looked down at Jake's quiet face, and then at his daughter's. "Your daughter is very beautiful." Running the barrel of the gun down Jake's cheek. "I should've just left you on that plane we rigged to explode. It would've

337

been easier, but I'll enjoy killing you and your daughter."

Jake quickly opened his eyes and glared at Anne. "I'd rather you didn't." He sent a vicious head butt into Anne's nose. Anne stumbled back with her hand over her nose. Jake pulled the last of the ropes off his feet and hands and stood up. Taking a step closer to Anne, he kicked her hard across the face. Anne fell back to the ground, her mouth bloody. Reaching down, Jake pulled Anne's pistol out of her coat. Flicking off the safety, he brought the gun to bear on Anne.

"How?" Anne asked.

Jake smiled. "The drugs you pumped me full of wore off about twenty minutes ago." He pulled the hammer back on the pistol. "You are not going to hurt anyone else, Anne. I'm going to make sure of that."

"Dad, no!"

Jake glanced behind him to see Samantha looking on in horror. "Samantha, this is none of your concern. Get out of here."

"No," Samantha said resoundingly. "You can't kill her. It's just not right."

"Yeah, Jake, listen to your daughter," Anne interjected. Blood from her nose was running down her face.

"Shut up," Jake said to Anne. "Samantha," he said, looking over his shoulder, "get out of here, now."

"No."

Another tremor moved across the alien base, almost knocking Jake off his feet. He quickly regained his balance. "Samantha," he said without looking away from Anne, "go now!"

"I don't think so, Mr. Silver."

Jake turned around to see Jannis holding Samantha in front of him with his gun to her head. Jake quickly brought his weapon to bear on Jannis. "Let her go," he said quietly.

"Put the gun down, Mr. Silver, or I kill your daughter," Jannis warned him. Jake smiled. "I don't think so."

Jannis cocked the hammer back on his pistol. "Why not?"

"Because of him," Jake said, pointing behind Jannis.

Jannis didn't believe Jake. This had to be some kind of trick. Slowly, he turned around to see Griggs standing behind him. Tossing Samantha away from him, Jannis tried to bring his weapon around, but it was too late. Griggs swung hard with the butt of his pistol and hit Jannis squarely between the eyes. Jannis fell to the ground like a sack of bricks.

Samantha rushed toward Jake and wrapped her arms around him. Jake looked up at Griggs. "Thanks."

Griggs walked toward Jake with a huge smile on his face. "I thought you were dead!"

Alex came around the corner followed by the rest of the team. She stopped dead in her tracks when she saw Jake. Tears instantly began to roll down her cheeks as she rushed toward him. Throwing her arms around Jake and Samantha, Alex squeezed them tightly. "How are you here? I watched your plane explode!"

Jake pointed down at Anne on the floor. "She

pulled us off the plane just after we boarded. I guess she wanted to make you guys think I was dead."

"I'm so glad you're alive," Alex sobbed.

Tyler was standing near the back of the group. The voice was growing stronger; it was becoming so loud in his head, it was all he could hear. Pressing his hands to his temples, he tried to block out the voice. Tyler leaned his head back and screamed. He fell to the floor in pain.

"Tyler?" Faith said, dropping to the floor next to him. "What's the matter?"

"The voice, I can't get it out of my head," he said in pain.

"What's it saying?" Tulley asked.

"It needs me to repair something, so it can communicate with the ships out there," Tyler admitted.

"Let's go fix it then," Tulley replied.

Tyler sat up and grabbed Tulley's arm. "It's not that simple."

"It never is," Jake remarked. "What do we have to do?"

"Just get me to the Moai," Tyler moaned.

Lifting Tyler up, Jake helped him walk toward the font of the room. The rest of the team, including Anne, was walking slowly behind, while watching for falling debris. After a moment, they came to a stop in front of the Moai.

"Tyler," Griggs said, "you can communicate with the aliens, right?" Tyler nodded.

"What the hell is going on here?"

Tyler looked up at the massive Moai before him. "This is the Keeper," he said, marveling at it. "It was built to monitor all life on this planet. Every five thousand years, the machine race returns to collect that data."

"They've been keeping tabs on us?" Samantha asked uneasily.

"We are their creation," Tyler said gravely. "We are nothing more than a grand science project to them."

"I can't believe that," Tulley argued.

"We evolved from a form of humanoid that used to reside on the planet Mars," Tyler explained. "Something happened there. The planet suddenly died and could no longer support life. They chose to save us, and moved us here." Tyler looked up at the Moai. "They've been watching us ever since."

"Why?" Alex asked.

Tyler's face was serious. "For no other reason than because they can." Tyler took a step closer to the Keeper. "They've encountered a problem though, the Keeper has malfunctioned. The machines need the data collected over the past five thousand years, or their experiment will be for naught. They're trying to clear away the ice to gain access to the Keeper in hopes of repairing it."

"What does this all have to do with you, Tyler?" a worried Faith asked.

"I have to fix the Keeper." A small portal opened at the base of the Moai to allow Tyler access to the communication circuits. "When I was taken by the aliens four years ago, they kept calling me 'the savior'. I thought that meant I would help eradicate The Yellow Death, but they meant I would fix the Keeper, and save millions of lives in the process."

"Let's fix this thing then," Griggs said.

341

"To fix it," Tyler said quietly, "I have to die."

Faith's eyes widened. "You didn't tell me anything about you having to die!" She rushed toward him and grabbed him. "I will not let you do this!"

Tyler pressed his hands tenderly to his wife's face. "I have to die to save the lives of millions of people. It's the only way."

Faith wrapped her arms around Tyler's chest and pressed her cheek to his. "I won't let you go," she sobbed. "You're all I've got."

Griggs began watching the scene as if he was somehow disconnected. Looking down at his hand, the answer came to him.

Tyler slowly pushed Faith back and kissed her passionately on the lips. "There's no other way." He looked into her eyes, "I love you."

"No!" Faith wailed. "Don't leave me, please don't leave me." Faith sank down to her knees in front of Tyler. "I love you, Tyler."

"There is another way," Griggs spoke up. Tyler turned to look at him. "What way?"

Griggs stepped forward. "I can go in your place."

Alex turned and shot Griggs a worried glance. "What?"

Griggs turned to look at the group. "I'm dying. My clone body is starting to break down," he turned back to Tyler, "you have your whole life in front of you. I have less than six months."

Alex ran toward Griggs and grabbed him by the arm. "You can't do this!" Griggs smiled sweetly. "I'm dying already, Alex. Let me go out with some dignity. Let me save the world."

Tears began to roll down Alex's face. "I don't want to lose you," she said quietly.

Griggs remained strong. "Please, let me do this."

"I...." Alex looked at the conviction in Griggs' face. She didn't want to watch him slowly wither and die. "I'm going in with you."

"No," Griggs said firmly. "You're healthy, you have a lot of living still to do."

"It doesn't mean anything without you, Jason. You are my soul mate. I am complete when I'm with you," Alex said with a smile. "If you're going in, I'm going with you."

"I can't let you do that, Alex." Griggs placed his hands on her shoulders. "I love you too much to let you die."

Alex leaned forward and kissed Griggs gently on the forehead. "I love you too much to let you die alone, Jason." Alex turned to Tyler. "Tell us how to fix it."

Tyler looked at Griggs, then at Alex. Griggs nodded at Tyler. "Two cables inside have broken loose of each other. You must stand inside and hold those two cables together."

Alex nodded. "Hold on a minute, Jason, I have to do something." Alex turned and looked at Jake. A lone tear had fallen down his cheek. She took a step toward him and stopped. "Thank you."

"For what?" Jake asked in a shaky voice.

"For everything." Alex wrapped her arms around Jake and hugged him tightly. Moving back just slightly, she kissed him on the lips.

Jake slowly pulled back. He looked into Alex's eyes. "I love you."

Alex smiled and nodded. Letting go, she took a step back from Jake. Turning around, she walked back to Griggs and stopped. Reaching down, she placed her hand inside his and held it tightly.

"I don't think so."

Jake spun to see Anne holding a pistol. "What is wrong with you? You want the world to die?"

Anne grinned and nodded. "That's about it." She felt a sudden pain in her chest and stumbled back. "It's not working anymore," she wailed. Jake started to move toward her, but she lifted her weapon toward him. "Don't move." Another wave of pain gripped her. She slowly returned her gaze to Jake and let out a gasp. There, standing amongst them, were hundreds of rotting corpses. She recognized Allen near the front. "No," she cried and squeezed the trigger. The group fell to the floor trying to avoid her wild shot. She lifted her gun to fire again. "You aren't real!"

Jake glanced up to see the fear in her eyes. "What the—" The crack of a weapon cut him off, but it wasn't from Anne's gun. Jake watched Anne drop to the ground. He quickly glanced around the room and spotted Jannis bracing himself against a wall, his pistol still aimed at Anne.

Anne turned her head toward her co-conspirator. "Why?" she mouthed as a trickle of blood escaped her lips.

Jannis laughed. "I don't work for a fucking clone." He dropped the gun to the floor as he fell to his knees.

Anne's eyes hardened. She began to reach for her weapon, when another gunshot echoed off the walls. Anne snapped her head around to see the barrel of Jake's pistol still smoking from the shot. Anne looked down at the bullet hole in her chest, then back up to Jake. "Fuck," she gasped as she crumpled to the floor dead.

"Go now," Jake said as he turned to Alex and Griggs. "While there's still time."

Alex and Griggs nodded. Turning their attention back to the Keeper, the two walked slowly toward the portal and stepped inside. The small room was circular, and looked to extend all the way to the top of the Moai. The walls and floor were both glistening gold. Griggs looked down at Alex. "Are you sure you want to go through with this?"

Alex nodded. "I am."

Looking around the small tube, Griggs caught sight of the two cables Tyler was talking about. Lifting them off the floor, he held one in each hand. The hair on his arms began to stand up due to the intense current flowing into both cables. Alex took a step closer to Griggs. Wrapping her arms around him, she kissed him. Instantly when their lips met, visions of their possible future flooded through their minds. They saw Alex walking down the aisle in her beautiful white wedding gown toward Griggs dressed in a black tuxedo, their honeymoon in Paris, the birth of their first child, their three kids playing together on the front lawn of their home, their daughter's senior prom, their son graduating from college, and each other, old and gray sitting together on the front porch of their home just before they died in each other's arms in bed that night. It was a final gift from the Keeper. A glimpse of what their future might've held. It was a gift to thank them.

Griggs slowly brought the cables together in

front of them. A surge of electricity began to build up around them. Tears were falling freely from each other's eyes. There was no stopping it now. The energy began to flow around them, and through them. Their two bodies became one in the flow. Each molecule that was separate, was now joined. They had become one, and they were content.

The energy burst from its confines in the tube through the top of the mountain and into the waiting armada. The tremendous blue beam began to shake the mountain to its very core. The wave of energy was so powerful, it began to destroy the Keeper. The hollow inside Mount Vinson began to collapse, sending tons of debris and rock raining down into the alien base. The mountain, which had stood for millions of years, imploded in minutes. The four ships hovering above the mountain finished downloading the data and stopped transmission. Angling themselves up toward the sky, they all hovered silently out of the atmosphere.

A lone helicopter went unseen as it headed off into the night. Six passengers sat in it quietly, mulling over what had just happened. That was the hardest thing any of them had ever done. Jake looked over at Samantha. She was lying on the seat next to him with her head resting on his leg. Looking out the window, he stared up into the heavens. The stars were shining brightly tonight. Picking two stars out of the endless sea, he quietly said "Thank you", to Alex and Griggs. The helicopter banked and headed out across the barren snow covered land of Antarctica toward McMurdo and home.

Epilogue

"...Ashes to ashes, dust to dust."

It was bright and sunny the day they interred the two empty coffins in the ground. Jake and Samantha stood quietly dressed in black in the front of the mourning group. Durard, via a pair of crutches, was standing under the shade of a willow tree just behind the tombstones. Faith and Tyler were standing quietly behind Jake, watching the coffins slowly being lowered into the ground. The priest, a gray-haired man dressed in a black robe, had just finished his service, and was moving away from the gravesite.

Jake knelt down next to Alex's grave and lifted a handful of dirt off the ground. Standing back up, he let the dirt fall out of his hand onto Alex's casket. Samantha was weeping softly next to him with a wadded up tissue in her hand. Tyler patted Jake once on the back, then he and Faith turned to leave. Durard was the next to go. Without a word, he turned and hobbled out of the cemetery.

Jake turned to Samantha. "Can I be alone for a moment?" Samantha nodded. "Sure. I'll stay close, just in case you need me."

"Thanks." Jake watched Samantha turn and walk away. He was glad she had opted to move to Nevada and live with him. He enjoyed having her around the house. Looking back at the two graves, Jake walked around to the foot of each. Alex and Griggs were being buried side by side in a small cemetery in Lake Tahoe. Jake knew they would've wanted it this way. Two small rounded gray headstones stood quietly at the head of each of their gravesites. Jake had felt it was appropriate to have each inscribed with just their names and one word: "Adventurer".

He hadn't cried since that day two weeks ago inside the alien base in Antarctica. He didn't know why, he just couldn't bring himself to the realization that they were gone. The pain was there, a dull empty ache in his soul that could not be silenced, but he wasn't able to release it. Six years ago, he'd started all this by taking a case to find out what happened to an eighteen year old high school student, and now his two best friends were dead. He couldn't help blaming himself.

Clasping his hands in front of him, Jake tried to think of what he wanted to say. "You two are my best friends, and I will miss you dearly." Jake reached up and took off his black sunglasses. "If it's any consolation, we beat them. We finally did it." Jake walked around to Alex's grave. "The funding for Area 51 has been pulled and the base is being permanently decommissioned. There's already word that a few Las Vegas tour companies are trying to get the rights to take tours there," Jake laughed uncomfortably. "Tulley and Durard are writing a book about our adventures together. I told them I wouldn't cooperate unless they paid me."

Jake walked back in front of the two graves. His emotions had been building for weeks with no outlet. He didn't know how to feel. "Why the hell did you do that?" Jake yelled. "Why did you have to die?" Jake slumped down next to the graves. Tears rolled down his cheeks as he looked at the two gray headstones. "I just wanted to let you both know I will never forget either of you," he said, wiping the tears from his eyes. "Thanks for taking the journey with me."

Standing up, Jake turned and walked away from the graves. He met Samantha at the tall iron gates. She leaned close to her father and hugged him. Grabbing the metal gate, Jake slowly pulled it closed behind them as they walked away.

***

Tulley was sitting in front of his word processor in his small office. He didn't know how to begin the story. He had racked his brain for days thinking of the perfect line to hook the reader. Laying his finger gently on the keyboard, he began to type. After a moment, he stopped and read over what he had just done. "Shades of brown and yellow painted the desolate landscape as the Great Pyramid rose magnificently from the Giza Plateau." A smile crossed his face.

THE END

OAK END